THE DESERT SEQUENCE

PUATERA ONLINE BOOKS 1 - 3

DAWN CHAPMAN

An NPC's story

Inspired by the cover
created by
Sarah Anderson
and set in *the game world of*
Puatera Online

For those who inspire me on a daily basis, my closest friends, my family, and the husband who puts up with everything.

For those who work with me, from cover designers to my editors—you're all awesome.
Sarah, Nick, and Rogena.
For those who talk to me daily, the Discord Crews.
Blaise Corvin, Stephan and Sam Morse, Luke Chmilenko, K.T Hannah, and Bonnie.
V, Zeb, Kajack, and Carl.

Special shout to my sprint buddy, Michael Chatfield for the continued push and sprints in MWC and beyond.

Thank you, all of you.
Dawn
x X x

DESERT RUNNER

PUATERA ONLINE BOOK 1

CHAPTER 1

*H*eat from the outside sun scorched the back of my head as I entered Dresel's office. He sat with his back to me, his head bobbing up and down as he talked.

I hated him.

Well, hate was a pretty offensive word for someone I once dated. I hated the fact he had this hold over me. Dresel managed all the Desert Runners in this vicinity.

When he turned around to face me, I wouldn't give him any satisfaction of looking his way. So, I sat down in the dog-eared chair I'd rescued out of a bin for him years ago. With a slight huff, pain shooting through my hip, I lifted my boots to rest on the end of his desk.

Tightening the laces, I listened to the tail end of the conversation and sighed.

"She'll be there in a couple of days."

He paused, his head still bobbing. "Yes, sir. Maddie's the best I have. There won't be any issues. She'll complete on time."

So he was talking about me taking on a quest. I was interested in the conversation even more now. If the pay was right, I'd do just about anything at this moment in time.

I glanced at my health bar.

HEALTH – 65%

Due to my past injuries, it had been steadily dropping over the last week. I needed cash for more potions, or I wouldn't survive much longer. I had one flask of potions left. That gave me two weeks at best.

That was when Dresel turned to face me. The greying sideburns did nothing to halt the years I'd known him. I kept telling him they looked stupid, but he never gave up on them.

I raised an eyebrow in his direction. As he listened into the phone, he mouthed, "Mayor Trellis."

My heart sank. Anything the mayor requested was doubly danger-ous... no matter how much I needed the cash. My growling belly was a testament to that. I would turn this quest down. I wasn't the mayor's gofer.

The pain in my hip worsened as I tried to heave my feet off his desk. Rummaging around in my pocket, I pulled out a hip flask. The pain relief I had wasn't going to last a few days, let alone the rest of this month.

Dresel put the phone down, meeting my gaze as I swigged from the flask.

With each sip, I prolonged my dropping health problem, but it never moved any higher. I needed regular potions for that. I also tried to stop watching my *Health Bar*... the more it dipped, though, the more I panicked. It was only natural after everything I'd been through.

"Hip still bothering you?"

I knew he cared, but it seemed forced, as if he knew I didn't have enough potions to keep the pain away and that it would be all the more to his advantage than the growling stomach of mine.

"You know it does. Don't be an asshole."

"I need you to go to Trox City, pick up a package, and deliver it to Port Troli."

"Can't cross the desert at this time of year, you know that?" I sat forward and glared at him. Everyone knew the desert was out of bounds this time of year, Tromoal breeding season. You'd be stupid to try to get across while they were at it.

But when I looked into Dresel's eyes, he slid the quest tag over to me. I looked at it, saw the flickering amount of cash it had to offer—fifty thousand. That was a huge pay-out. I didn't want to take it, but if I didn't, it meant I might be surfing the scrub lands for food or more importantly, pain relief, and they were never good places to draw gear from.

I picked up the tag, the small item vanishing. Instantly, a screen popped into my view:

QUEST ACCEPTED
PICK UP A PACKAGE AND ESCORT TO PORT TROLI

Yeah, this could get very interesting. Almost a quarter of the allotted funds transferred over to my account. At least I could get some supplies in, which meant a quick trip out of town and towards Alstead village.

I stood to leave, the pull on my hip bearable. If I needed to, I could down the rest of my potion. I'd manage quite well without any pain today. Sometimes, though, I liked to feel that burn. The injury reminded me not to forget the past. The past and its consequences were what made me who I am today. A survivor.

"Maddie," Dresel called after me. I turned to look at him. "Be careful out there."

The way his eyes roamed my body made me feel sick. "Always am," I replied, stepping back out into the heat of our summer's day.

First stop, fuel.... and I meant for the groundhog, not me.

My fuel would have to come later. Much later. First things first. I needed full tanks to get across the desert. I could get whatever else I needed after that.

I rounded the corner to see the usual horses, ebolos, and patrons milling about the car park. I still called it one, a car park, even though there weren't many of us around who had working vehicles. The Hog took most of my cash flow, but he was much faster at getting places than any horse. That meant the larger more attractive quest offers came my way first. If I declined them, and they were okay with a longer trip, the horse jocks got the offer.

With nothing more than a thought, I strode forwards, a couple of the guys looking my way, one even nodding his respect, but the other turned away from me. I wasn't well liked despite my prowess. After all, a gal shouldn't be able to hold power over men, should she?

I'd earned the right, fair and square.

Feeling the inside of my wrist, I clicked the tiny button stitched into me. The internal core ran off my biorhythms. The Hog wouldn't open for anyone else but me, and that was a blessing. I'd discovered many a time some idiot thinking they could steal him away.

Not now, not ever.

Magical wards hummed about him when activated and were very notable. After a try or two, most thieves gave up.

As I approached, one of the guys I knew, Dail, dropped the reigns to his ebolos. Taking his time, he wandered over.

"Hey, Maddie." He grinned. "Good to see you." I noticed the other guys' watching him. Had he been baited to say something? I wasn't sure, so I paused by the trunk of the Hog.

"Something up, Dail?"

"We heard a quest came in. A *perilous* one."

I left my face blank. I wasn't going to give him any answers. Besides, why should I? I owed them nothing.

He moved a step closer to me, close enough I could smell the fresh leather wax on his skin. I did love that smell.

"Maddie, if you need backup, you know you can ask me, right?"

I wanted to believe him. I wondered how many of them would actually come if the price were right.

"Your ebolos, can't. You know that."

He nodded and blew out a sigh, then reached in his pocket. "Seriously, if you need a friend, call me."

He held out a com card. Not unlike the quest tags, this would allow us to communicate internally. I'd removed his com from my system after we split up a good few years back. The system itself was pretty good, but I hated to use it.

"We're friends now, right?" Dail motioned to the card once more. "I don't give them out often."

I reached up and took it. The loud clicks as the info was added to my internal memory banks resounded in my head. "That doesn't mean I want any late night booty calls," I retorted with a wink.

When his face dropped, I knew I'd hit the mark. I don't think any of the guys here would try to initiate anything bar maybe an arm wrestle or shoot out. I hadn't been hit by a chat-up line in years. I preferred it that way. If I needed anything, I had the right person to call, and he never refused me, drunk or horny.

"How is Jade doing?" I asked, turning the conversation.

I knew Jade had been hit by a Tromoal flare six weeks ago. Her left flank still looked red raw, but she was prancing about with eyes on her master.

"She's almost healed." He grinned at her and pointed to the feed bowl she'd pulled her head out of to look his way. Within a moment, she was munching once more.

"And what about you?" I looked him up and down. His tattered clothes didn't do him any favours.

"Our injuries wouldn't stop me coming if you needed me. She'd be fine here until I returned. One of the guys would look after her."

I snorted. "You've no idea what the quest is, and you're pushing yourself on me. Why?"

Then I realised the *why*. Closing the distance once more, I stared into his eyes. They looked gaunt, tired, his leathery sun-kissed face cracking in the heat of the day.

With a flick of my hand, I opened the side of the Hog. "Get in," I ordered. Not waiting to see a response, I moved to the other side, sliding into the driver's seat.

I didn't have to wait long. Dail was beside me within a moment, the door closing with a soft click. I kept the Hog nicely oiled, and it showed. Placing my palm on the panel, I started the engine. It roared to life with a splutter, and a tiny red light flicked on the dashboard once, then stayed lit. I really did need this quest. There would be just about enough fuel to get it to the refill station.

Many years before, there'd been gears attached to a small stick at the centre of the cab, but with my hip playing up as much as it did, I had the Hog retrofitted. Fully automatic now, it was a case of pointing him in the direction you wanted and keeping your foot on the gas pedal. I much preferred this mode to lifting my leg on and off the clutch.

"Where we headed?" Dail asked. I turned to see the look in his friends' eyes as I backed the Hog away from the animals. Ebolos didn't care about the noise, but their counterparts did.

"Alstead Village. I need fuel, and then we can get something to eat. You can decide if you want to join me."

"Heck, Maddie, just tell me what the quest is. Can't be that bad, can it?"

I wanted to laugh at him, but I couldn't. "What time of year is it?"

"Oh crap," was all I heard. "Seriously?"

I didn't need to answer that one, but I noticed he rubbed his hand on his trouser legs, the rip along the seam exposing skin almost as burned as Jade's had been. "So you need the cash for your potion costs? I need it for fuel and food."

"Looks like we're both in the same boat," he said with a hint of sarcasm.

"I can't take you with me," I said. "But you've always looked out for me. I'll remove the med bills and get you some food on the table. There should be some quests portside before the end of the month."

"Maddie, you don't have to do that."

Reaching over, I tugged at the rip in his clothes. "We've all had some bad luck lately. So it's about time someone had a decent pay-out to tide the gangs over."

"It shouldn't be you, though."

"Why?" Yet I held up my hand. I didn't want the answer to that.

Turning the corner, I pulled into the lot at the fuelling station. The patron walked over, and I rolled down my window to the usual question. "How much?" he asked and held out a reader for the transfer of cash directly to him.

"Fill him up. Everything he'll take. This will be a long trip. Pack me two canisters for spares too," I ordered.

I ran my palm over his reader, the click of our agreed transfer passed between us. I'd feel comfortable once the tanks were full.

Dail stole my gaze by placing a hand on my leg, a gesture I might have slapped any other guy for, but we had been lovers—had been more than that. I'd almost married him a few years back.

"What can I do for you?"

"There's only one thing you can do. Keep the peace till I get back. The boys will be restless without someone to pick on."

Dail laughed. "Don't I know it. You really do keep them in line, Madz."

Almost full to bursting, the green lights on the dashboard lit. I made sure the patron hadn't taken more than his share, leaving him a nice 'paid forward' amount so on my return, I had another full tank. Always best to spend it on the important things now, and then worry about the next quest after I'd blown half the cash in a local bar drowning my sorrows.

"When do you leave?" he asked as I parked the Hog next to a tavern. "I have a couple of days to get to the city to pick up the package."

"Do you even know what it is? What it's for?"

I shook my head. I'd seen many a quest lost because the runners asked too many questions. "No, I never want to know. They've their reasons. All I need to know is who is paying and how much."

"Must be really important with it being this time of year."

"Yes, very much so, especially with cash upfront payment as well as the final amount. Don't worry. I'll be fine." I met his gaze of concern. "I've done this before, you know."

He nodded. "But what happened that time might well happen again."

I rubbed the side of my hip. I knew it could. I'd not escaped the desert or the Tromoal unscathed. They were deadly creatures. Still, nothing compared to the bone shattering dive I'd taken years before and the burns from the Tromoal to them both.

A shiver ran through me, as did the pain. Popping the door open, I moved to stand outside, sucking in the harsh air from the sun-stroked lands.

"Summer isn't getting any cooler," I added, wiping a sleeve across my brow. "Hope the beer is."

The tavern, called *Bow-makers*, smelled just like any other overripe used alehouse. The sticky floor pulled at my boots. Making my way to the bar, the guy behind it smiled at me. "Madz, happy to see you back." He looked at Dail last. "Heard you took a rough tumble from Fril's rock."

"The Tromoal are getting earlier each season," he replied, pointing to the kitchen. "Two of your specials, Val. Two pints of ale, also."

Val smiled and was soon in the kitchen. I took a seat at the bar, but Dail tugged my arm and pointed to a more private area in the room. I wondered why until he sat me down, taking the seat next to me.

"Maddie, I don't want you to do the quest alone. Please let me come with you."

With a finger, I gently ran across the scarring over his exposed thigh muscle. He didn't flinch at my touch. I'd expected something from him. Instead, he edged closer and wrapped an arm around me. I was tempted to push him off. "People are watching," I said.

"Don't care..." Then he held me close. "Maddie, the last six weeks gave me time to think. I don't want to lose you again."

I spluttered, "I'm not going anywhere." I managed to shrug out from under him a little. I suddenly felt overwhelmed, emotions flooding my system, feelings I'd pushed back the day I turned him down. The day I'd hurt him, stormed off into the desert, and almost died.

Then I noticed he had pulled out a small box from his pocket. I swallowed remembering the box. "Dail." I tried to stall, but he opened it, revealing the stunning pink gem inside.

"Maddie, I'm not taking no for an answer this time. You love me, I love you. Accept it."

The last few years flittered through my mind, all the times I'd just plain avoided him. Yet the day I'd heard about his mistake out on the desert plains, I had rushed to his hospital bedside. "Xia told you, didn't he? That I'd been to see you."

Dail nodded, holding the box up to the light, and the ring it glinted around the room.

I reached out, touching the pink stone, feeling its warmth as we connected. It had magical enchantments, its stats flashing up.

STRENGTH + 5
INTELLIGENCE + 10
CONSTANT HEALTH BONUS + 10
EXTRA BONUS – HEALTH BOOST + 10 – To activate, twist the ring twice

I'd not seen this when he first tried to propose to me. The fact was, that day I'd just turned and ran. Ran away from the only man who I knew cared about me.

Now I noted its potential. What it actually might mean for me, especially out there on the plains. My thoughts were purely selfish, though. I pulled back.

"I can't."

Val brought over two steaming plates of food and then two tankards of beer he brewed himself. The fresh smelling bread he'd plonked with the food had my mouth watering.

Dail picked up a fork, tucking in. I could see how hungry he was. Heck, my own stomach was growling. My mouth watered beyond measure. The ring sat between us now, like a glass wall. I couldn't bring myself to push it away further or ask Dail to pack it away once more.

The more I stared at it through my mouthfuls of food and contemplation, the more I realised I wanted it, but it was for all the wrong reasons.

The food tasted a lot better than I remembered from just a few weeks ago, so I mostly ate it without talking. I listened to Dail chatter about his healing costs. I wondered if offering to pay it off was another reason to bring out the ring.

The beer slid down, and without a thought, I picked out the ring from the box. When I met his gaze with my own, I licked the beer foam from my lip. The words tumbled out before I even realised. "If I make it back alive," I stuttered. "I'll marry you."

CHAPTER 2

I hadn't quite expected his response, but he grabbed me, pulling me to him for a kiss. I'd almost forgotten how muscular and yet vulnerable he'd become.

His kiss was just as I remembered. It wasn't sweet or romantic—it was sloppy. A few claps and whoops came from the patrons of the bar. I grinned at them. I could be a badass runner and love someone, right?

Dail took the ring from my now shaking hand, placing it on my finger. The instant boost to my energy levels was intense. I knew he saw it.

HEALTH – 75%

"I've been having it enhanced. Knowing your line of work, it only seemed right."

When the ring was on, he leaned in, kissing me again. "Come back to me, won't you?"

I wanted him to go with me, but the thought of putting his life in that amount of danger so soon after the injury was a definite *no*.

Pushing myself up, I tapped the side of my head. "If I don't go now, I'll never leave."

Dail nodded. "I understand." He stood with me, but I strode to the door alone. I was never good at saying goodbye. I didn't want to say it now. Awkwardly, I opened it, the heat slapping me in the face. "I'll call you from Trox," I said as I walked away and never looked back.

I knew he watched me, but I couldn't do it. The pain now in my chest was for different reasons, the aching of our past relationship, the reasons why it went wrong. Survival and love.

Whatever this darned package was, I'd better go fetch it.

The water tanks and internal battery systems needed a good overhaul, so that meant at least a short trip to the garage while it was in there for a check I could possibly see the local wares of the market.

Walking down the main street, I was greeted with sellers galore. It was a beautiful day. Many of the stalls were decorated in fantastic summer shawls and clothing, all handmade and stitched by the town's local crafters. I didn't have much in the clothing department, but I hung back after I'd spotted a new jacket. The one I wore had far too many patched holes. I smiled at the stallholder, who smiled back. Picking up the jacket, I tried it on. Perfect fit.

"Suits you," he said. "Be good out in the desert."

I shrugged it off. "How do you know where I'm going?" I asked, instantly worried someone else knew the plans for my run. Then I shook off the concern. He couldn't know anything. The visitors here called us NPCs. Non Player Characters. I hated the term. They laughed at us, used us. We were programs to them, nothing more. Knowing I was programmed, I fought every day to go against it. That included the 'falling for everyone I meet' trope.

The man tried to smile at me, adding, "Just see it in your face, miss."

"Oh, really?" I clung to the jacket. "How much?"

He grinned. I wasn't usually so great at knocking these guys down a peg or two, but I apparently wanted it.

"Make me an offer." His toothy grin gleamed gold. No wonder he could afford teeth like that with such high-quality items. So I looked at the tag, seventy-five silver, and then offered him fifteen less.

"Make it sixty-five, and you can have the gauntlets to cover your arm tags."

I looked at where he now pointed. There were indeed two gauntlets to match. I held out my arm for the transfer of the silver. "Pleasure doing business."

I had all my other gear stored in the boot. There wasn't much—spare boots, underwear, tops. I'd never needed them, never been stuck bar that one terrible year. No matter the water or the stores I'd kept as backups, there would never be enough, hence my fight with the Tromoal. I wanted what it had, food. It wanted to eat me as well. I was lucky to get away.

My internal clock pinged. The Hog would be ready to go. I made my way back to the garage, checking over their work just once before I paid and drove out. The Hog always got stares as we made our way out of town. After I made a quick turn, I stopped by the main food store, loaded up and packed tight into the boot. There wasn't going to be much room for anything else.

Whatever happened, this might be the only time I'd see Alstead Village and its fascinating ways. Onwards to Trox and to the mayor's home.

As the setting sun moved its way through its cycles, I found the roads narrowing and the terrain becoming more uneven. There was a time I'd never thought of going off road to where I needed to, but with the AI system I'd enhanced the Hog with, I found tracks easy to store and use. Of course, sometimes I'd have to backtrack. They were the runs I really needed my wits about me. Doing quests that were time restricted were tough. I knew all the areas around Trox, the villages and through the desert cave systems to Port Troli. If there were a better one, I would dare anyone else to find it. I'd spent years getting to know every nook and cranny of this land. As treacherous as it was, I knew almost every danger, every lurking creature from the ground to the skies. It was the Tromoal that were worst. They came every year from faraway lands to breed, the cave systems ripe with their fighting, gorging on the local animals, and generally causing mayhem.

Some hunters tried to tame them, but so far, no Tromoal had ever been caged, tamed or otherwise. They were creatures that no one should have control over. Especially us. Or the 'visitors' we had now and then.

The visitors were people just like us, but then they weren't. There were a few who we'd crossed paths with over the years. Dail especially. The visitors came, asked for quests or to be taught skills. They caused mayhem in local towns, taverns, and brothels then went off on some quest, and mostly, we never saw them again.

It was something I'd never gotten used to. I'd met many visitors along the way, but the only one that meant anything was called Leon Boki, a young man who vanished from our town after going out hunting the Tromoal during their breeding season.

My problem... programming, I'd fallen in love with him. Not only that, I was besotted. More than besotted. Afterwards, I'd questioned all of this. It was in my programming, right? To fall in love and then lose them. I could see it. I couldn't, however, change it. It frustrated me to no end.

So Leon managed to convince a few others to join him, but no one had returned. It was after that I vowed never to get involved with any of them again. They seemed to just breed distrust amongst the locals and death among everyone else.

I flicked the low headlights on, steadily increasing my pace through the night. The creatures that roamed the world at night always made me shiver. They were mutated, horrific, and even made me cringe. It was tough to do as I'd seen everything Maicreol had to offer. Not many creatures would be attracted to the lights from the Hog. If they were, I could soon stop and take them out with the external harpoon.

Fighting the draw of the night sky, I forced myself to keep awake.

Driving always made me sleepy, and thinking about the journey ahead of me to Port Troli made me want to sleep even more. I'd not had a decent sleep for days. The idea I might be able to get a bed in a charming inn before picking up the package actually made my day.

Twisting the ring on my finger, I felt the renewed energy it lent me.

HEALTH – 85%

The boost to my overall health and well-being despite feeling so run down was worth saying yes to even if I felt guilty. Would I actually go through with it if I returned alive and well? I didn't honestly know the answer to that. I did still love him, I always would.

Steel gates twinkled ahead from my view, and with a *ka-thump*, the Hog touched the gravel pathway leading to the vast city of Trox. I'd been here many a time, but each time I came, it actually made my skin crawl. It was nothing like the homey area of Alstead village and its local towns. I rolled up the window, not wanting to smell the dank waters of their moat as we crossed it.

The wooden decking creaked. I saw its supports and metallic systems and cringed as the Hog drove on it. The guards at the gate moved up the portcullis. Either they recognised the Hog or the mayor had sent them.

Once nearer to see the guards, I rolled down the window again, settling back while the shorter one with a red helmet approached me. "The mayor's got you a room in the Scoth hole. You'll be well fed and watered for tonight, miss."

Relief washed over me. I knew the inn well. I'd had a room there once before a few years back. I looked forward to seeing the innkeeper and his wife again. Plus, they had a bathing area inside the ground that ran from a natural spring. It was incredible. I had never felt so clean afterwards.

I looked forward to it as I slowly drove past the guards into the main road systems of the city. I took the roads to the left, heading to where the inn used to be. It was lovely to see people still milling about and the late night not scaring them all off. The walls were protecting them. The drinking inns stayed open until the last person fell out, no matter who or how smashed they were. I'd always made them stay open till dawn for me, even if I couldn't walk out. I wanted to know I'd been up all night, safe somewhere, not where the dreams would haunt me, where the pain hurt more than the physical.

I shuddered, hoping there was a bar tab as well as food. I would love to sleep in a bed for the night, but I also wanted to keep the pain at bay without the need for using potions. Before going for the Mayor's package, I would pick some up from the alchemists in the morning.

Parking the Hog, I found the inn easily enough. There were a couple of people outside, drinking and chatting. I walked past them, putting on a brave face It was important I didn't show any signs of weakness, even if I was curling up inside, wanting to just hide from them all. After concentrating on getting over here, all I wanted was a few drinks, some food, and a bath.

The place hadn't changed much from my last visit, apart from the décor. It was bouncier—at least that was the only word I could come up with. The seating areas were the same, and the bar curved into both rooms of those who were staying overnight and those who were just regular drinkers.

I didn't see anyone I recognised, but I moved to the other room, waiting for the waitress to notice me. "Miss," she said. "Miss Vies?"

I nodded.

"There's a room with an open tab for you. What would you like this evening?"

"The strongest beer you have. A plate of the local specials an' a quiet table, please."

She pointed me towards a table in the corner of the room, and I took a seat. A couple sat at the other end of the chamber. Four guys at the bar were being served drinks by another barman. Again, I didn't recognise anyone, but that might have been a good thing. Sometimes, it's best to leave old memories in the past.

Within a moment, the waitress returned with my beer, a large jug, and a glass. A little posher than I was used to, but I thanked her.

Contemplating my next few days, the beer slid down well enough while I listened to the conversations. A couple was discussing moving into the city. This was an exploration for them. It was nice to hear some of the good sides this huge place offered. I only knew the bad sides, the seedy underworld of trafficking, and of course, the potions. I wouldn't be where I am without them as far as the pain I live with is concerned. As much magic as there was in this world, no one wanted to live in constant pain. No amount of magic could have put me back together, though they tried.

Scraping my plate and polishing off the beer, I was ready to retire, wanting to avoid the guy at the bar who had been eyeing me for a few minutes. I didn't move fast enough. He sat across from me. I was about to slip my knife from its sheath when I noticed a small tattoo on the side of his wrist. It was an older mark, but still one of a Runner.

"I'm Kraal," he said. When he spoke, I'd half expected slurred words, but there was none. "I was polite enough to wait for you to finish your dinner. Hear me out, Maddie."

I let the knife slip back into its sheath, placing my hands on the table with a nod. To him, a sign of trust. For me, a sign I wasn't going to take him out—yet.

"You've taken the quest for the mayor, right?"

I never answered, so he continued. "I knew there would only be one person willing to do it. I hoped you wouldn't, though."

"Why? What is it to you what I do?"

"This is a political game, Maddie. One you're not fully aware of."

I smiled, knowing this would end badly. I neither wanted to know or to understand their politics. All I knew was whatever their agendas were, they didn't involve real people, those who suffered on a daily basis.

"Look." I started, "I am going to bed. I'm a light sleeper." I warned, but I doubt he needed it. "I don't have time to get caught up in your politics here. I'm doing a quest, and that's all there is to it."

He looked back to the others at the bar. I really didn't want to fight, especially against four men, but if they came at me, I would.

"You're an old-school runner like me. Whatever it is, let it go," I said, moving my hands to my lap.

"I know Dail. He asked me to come see you. Tell you the finer details. It was offered to me, but I turned it down."

That surprised me, but I couldn't back out now even if I wanted to. I'd end up in jail for breach of contract.

"Give me the run down."

I listened while Kraal gave me the information on the quest. It wasn't a regular package I'd be taking to Port Troli. It was a person. This individual held vital information about the local lands, layouts, and all trading routes. It was a plan of action between the mayor and the Port's lord to negotiate better passing trades. It seemed not only would I have the Tromoal to get around, but there might be other bounty hunters on our asses, trying to get the information I'd be carrying. This might be one fascinating trip for sure, and in a brief flash of regret, I wish I'd let Dail come with me. The backup might be nice right about now.

It wasn't that Krall wanted to put me off the quest. It was a warning. A fair one. I thanked him, and he left with his friends. Knowing they wouldn't bother me, I made my way to my room. Dreams of my coming days haunted me, though, along with my hip pain. First thing on the agenda for the morning was getting some much-needed pain relief.

CHAPTER 3

*B*rightly coloured jars and vials adorned every nook. The alchemist's store was fit to bursting, and I loved the place. There were many treasures to be found within these walls. It was a great place to nosey around with money to burn.

The owner, Miss Curthao, had let me in at first light, something she would only do for those returning customers who paid out a lot for regular potions, even if they didn't always visit. Miss Curthao would deliver, for a price.

I picked up several potions I knew would be useful for general healing, some fire wards to hopefully stop the Hog getting burned, and one more expensive healing mix. I was hoping I could keep off the main desert paths. Sometimes, the younger Tromoal couples stayed away from the main breeding zones. Heck, if I was a Tromoal, I think I would too. I wouldn't want my head bitten off by one of the larger groupings, stay away... simple reality.

I placed the products on the counter, lining them up in order of how much I needed them. Miss Curthao pulled out a set of silver flasks. These held the product I really wanted, the pain relief I was so addicted to.

"How is the pain?" she asked as I picked up the first flask.

I tried to feign a smile, but she saw through it right away. "You've no need to lie to me, child."

How I hated that she still called me a child. "Sylvie," I replied, "I'm twenty-four suns past. Not really a child anymore."

She let out a real old lady laugh, her greying hair usually tied back bouncing about her small frame. "You're still a child to me, my dear."

I wanted to open the flask, to drown in some of its contents. The pain hadn't eased off through the night, and the beer hadn't masked it. It never did.

"The pain is the same," I eventually said.

She slid the flask towards me. "How long since you have had your potions properly?"

"Consistently, about three weeks."

"You're pushing your limits." She sighed. "My potions need to be in your system constantly, my dear,"

When one flask cost more than a week's supply of food, it wasn't possible. "I know, Sylvie," I said. "Things got tough on the plains."

"You could have come sooner."

I knew this, but then I'd be beholden to no more than a drug dealer, even if a legitimate one, and running through the city with the kinds of loads she would ask me to wasn't what I wanted, either. The potions were the real danger zone here. Tromoal out there was something you couldn't avoid, but the sewer rats, the actual users were the craziest, most deadly underworld in any city. I shook my head. "Thanks, Sylvie. You know I would if it got that bad."

It was entirely a lie, and she knew it. Yet she still smiled at me, patting my hand. How this frail and mild-looking woman could be the underground drug lord of this city I never quite understood.

She packaged up my order, and then slipped in something else. "I think you'll need this. Just be very careful if you do decide to use it. It's on me."

I didn't see any marking on the jar, but it was small, maybe contained pills instead of a liquid.

I slid my palm across her reader, paying for the goods, the usual ping and new denomination. I'd almost spent two-thirds of my funds. That made me frown. I knew some of it went to Dail... but even so.

Sylvie tugged my hand back to her. "What's this?" She pointed to the ring.

Not something I had thought much about since last night. I had almost taken it off to sling around my neck leather instead.

I met her gaze, seeing something odd twinkle in her eyes. *What?*

"Where did you get it?" she asked, raising an eyebrow.

I hadn't known the origin of the ring at all or how much Dail had salted into it. In fact, why the hell hadn't he sold the ring to pay off the med bills? Then I knew why... me. He really did love me.

"I don't know," I stuttered. "Why?"

Sylvie moved to the back of the counter, pulling out an old tome. The dust blew up in my face as it slammed down. She flicked through several thick pages before settling on a picture.

"This is why, my dear." She pointed to the central picture of a young woman. "This is Lady Mysiol. She was rumoured to be the ruler of Trofoth before she took a sailing crew around the other islands many centuries ago."

I stared at the ring. It did look similar. "You really think this was her ring?"

Sylvie nodded. "May I take a closer look?"

I slid the ring off my finger and gave it to her, the instant dip to my health quite noticeable.

HEALTH – 60%

She drew out some pieces of equipment and examined it for a few minutes. "You have a rare item here. Would you be willing to sell it?"

"No, thank you. It was a gift." I snatched the ring from her hands, slipping it back on. "It's staying with me."

HEALTH – 75%

Because I'd twisted it, another popup appeared.

HEALTH BOOST – 85%

That 10% boost, instant and amazing. I'd get too used to it. I was sure. Maybe I shouldn't wear it, but for now, it helped. A lot.

"A gift from a lover, I can understand why. If you ever change your mind, do come back."

With a heave, I lifted the sectioned box up. "Thanks, Sylvie, I sure will." Though I'd no intention of coming back to sell anything—to buy, of course, she was my ticket to a pain-free life.

I placed the box on the passenger seat floor, starting the engine. I had just enough time to get to the addresses on the mayor's quest listing. It wasn't too far away and further on the smarter side of the city. The Hog roared to life. Sipping from a flask, I eased back into the seat. I took my time driving through the busy streets. Several people looked my way as I eased over the cobbles, carts and horses shying away from the roaring engine. Braking to a stop, I waited until they were out of the way despite the daggers in my head.

I paid little attention to the houses I passed. There were a few curtain twitches, but when I reached my destination, all I could see were two guards. They stood in casual black uniforms, their chainmail stretching over their massive physiques. I slid out of the Hog and spoke with them.

"Miss, your quest is inside. Good luck." That was it. They wandered off, leaving me staring at the front door of a small home. I took a step forward and gently knocked.

There wasn't an answer, so I pushed the handle down, stepping inside. The room was dark, for the most part, but a small light illuminated a side wall.

"Hello," I called out. There was indeed a parcel on the table. Maybe there wasn't a person after all.

No sooner had I stepped to the table, I felt a knife at my back.

Quick reflexes and a moment later, I was looking into the green eyes of a young man, my knife at his belly.

"Nice job." He smiled, then pushed away and held out a hand for me to shake. "I'm Alex."

I looked him up and down, then a small icon popped into the corner of my view.

ALEX DUBOIS – VISITOR – HEALTH – 100%

Oh no. Oh hell no. This changed everything. I started to back away. "Sorry, Alex. This quest's not for me."

I moved to the door, but he got there before me, blocking my path. "Hey, what do you mean, not for you? You've already been given the funds. The mayor's promised me you'd do this. You can't back out now."

The hairs raised on the back of my neck. "Find someone else. You can have your money back."

Alex grabbed my arm. His mistake. Within a second, he was on his knees pinned with his hands behind his back.

"Hey, hey…" He squirmed. "That's not fair."

I leaned over and whispered in his ear, "What's not fair is you, playing in the affairs of our world. You've no right to do that."

I saw the confusion breach across his face. "You know what I am?"

I flung him away from me, grabbed for the door, and was out in the early sun before he could follow.

With the door to the Hog open, I slid in. A hand grabbed my shoulder. "Please, Maddie, can we talk?"

I didn't know what I wanted to do more—run away, hit him in the face, or reach over and throw all the stuff I'd just bought at him. I got back out of the Hog. He placed his parcel on the roof.

"So. Talk. What is it you're doing here?" My voice was raised, heart beating faster than I wanted. I could see the tension in his shoulders as he looked around. "Why the hell do you want to get across the desert to Port Troli? What's in it for you?"

"I really do have to deliver that parcel. What I get from it is the next stage in my journey. I get paid, gain experience, and hopefully, learn some more aptitudes to boot."

I was shocked he actually told me this. Leaning back on the Hog, I swallowed, waiting for him to continue.

"Maddie, no one else would take this quest. No matter what I offered. I need to get that package and the information I'm carrying to Port Troli. It's of vital importance the information is passed over to Shiroth as soon as possible."

"You want to take a boat?" I was interested in this. I'd hoped one day to leave Maicreol.

But he shook his head. "Someone else is doing that part of the journey, but they can't cross the seas if I'm not there."

"You guys are about three months too late for both sides of this journey."

"Exactly, I'm desperate. Help me."

The plea on his face changed, his eyes losing their anger and frustration. I saw the desperation within as his lip twitched. I moved off the side of the Hog. Its metal sides were digging into my flesh. "Get in. We've a lot to talk about and a hell of a long way to drive."

Alex picked the parcel off the roof and moved toward the back of the Hog. "All supplies in there, passenger side," I ordered him.

I watched him open the back door, place his parcel amongst the supplies, and then move to get in the front with me, wedging his feet in amongst the alchemist haul. "We really need all that?"

I closed the door, resting my head against the window, now able to get a better look at him as he sat next to me.

"Yes, we need all that." I noticed the clothing he wore and how the leather stretched across muscles, seeming too neat, tidy. His hair was freshly washed, but not a speck of grime anywhere, even his boots polished. I let out a sigh. "Have you ever seen a Tromoal?"

With no answer, I was quick. I unzipped my pants, easing them off my sore hip. The exposed angry gashes there never went away. The torture I got from looking at them was always the same.

I watched the reaction on his face then motioned down my leg. "Picked up and tossed about like a rag doll," I said. "Six years ago. The toxins in their mouth don't allow healing. The damage done to my body from falling sixty feet will never heal, either. We're heading into the most dangerous part of the world where no one dares go. They're breeding, which makes them even nastier than when they're flying around looking for food. If we're spotted, we're dead. If we get attacked by the matriarch, or the male lead sees us, we're dead. You will do everything I say when I say it. No questions. Understood?"

"I don't want to die. I'll do everything you say. Runners honour."

I started the Hog, the low rumble of his engine an instant comfort. "Today, we get out of the city, drive through the villages towards Hanson's Estate. Hanson owns most of the north side of the cave systems. He farms there. He also provides food for the Tromoal at this time of year. He's highly ranked in this area, but also has many bounty hunters about. I've already been told there's a price on the information you carry. So the route I had planned for us, I'm changing. We're more off-road than I wanted, which means the tracks I am using aren't protected. You'll need to man the weapon when I say, keep a look out at night. We'll be sleeping in the Hog. I'll ditch the other supplies."

"We were going to sleep rough?"

"I hadn't planned on much else, being stuck in here with a stranger. Just not my idea of a good time. No offence."

A wicked grin spread across his face, but he swallowed it.

"How long will it take to cross?" he asked.

"Approximately six weeks on horseback. With the Hog? Three days."

"I can see why they're highly sought after. Don't you have trouble with thieves?"

I looked at him, briefly considering not telling him. "No, the Hog's linked to me. No one else can get in or out without my say so."

"So, it's a magical item then?"

"I don't understand all your terms." I laughed. "But there are only

27

four on Maicreol. Their inventor tied the systems up with DNA strands, so the users are unique."

He listened, glancing over the mechanics of the dashboard. "Seems a blend of technology from home and something else entirely. It's been modified, but by who?" The more he looked at the Hog's dash, the more his eyes widened. "And a hell of a lot by the looks of it."

I knew this. I'd worked on a lot of the mods myself. "That it is."

"So," he looked at the dash board's map. "Three days, two nights? Do we have travel speeds, distance?"

"I have everything I need in here." I tapped the side of my head. With the flick of a button on the edge of the dash, a screen popped out for him to view.

"Wow, I've never seen anything like this in Trox. I didn't even know tech like this existed. It's supposed to be a fantasy world."

He made an awful lot of blanket statements. I grinned. "There are enough of us about who like tech to keep at it, despite you 'visitors' who always want to repress us. You think we're all programs? Well, some of us like to program too."

He contemplated it for a moment, and then added, "The red lines are the path we should've taken then?"

"Yes. Now we detour. It'll add about half a day, but if I can keep a good pace, it won't matter. The only issue is when we're on the central plain. Skirting the forest side isn't an option. We need the mountains now, and the terrain there is much more uneven. If the Tromoal have been fighting a lot, there could be more debris."

When he met my eyes this time, he whispered, "Thank you. I hope you'll learn to trust me, Maddie."

The next three days with this guy already seemed like it would be a lifetime too much.

I looked back at the road, concentrating and thinking on which route was best out the city. "Don't thank me for anything. In fact, don't talk until we get out of the town and onto the central plains. I need to think."

With that, Alex went quiet.

CHAPTER 4

The city guards let us out through the gates, and we drove southwest. We still had plenty of daylight, and I fully believed we could get through the outer villages and towards Hanson's estate before nightfall. Alex kept quiet, but he fidgeted a lot. I wasn't used to passengers sharing the front of the cab with me. "You going to fidget all the way to Port Troli?"

"Sorry. First ride with a deadly NPC. I'm nervous you're going to kill me."

I almost hit the brakes to dropkick his ass out the door. But when I looked at him, he was still smiling. Something about him made me want to laugh too, so I did. "Please do not call me an NPC." The burning hatred for that term was deep seeded inside my brain from some of my previous encounters.

"Can we talk about this world?" He skimmed his thick head of hair. "I've been quiet enough, but you're the first..." He almost repeated NPC, I was sure of it. "...person who understands all of this." He indicated to the world outside.

"I believe there are very few of us who are aware," I said. "It's not something we often talk about or speak with *visitors*. But we know you're here. We know what you do and why you do it."

"It bothers you?"

I flexed my fingers on the steering wheel, seeing the ring flicker its pink hues around the cab. "What bothers me is that sometimes, there's a lot of damage done because one of you doesn't know what they're doing. This world we live in has many rules, some we don't understand. But they're there. Even for me, the rules are there, my programming is there. It's a constant battle to bypass it."

"But you're getting around it, though. That's very interesting."

I tried to push the thoughts away of the constant battles in my head. Falling in love, the quest... Usually, they come in, I accept, I do them, no questions asked. Now, I ask questions, and I don't always do the quests. The fact I was out of money was the only reason I took this one on, and Dresel knew it.

"When do you need a rest?" Alex let me be silent for quite some time. "I'll do some of the driving if you'll let me."

"And give you access to something I hold dear? No..."

"I won't betray you. Can't you see how sincere I am?"

I watched his eyes. They were the window to his inner being. They didn't tell me he was going to double cross me. "Have you driven one before? It's a bit of a strange thing to get used to with all the modifications."

"I won't know unless I try. When we swap over, maybe you can find a home for this box of goodies. Bag of holding or something?"

I glanced at the floor. I could see how awkward it might be there. "Sorry. I broke my last one, besides I like to see what I have."

"You mean the Creolin?"

"You're an alchemist?"

"I've a few aptitudes I think are useful. If you start to trust me, I can open them up so you can see them."

I thought about it for a little while. Knowing more than his general skills might well come in handy over the next few days. But that also meant he would see everything I was. I hadn't shared myself with anyone in a very long time. Not even Dail.

"You do realise how personal that is, right?"

"Yes." He rubbed his hand down his leather pants. "Sorry, if it's too personal yet. I just thought it might help."

"No, you're right. It might well help. We're doing the most dangerous quest I've done in many years. I just wanted you to realise that if I do let you in, it's been a very long time, and it changes the quest somewhat."

I could see he was confused, but he didn't press. "I understand. The offer is there if you need it."

Spinning the wheel slightly to avoid a pothole, I cursed as the bottles clinked beneath his feet. "I'll pull over as you said. We'll find a safer place for my things. You can take the wheel till we get to Hanson's estate. They're a few hours out. It'll give me a chance to rest for a while if you can handle the Hog."

Alex nodded. "I'll be fine with your instruction." Then he laughed. "I love the name Hog."

"It was his first kill," I said. "Soon after, I obtained ownership. Damned thing nearly killed us both. Ran straight out in the middle of the road, large as an ebolos, and we hit it. The hog bounced off the roll bar, smashed the screen, landing a few hundred feet up the road. When I stopped shaking and made my way out to see what we'd hit, I was shocked. I roped it, strung it to the roof, and we headed home. The local villagers started to run after us as we drove in, shouting for the hog. It kinda stuck."

"Well, it suits him, and you."

I pulled the Hog to the side of the road away from the tree line I'd followed for a while, and Alex hopped out. I stretched my legs, walking around to his side then he handed me the box. "Thanks." I took it, finding a nice place to wedge it with some clothing wrapped around the tops. Taking one of the flasks out, I opened the top and swigged it.

"Does it taste as bad as they say?"

I swallowed, remembering the first time I'd been handed this for pain relief. I grimaced at the memory. "Yes, it's really awful stuff."

"But your hip?"

"I need it, yes. It's addictive to some and has killed many. But I restrict the use, gotta keep my mind clear and my body healing."

"Then I won't ever touch it. Unless I'm in dire straits. Any water in there?"

I pulled out a bottle, handing it over. Our hands touched for the briefest moment. "You're engaged?"

"A little personal for our first day on the road, no?" I seemed to like drawing out his embarrassment and smiled, trying not to be the harsh woman I knew most guys thought I was. "Yesterday, my ex decided he didn't want to lose me ever again, so he gave it to me."

"You accepted his proposal though, right?"

I guess I did. I said I would marry him on my safe return, so I just nodded. "You? Do you have a someone back home?"

He shied away. I for once wasn't sure on getting an answer. "Can we leave my home life out of this?"

I slid past him, deciding myself not to part with any more personal information. "Sure, if that's what you want." He may be good looking, but he was an ass.

The passenger side of the Hog was more comfortable for my hip than driving. I quickly ran through the instructions with Alex. Soon, he was slowly pulling away with a grin on his face. "I'll be fine, just tell me which direction. I'll stick to it."

I flicked the side panel viewer towards him so he could see it better and traced a new red line down the side of the screen. "The little blue image, which is us, is here. Keep following the line, and you'll be okay. Sound good?"

He nodded. "I can do that. Rest your eyes. If you really need to take over later on, you'll feel better."

I wasn't sure if this was a genuine concern of his that I was actually fit enough to drive him, or if it was his need to complete this quest. Maybe a little of both.

I eased back in the seat, drank some water, and closed my eyes. The driving had calmed my thoughts. We were already making some real progress. I had everything we could ever need, so sleep took me. Driving and the rocking motion always made me feel better, I loved being on the road like this. Flitting memories of being with Dail swept through me, turning to dreams.

It was a little while later I noticed the movement of the Hog had slowed somewhat. I opened my eyes, glancing out at the road.

"Welcome back," Alex said. "I was just going to try waking you."

"What's going on?" I asked, noticing the droves of people walking towards us from up ahead.

"I don't know, but it doesn't look so good. Should we pull off the road?"

I nodded, pointing towards an open grassy area. I checked the map. "You haven't deviated at all?"

"No, followed the plan the map directed me on. It seemed easy enough, but getting here, there were more and more people about. Then I saw those ahead."

The number of people was what worried me the most. Hanson's estate had a lot of workers, but not this many. These looked to be refugees by the amount of gear they had strapped to their backs, and the small carts of children they tried their best to push onwards.

"I need to go ahead and ask someone what's going on. Will you stay with the Hog? Do you have any weapons or know how to use them?"

Alex loosened his jacket. I could see two daggers, probably one of which he had at my back earlier. I nodded. "Good. If anyone approaches, don't speak to them, don't say anything about where we're going, or what we're doing. We've no idea who they are, or where they're from, I don't suddenly want us being mobbed on the roadside."

"Is the Hog sturdy enough to stand on?"

"Yes. We modified it a while back. There's a harpoon we'll need to set up later before the plains. It's seen as a threat in the cities. I keep it under the seat until I need it."

"I'll watch you from the rooftop," he said, moving to climb out.

I made sure the Hog was totally secured, and he was safe where he was. I walked to where the nearest approachable person was sitting with her small children.

No sooner had I approached the woman had she grabbed her kids, pulling them to her. I made sure my hands were visible in a gesture to show I meant no harm.

"Hello there," I said. "Mind if I ask what happened? Why are so many people on the road?"

"Hanson refused to put the cattle out early this year. The Tromoal are restless. They started to come in. There was no food for them, so they turned onto the estate."

"What? Why would he be so foolish?"

The smallest of the children started to cry, and the woman hugged her tighter. "I don't know. He'd been going on for months about us not pulling our weight, making us work longer hours for less pay. He'd said there wasn't enough money to buy the extra food for them. When the first Tromoal came looking for dinner, he attacked the nearest farmstead with cattle. Their owners all died in the initial wave. We're not sticking around if he can't provide the food for them, as we would become their food."

A shiver ran through me. This was awful news. "When was the attack?" I knew by the distance we'd travelled it must have been a while ago, but I needed confirmation.

"Two days ago. We've been looking for somewhere to go ever since."

I glanced back at the Hog, worried for Alex, but he was okay, just watching me like he said he would.

"There's not much on this road for miles," I said. "You're better taking the kids and turning east, going across the land into the forest. There are some decent towns out there. Maybe you'll find refuge. But if the Tromoal aren't getting fed, they'll come looking either way. I'm not sure anyone in this region is safe."

The woman looked at her two kids, a girl and her older brother who stood listening. "You can't take them with you, can you?"

I knew this might be an issue. I could see it in her eyes. "I'm crossing the plains. They'd be no better coming with me. Get them east."

I turned, walking back to the Hog, my mind heavy with the worry of our next few days.

Alex hopped down in front of me, his eyes full of concern. "What is it?"

"There's no food for the Tromoal."

I saw his face drop. I moved to the side of the Hog to rest my aching hip on its backdoor.

"What can we do?" I felt the weight of his body ease against the metal work, and I looked out to the horde of people heading our way.

"Our quest doesn't change. We can't do anything for them. I sure can't find food for a thousand Tromoal. We'll drive through them and just keep on going."

"There's no food at all?"

I shrugged. "The woman didn't seem to know, but once the local villages started getting attacked, they thought it best to run."

"Seems odd, don't you think, that there's nothing to give them, with the number of years he's held onto this land?"

"I couldn't agree more. But we don't have time to figure any of it out. I need to get you to Port Troli."

Alex nodded, but his lips curled down. "I wish there was something we could do. There are whole families on the roadside."

I couldn't help it and snapped. "Why the hell do you care? They're no one to you. Just food to keep the Tromoal from biting your ass."

He looked shocked, red rising up the sides of his neck.

I tried to retract it. "Sorry, I didn't mean it. I—"

"Look, Maddie, I don't know what bad experience you've had before with my people, but I promise you, I'm really not like that."

With swift reflexes, Alex opened the back door. He pulled out the package he'd brought with him. The package and virtually nothing but the clothes on his back was all he had with him. "You never asked me what was in the box," he said, handing it to me.

Taking it, I could tell it didn't weight much. I opened it carefully. Inside was a note, a cuddly handcrafted toy, and a jar. Written on the front of the jar was the word Mytoxoloth. "This is a potion for a sick child?"

Alex took the box back from me. "I met her when I first entered Troli. It was my starting city."

I felt my hand shaking, holding onto it with the other. I was really not sure if I wanted to hear any more. My experience with visitors was so vastly different than this. He couldn't be this nice a guy, he just couldn't.

"You didn't need to do this, did you? Take her the potions?"

Alex shrugged. "I was out of my depth. Melee's older sister, Jenni, helped me. I owed her something. When I heard Melee was sick, what she needed and that I was heading back to Troli anyway, I had to pick it up."

"It's expensive," was all I could manage to fumble out. These potions were vastly more costly than the addictive ones I passed about, or even the one I drank daily.

"I know. It doesn't take away how important to Melee and Jenni they are though, does it?"

I watched him put the box back in the Hog. "Come on," he motioned. "We've a long way to go yet."

CHAPTER 5

I drove steadily through the growing tide of people who were leaving Hanson's estate.

There were such vast differences in the appearance of some of them that I wondered what the living conditions were like. Half of them looked starved. How could a guy with his amount of money and power grow so desperate to not feed his staff?

About an hour later, after we'd passed the last of the fleeing workers, I noticed the ground had changed colour. Not so green anymore. Was there a reason things had taken a turn for the worse? Had no one noticed or offered support to Hanson?

Without seeing anything untoward, Alex placed a hand on mine, easing it back from the steering wheel. "You'll injure yourself if you grip it any tighter."

I saw the lack of blood flow as he massaged it gently with his own. I pulled away from him and jerked the wheel to the left. "I've got to go see ole man Hanson. I promise it won't add any time to the journey at all, and then I'll message Dail."

"Dail?"

I tapped the ring on my finger, watching as Alex turned to look out the window.

A moment later, I pulled into the long driveway of the Hanson estate. I'd no idea what I might find or where Hanson might be. Had he abandoned the place like his workers?

I opened the door and was about to get out. "Want some backup?" Alex asked.

I leaned back. "If you let me do the talking."

After he opened his door, getting out, I locked the Hog. We walked together up to the estate's main door, finding it open. I placed my palm on the panel, either way, just to see if anyone answered the call. Nothing.

"His office is on the fourth floor." I stepped inside. "Just keep your eyes open. Maybe we'll find some answers."

The answers I hoped for were strewn around the hallway. Discarded remnants of food jars, pans, even cutlery. This stuff was still worth a fair bit on the trade market.

I edged closer to the stairs. It was eerily quiet. I didn't like it. I took one step up at a time. A beautiful double-edged stairway stretched into one smaller hallway. Then led up three more flights. It had been a while since my last visit, but I knew the layout to his office well enough. My heart rate was rising with the staircase. Coming to the fourth floor, we realised we'd not seen a soul or heard a sound.

The large wooden office door loomed ahead, allowing light into the hall, dust motes floating in it. I loved this home. I'd been here many times crossing the desert. Spent some good days in his bath spars and of course his bars.

Forward I went one step at a time, my hand ready to flick out my blades if anything ran at us. When I got to the door, Alex stopped me. I watched as he took the lead. He stepped inside the room and then popped his head back out. "Maddie, you don't need to see this. I'll go to the desk. There's an envelope on it."

I almost pushed past him but decided to trust his judgment,

catching a whiff of the stench that breezed into the hall. Whatever was in that office was dead and had been for quite some time.

Alex returned a moment later with the opened envelope.

It wasn't addressed to anyone, but it was in Hanson's writing.

I took out the letter, reading it.

"The farm's being poisoned. The cattle are all dying. There's nothing I can do to stop it. We'll all be dead by spring, if not when the Tromoal arrive. There's nothing left. I've tried. I'm sorry."

"He committed suicide. Looks like he took his family with him."

I felt a burning at the back of my throat. "He had three daughters and several grandchildren?"

Alex swallowed and then shivered. "I hope I never see anything like this ever again. Let's get back on the road. There's really nothing we can do here."

I followed him back down. Numb. The stairs seemed steeper than usual. I felt Alex's hand on my back when I wobbled, nearly losing my footing. He helped me into the passenger seat of the Hog, and I strapped myself in tight. Memories flooded my mind, eating with Hanson's family, laughing, drinking. If he could do that to those he loved... I couldn't process it, at all.

I slipped off my ring, instantly feeling the drop in energy and buffs. I placed it on the dashboard. If someone could murder his whole family, then what chance of real love did I have? I was better off without the ring and without Dail. I reached for the only other thing that might ease my pain. Alcohol.

Alex didn't stop me. He started the engine, driving us off the estate, following the alighted path once again, even though it had begun to get dark. I offered him the bottle. "It's fine. You drink. I'll drive for a few more hours, then we'll stop. Sleep."

I took one more swig and put the bottle away. I couldn't get that drunk, or I wouldn't be able to defend us if the situation arose.

I tapped the screen, changing our heading. "Follow this route. It will be even closer to the mountain range, but with the Tromoal looking further inland for food, we'll be safer."

"Their loss is our gain." He sighed, and it was his fingers that gripped the steering wheel this time. I took the plunge and reached for his hand, tugging it off the wheel.

"Neither of us can lose our focus," I said. "We'll get to Troli, I promise you. Melee will have her potions. The quest will be completed."

Alex focused on the road. I let go of his hand. Reaching inside my mind, I called my screen up. I ran through the small list of people I had in my contacts for Dail's personal number. I tapped it with a thought, and it popped open.

I typed the message I wanted to send him, calling off our engagement. Then I deleted it, and I typed: *There's no food at Hanson's estate, everyone there is dead. The workers have abandoned the fields and are heading inland. There's nothing to feed the Tromoal. Get everyone you know to a safe haven, out of the runner's quarters. Stay safe. I'll be there as soon as I can.*

When I hit send, I shivered and reached for the blanket.

I saw Alex shiver too. "Pull over there." I pointed to a small copse of trees. "We'll stop for a while. We'll eat then we'll get some rest. When we're both feeling better, we can drive on."

Alex eased the Hog off the road, under the tree line. I rummaged in the back and found some dry rations. Handing him some of the packs, I opened one myself. It had been a long day.

"Thanks," he said, when I passed him a water flask.

"No, thank you. I think I'd have lost the plot if I had gone in Hanson's office."

"Did you know them well?"

"I've been running through his estate through to Trox for many years. His daughters were about my age. We'd had some fun. The fact he took their lives as well as his own, I can't..."

"I'm sorry," was all he could muster. "Do you have any idea why?"

"I think it's down to shame. He couldn't provide for any of them. He tried, but couldn't. Pride, money and loss, they were all too much. I'm just glad he didn't poison the whole estate. At least when the workers found him, they fled, and then word spread with the attack on the outer fields. It seems this has been going on for some time. There had been some attempt to cover it up. But no amount of that would ever take away the fact that the place here was dying."

"A neighbour trying to start a war? Maybe?" he asked then retracted it. "No, I think that would just mean the Tromoal would make the choices. After all, what are they going to do now?"

"They'll still find food. There's plenty about, just further out of their zones."

"Exactly."

When Alex quieted down, I passed him over half the blanket and the bottle of booze. He took another swig, and I followed with some pain relief.

Sleeping in the Hog had never bothered me mostly because I kept the potions at hand. Had I ever considered I was an addict? Of course. At the earliest stages of my treatment, I was supping it like water. Now, it was barely every few hours, and so there was only a dull ache instead of that constant nagging and the urge to hit someone.

A ping in the side of my vision alerted me to a message.

"Was that an internal message?"

I nodded, not knowing how he knew that and opened the message: *Maddie, what the hell is going on out there? Hanson's dead, his whole family? I can't believe it. Are you okay? Sod taking that damned package. Head back here, now. The Tromoal will be one hundred times more likely to go for the Hog without a food supply.*

"What's he saying?"

I noted the turn in Alex's face. "He wants me to head home, not to follow on with the drop."

Alex nodded. "If you were my fiancée, I admit, I'd want you home too."

I couldn't help but take offence at this and threw the cover off storming out of the Hog. I couldn't take his stupid comments any longer. I pulled open his door, dragging his ass out. "I'm not some

41

feeble woman you know back in your world, Alex. I've been through a lot, and I won't take any shit from some hyped up visitor."

"Hey, hey, calm down."

I wasn't listening to him. I needed to walk, to get rid of him. But Alex followed close behind me.

"I'm sorry. I didn't mean to offend you. Please don't call me a visitor. I'm a player. I came here to escape the things in my world that I can't stand. I try to help, though I don't think I'm doing much of that at the moment."

I saw his breath in the air as he let out a sigh, his green eyes twinkling with the lights from the Hog.

Taking stock of what I'd done, I heard a faint noise at my back. I felt a twinge in my gut. I'd done the one thing I knew I shouldn't, especially at night, opening us up for an attack. There was no way of knowing what kind of creatures were out here with us.

Behind Alex—I saw it. A ghostly shape drifted by. I stepped in closer, pulling his frozen body against mine. I whispered in his ear, "Keep calm. When I tell you to run, you run!"

He didn't answer, but I took a few steps backwards. He followed me. I could hear the beating of his heart in his chest and feel his quickening breath in my ear. Whatever he'd bathed in that morning filled my nostrils. Stupid programming. I pushed those thoughts aside.

"Now!" I shouted. He ran toward the Hog. I heard the door slam. I reached for my blades just as the creature made a run at me.

I sidestepped and slipped the knife in between its shoulders. The bellow it made hurt my ears, but I turned around as I felt its claws rake against my trousers. It, however, didn't make it through to the flesh. Bouncing off my bad hip, I struck once more. This time, I hit it in the face, piercing its eye.

Blood splattered. I yanked hard to get the blade back out. The creature slumped to the ground, not quite dead, but roiling in pain. I took my cue and ran for the driver's side. Alex threw open the door for me. I piled in, catching my hand on the outer metal. Dang! The creature didn't get me, but the Hog did? I swore, slammed the door, and started the engine. "No rest for the wicked, the whole continent would have heard his roar. We need to get as far away from here as possible."

I glanced at Alex who still stuttered, "I—I'm sorry."

"I'm sorry, too, I shouldn't let the past dictate what happens now. Can we start over, really start over?" Alex met my stare with a nod. "Good. Reach under the seat. There's a first aid kit. Get me a bandage and some wipes. You can clean off and wrap it while I drive, okay?"

I watched as he fumbled under the seat then pulled out my small kit. I held out my hand, and he took it gently.

"It's not deep," he said. "But it does look nasty. Was that the creature?"

I laughed. "No, the side of the car."

He started to wrap gauze around it, and it felt better. However, the intimate contact with him didn't. As soon as he finished, I pulled away.

I wasn't sure if I could like him. He's paying me, nothing more. So why did I have a gut ache? I looked over at him, caught his smile, and then I focused on the road ahead.

About an hour later, I found a place to pull in and rest. Driving through the night was never a good thing, even if I knew the terrain.

I turned the engine off and settled back to pull the blanket over me. Alex had fallen asleep a while ago. His snoring settled my nerves. Putting my head back on the rest, I watched as he breathed in and out, the slight mist filling the cab.

The only light now was from the moon. There were several unanswered messages from Dail, but I had ignored them all. When I finally clicked them open, I read the last one only.

The package is a visitor named Alex, I wrote out. *His quest, I can't ignore. Nor will I, or, your debt to the healers guild and my life are forfeit, I'm sure. I'm safe. We've stopped for the night now. I'll message you when we've crossed the desert.*

I knew I'd already said too much. I wasn't sure how he'd react to someone else in the Hog with me, let alone a visitor. The last one we'd both been involved with caused so many problems.

Alex moved under the blanket. I felt his leg brush mine. There

43

wasn't much room in here, but I didn't mind. The heat from us both steamed the windows on the inside.

I turned off notifications so I wouldn't be woken, clicked the *safe* mode on the Hog, and locked all the doors.

Closing my eyes to the night, sleep soon came for me.

I didn't know how long I slept, but Alex gently woke me the next morning. The sun was trying its best to get through the Hog's night windows, a feature I'd paid a lot of money for.

"Sun's up. Thought we'd best drink, eat, and get back on the road."

I nodded and took a breakfast ration from him, then slugged back a load of water. "I'll just be a few," I said, exiting the Hog to relieve myself—behind the nearest bush or tree. When I got back to the Hog, Alex left too, no doubt for something similar. I wished there'd been a function for us to not have to go. But, yeah, peeing in a bush, great fun.

I programmed the Hog for daylight driving, watching the tinted windows lighten so we could see ahead.

"I love this vehicle," he said. "Looks like something out of a movie, but it's so much more versatile than anything I'd ever dreamed of."

I grinned. "In total, this has cost me more money than most people spend in their entire lifetime."

"Damn, I can see why. You and the Hog are unique."

That we were, and the quests we took on were too. Everyone knew it. Don't mess with Maddie and the Hog.

The road ahead was littered with boulders as we edged off the forest trail and back closer to the mountains. No matter where we were, the heat from the desert and the fact it was summer plagued us. I tapped the control system and cranked up the air con, even though I knew it used more fuel. We needed the respite.

Alex looked out to the beyond, and asked, "What does a Tromoal look like?"

"They're huge," I replied. "The females are bigger and heavier than the males. They're sleek and fast, but the females are in charge. The males do their bidding, so they're wild on approach and quick to hit you with fire."

"Fire?"

I nodded. "They have both abilities—that of red-hot fire and of ice —both are deadly."

"Wow, ice as well. I can't imagine getting struck with a fireball let alone something made of ice."

"That's the one that got me. Fire would have burned my skin, the ice penetrated into the bone in thick slices. Worse than being hit with a thousand daggers all at once."

"And they fly?"

"Yes. They're born only to land when they breed or feed. Otherwise, they retreat to Trofoth. We believe their lands are a mixture of solids and air-based floating islands."

"Trofoth is the place where no one's been so far." Alex nodded back to where we'd come from, although Trofoth was much further away and many hours in the water or on land.

"No, there are only rumours of people living on Trofoth. Maybe one day I'll get to travel the seas and see where it takes me, but not now."

"Why not? Is it because of Dail?"

Were my travel plans on hold because of him? I'd not thought of that. I'd refused to marry him. Yet I'd stuck around as a runner, using my excuse of the potions to tie me to the village. I glanced to my ring, it was still on the dashboard. Really, I knew I'd been scared to head out alone. What if I couldn't find fuel for the Hog? What happened if, and if—

Alex shrugged. "Sorry, just trying to understand the creatures we'll have to face."

"I don't think facing them is an option. I'm going to try to sneak in without them even scenting us. I don't want to tackle one, even a young male or female."

"Understood, they sound like mythical creatures we call dragons.

They fly, breathe fire, and are nasty. Do you know if anyone has ever tamed one?"

I laughed at this. "You're one crazy player." When I realised he hadn't been kidding, I added, "There are rumours for every occasion, for the people who actually live with them on Trofoth, and for the individuals who have managed to kill one. Yes, even to tame one and to fly on their backs. But I wouldn't believe any tale that involved one. If you see them up close, you will know and understand why we don't go near them."

Alex nodded, rubbing his wrists. "Understood. I just think we players like the sound of them. They're a challenge."

"That challenge will get you killed." I noticed the grin but then laughed. "You said you didn't want to die. What is it like?"

"From the day I woke in this world, I knew it was going to be a bad thing. I came close that first day when I met Jenni and her sister. I'd picked the wrong city location. There were gangs of players waiting to kill me for all the wrong reasons. If Jenni hadn't saved me from that beating, I wouldn't have made it past day one in Puatera."

"I can see why you want to repay the favour."

He smiled. "They were the nicest kids I've met, so yeah, when I heard she wasn't going to live without this potion. I had to get it for her."

"No matter the cost to you?"

I could see why he'd taken this quest. This quest to Port Troli wasn't just because of politics, whatever the politics really were—they were a side quest compared to getting the potions to his friend.

There was no answer to my question, and that made me even more curious about his circumstances. What man would risk all for a child, especially a visitor?

I reached out placed my hand on his, squeezing. "Then I'm glad I didn't back out and that we're doing this. The potions will save her life."

Our eyes locked for quite some time. I didn't move or pull away. I wanted him to be close to me. Then I reminded myself, he was a visitor.

He'd do this quest, then be gone. What was going on in my head? Stupidity. He wouldn't stick around. Not for me.

I pulled my hand away and focused on the driving. "Get some rest, while you can," I said. "You can drive in a little while."

But he didn't settle. He reached over, tugging my hand back to his. "Don't take this personally, I'm freezing. I could do with the body heat."

I panicked as I looked at him and noticed how much he actually was shivering. "Did you get caught by anything? What did you touch in the estate?"

Panic filled my veins as I noted the colour to his cheeks. They were pale blue. I stopped the Hog dead. Pushing myself back in the chair, I slid over the gear stick to sit on his knee wrapping my arms around him to pull him tight against me. He really was cold. I could just reach into the back of the cab, to where he'd placed the alchemist's box. I rummaged around in it. I found what I needed, dragging it towards me. I popped the lid.

"You need to drink this. Now."

"W-w-wha-at is it?" he stammered. "W-w-ha-a-at's wr-ong w-with m-e-e?"

I didn't have any real answer, but I wasn't waiting until he turned completely blue and passed away. I put the vial to his lips, forcing him to drink. Rubbing his throat so he'd actually swallow, and then I curled around him.

"Close your eyes, think of how warm you are. Don't let the cold inside anymore."

"It hurts," he stammered.

I blew my breath across his brow. "I know, but you can feel me against you, yes?"

"You're so warm... I'm not pervy, I swear." I felt his hands reach up inside my jacket. They were so cold. I wanted to slap him across the head. How dare he touch me like this, but I also knew he needed it. "Shh, it's okay. I won't hold it against you."

"Maddie," he whispered. His voice low, so low.

"Yes."

"Don't let me die. I don't want to die. I want to live, live better than I ever have. Do so much, life sucks back home. Let me live."

I leaned in, placing my face to his, letting the cold seep across me. My warmth settled into him. "You are living," I replied. "You can do anything you want here. I'll support you. You're my friend and charge. I'll get you to Troli. Melee will get her potions. We'll be home before you know it."

CHAPTER 6

*W*aking sometime later, I tried to move. Couldn't. Sleeping wrapped around another human being in the Hog was not a good idea.

I pulled on the door catch and sprawled out onto the desert floor. The jolt made my hip hurt all the more.

I bit down, trying my best not to swear. Forcing myself to stand, though the pain in my leg and hip was horrendous, I slammed my hand on the roof, cursing.

I felt Alex wake as the Hog moved. "Sorry," I muttered.

When he poked his head out the door, at least he had more colour than he did last night. He reached down to pass me one of my flasks. "Here," he said passing it to me.

I took a swig then downed a lot more than I probably should have. "How are you feeling?"

"Like I said things last night I shouldn't have."

I looked away because he had. He'd said too much, and I'd felt a lot more than I should have. Damned programming. But then, remembering how this time, I didn't want to fight the programming, I almost let out a laugh. I covered my mouth before he tugged my arm back to look at him.

"Don't be mean."

"I should feel weird about being so close to you last night," I said, drinking in his stunning green eyes. "But I don't."

I wasn't sure what emotion I saw, his eyes twinkling and darted left to right, but I don't think he knew either. I was the one who turned, walking away. I needed to stretch out and get the feeling back in my body.

I also wanted to take in the surroundings, to see where I'd actually driven us. We were slightly off where I'd wanted us to be and time was ticking.

Getting my bearings didn't take long as I heard a humongous bellow above us. Instantly, I flattened on the ground, hoping the Tromoal hadn't spotted the Hog or me. I flipped myself over and pulled my goggles over my eyes.

I could just make out the creature in the sky, its long wingspan flowing around it for what looked like miles. This one was the largest I'd ever seen. The underbelly of the creature was so huge. I realised suddenly this was a female. I swallowed, not just a female... *The female!* I was looking at the underbelly of the matriarch, the biggest of them all. I clicked a tiny side button on the goggles and zoomed in so I could see her in all of her glory.

The details of her scales were stunning. Reds and blues mixed with silver and black edges. The more I watched her, the more I was in awe. Then I noticed. Her belly actually moved, but they didn't bear live young. They had eggs... What the...? I patted myself on the back for money spent well on this enhancement.

I felt something at my side. Alex poked my ribs. "Everything okay?"

I looked at him. His face went right out of view until I pulled the goggles off. The Tromoal had passed over. We'd not been seen.

I smiled at him, noting the features on his face, deep laugh lines and the odd grey hair. "I just saw the matriarch. She's huge! But something was off." I pushed myself up, and he helped me to my feet. "Let's not hang around as the rest of the gang will be on their way too. They're never far behind her."

"How many usually come to the plains?"

"I think there have been counts in the hundreds, maybe a thousand. Usually not many volunteers for that kind of research."

"Yeah, not sure I'd want to get too close."

"You know you're going to regret saying that." I moved to the driver's side and pointed for him to get in. "Breakfast is on the move. We've got a lot of ground to cover today. She's at least going in the opposite direction, so that's a good thing."

Alex climbed back into the Hog, and I pulled us out slowly, getting us back to some semblance of our route. The Hog bounced a little too much, but the pain relief spread through me. I wasn't worried. Alex hung onto the side door and the dashboard.

"Not scared of a few bumps, are you?"

I watched as his face frowned, then he laughed at me. "No, it's just women drivers, you know, they suck."

Oh, I saw a nice pothole... which I aimed for. "We suck, huh?"

He reached over, placing his hand on mine, easing me away from all the holes. When he let go, I flexed my fingers on the wheel and concentrated on what I actually needed to do. Drive.

The plains started to stretch ahead. The Hog dipped down then rose again to let Alex see how truly vast they were. He let out a gasp. "I never knew..."

"They're something else entirely, aren't they?"

He rummaged around for something then pulled out a set of binoculars. Looking through them, he spoke openly, "I'd not expected this, no."

"Nor me. I remember the first time I saw the plains. I was coming down here on an ebolos back with Dail."

I knew he was gazing at the colours. The veins that stretched through the miles of the desert were something unique. Many came here to view them alone. Some tried to do more than mine the cave systems, but at this time of year, they had something else inside them, something the Tromoal needed for their young, then something we could harvest after they'd left. *Hismaw.*

The cave systems that also ran alongside the veins were noticeable even from this distance. I pointed to the left central vein, its silver and purple lights flickering into the sunlit sky. "Most of the Tromoal will inhabit those systems there. They offer great places to shelter and hatch their young. I'd imagine the matriarch will be leading them there later, after feeding."

"There's nothing for them to feed on though."

I knew that and hoped they would find a herd of forest creature, or something else, preferably not the humans who had left the estate. I couldn't do anything about it now. I had to keep driving and hope Dail would get word to the other cities that they needed to keep livestock away and set out some sacrifices.

"I think they'll be back soon enough. There's usually a two-week mark from them arriving for their egg birth, then another week before they feed once more to return to Trofoth."

"Let's hope this journey is quick. I really don't want to be here if they return."

I drove faster. "We'll be fine."

I wished I hadn't opened my mouth, though. No sooner had we managed to get on the flat of the longest stretch of the desert when the passenger front tire burst and Alex screamed.

The wheel spun to the left, causing the Hog to swerve. I just managed to stop it from rolling over, but my heart pounded in my chest... I slammed the steering wheel, flinging the door open.

"Have we a spare?" Alex asked joining me on the desert flat.

"Of course, I carry two. But this is not good. I pointed to the sky, noting there were quite a few clouds in the distance. "Do you know how to change one?" He nodded. "Under the driver's seat."

He moved quickly. I could see the panic in his eyes as he jacked the Hog up. I helped him with the main nuts, then found the spare under all the equipment we'd stashed.

Distant rumbling spurred me on. I knew this wasn't any ordinary rain storm. "Faster," I said.

The wheel came off a moment later, and I put the new one on. Alex dropped the jack then tightened all the nuts—just as I could see several tiny black spots appearing behind us. I jumped in the cab, and Alex followed me. I hit the gas, the Hog roared to life, and I floored it.

"How fast are they?"

"I told you where the harpoon was, right?"

He nodded. "I can't shoot. My aim is awful."

"Then you'll have to drive if we need it. Okay?" I pulled the goggles from my head and passed them to him. "Use these. There's a catch on the right side. It will zoom in. Keep me informed on their progress."

He slipped them over his head, and for a second, I had an even closer look at his eyes. They were green, but also, there was something else there. A fleck of red? I'd no idea what that meant, but I'd only ever seen people from my world with that problem. I pushed the thought aside as he started his running commentary, letting me know what was going on ahead.

"They're not gaining on us. They seem to be heading east."

"No." I let out a sigh. They were going to the one place I hoped they wouldn't, where I'd just sent half the estate's refugees.

"That's the forest area, isn't it?"

"There's nothing we can do. Nothing."

Tears burned my eyes, their hot wetness dripping down my cheeks. I wanted nothing more to do with this darned mission. Aiding him meant so many lives I could have helped and now would be lost.

"I'm sorry," Alex said. "I wish there was something we could do. Can we save them if we go back? Maybe this quest wasn't meant to be."

I shook my head. There was no going back. We'd most likely die with the refugees. I felt a finger brush my tears away. I snatched his hand from my face. I did not let go though. I placed it between us and just held onto him while the dirt and dust billowed behind us.

I was sure the Tromoal could see the trail, but they had other thoughts—they needed food. They'd not survive being here without it, then I guess neither would Puatera. That thought was as erratic as I felt. What if? No, I pushed it away. Dail would get them as much of a supply as he could. They'd be okay there, and it would be enough for them. They'd lay their eggs, stick around till they hatched, then they'd be gone. Nothing unusual. Just a little harder on our community.

While the sun stayed high, I drove as fast as possible. The plains were chiselled almost like pure glass out of a furnace. Polished by the years of Tromoal fire and ice breath. There was a fine dusting of what I called sand, but I don't actually think it was. I believed it to be leftover remnants of the egg shells.

Finally, my hand grew tired on its own, so I let go of Alex's hand. He looked my way and asked, "Hungry?"

Then he reached back, digging out some rations. I chugged down the water faster than I should have, and it went up my nose. I choked, and the wheel moved slightly. "Easy there." He patted my back while I coughed.

"Thanks." I pointed up ahead. "We've made it almost halfway. There's a cave system we have to stop in there. Usually, there's no Tromoal about. We can tuck in, and the Hog can rest while we do, then after they've returned and settled in for the night, we'll go the rest of the way."

"We can't do it all in daylight?"

"No, the Tromoal never stay out all day. They tire easily because of their weight. Heavy females aren't good at flying too much."

"I guess so. Have you ever seen an egg?"

"Yes. The first time I came out here, I stopped in a cave that had their attention. It took me a few trips to work out where they didn't rest. I was mesmerised at the sheer size of them, but also because they're almost see through."

"Really? I'd never thought about that. Usually, dragon eggs are solid."

"They're not dragons, though. Your creatures aren't what we have here. Our world is vastly different."

He grinned, and I wanted to ask why but didn't follow through. I knew players sometimes spouted out stuff to do with programming. The only programming I was used to was what we did with the Hog and her systems. They almost had a mind of their own. Then wondered if that was how we started out. Did we all have minds that worked like mine? Or were we all just programs, like I'd been programmed to fall in love so quickly. I shuddered.

I was silent in my thoughts for a while. "Alex?" I asked. "I know we're called NPCs, that we're characters. But do you feel that I'm just a character in this world?"

"Honestly..." He stared at me, and I kept looking back as I drove on. "No," he finally said. "There'd been rumours that the AI system had been developing, that some of the people had become semi-sentient. That they were doing things not scripted, designing things that the programmers had never even dreamed of before."

"That scares you?"

"It might make some vast changes to my world if it's true."

"How would you decide it was true?"

He looked away from me this time. I could tell he was nervous. The way he rubbed his trousers smooth. Something he'd done quite often since getting inside the Hog.

Alex's eyes met mine once more with a fierceness I'd not previously seen. "The only true way to know if you are real is if you die and respawn to carry on with life as you know it or if you actually remembered anything."

I thought about it for a moment. "I could have died with the Tromoal many years ago. I didn't. At least, I don't think I did."

I eased off the gas, negotiating closer to the rock formations in the caving system. I knew it so well, I didn't need to concentrate on it much —where to drive, where the floor dipped, and where I needed to brake on the way in.

I slid the Hog into the hole, turning off the engine. "Take the light, look around, and make sure nothing else has moved in for us. I'll unpack and reload the back of the Hog seeing as we made such a mess."

Alex opened the door and slid out. I could see him stretching in the light from the Hog's headlights, but I would need to turn them off soon. It wasn't good to let our only battery drain. No, I never had a spare on that. It was a bad thing if... I pushed the thought out my head straight away, though and then went to turn off the lights.

I wasn't chancing it.

I wanted to shout to him, but maybe he'd realise something was up when it went dark. He came back over to me with the light shining on my face. "Saving the batteries?"

I nodded. "Shine the light for me. I'll unpack us enough to settle in for a few hours."

He did so, and I was quick to move everything around, then re-packed it. We'd done really well without the need for many things. I knew I was always over cautious, but that wasn't a bad thing, was it? The sleeping clothes and packages I knew I needed for the cave, so I hauled them out and over towards the edge of one of the walls. I set them up, throwing the blankets over them.

When I looked at Alex, he blushed. "Don't worry, you're not freezing to death now. You'll be safe in your own bed."

I walked back to the Hog, pulling out a small box. This had a special light inside to heat up a package of food. All I needed was water... and we had plenty of that.

I moved to the largest of the water butts and turned the tap.

Nothing came out. *What?*

I tried to lift it. I'd put it in the Hog, so I knew it was full. It lifted right out of the seat. A slight amount of water at the bottom rattled inside it.

I swallowed. Maybe there was a hole in the tank, but that seemed impossible. They'd been stored really well.

"Something up?"

I motioned to the seats where he'd stuck his head in. "How many flasks of water do we have left?"

He shrugged and moved to count them. "Seven."

"Fuck." I actually swore. "I don't know how. I don't understand this. It's empty?"

Alex picked up the tank and shook it also. "It was full when you put it in?"

"I packed it myself, yes."

"Then this is the strangest thing. It seems intact." He turned it over on its side, allowing the last bit of water to float till he saw a drip. There was a puncture hole.

I took the light from him shining it at its edge and saw it. Inside the water was a creature... "Did you drink from the bottles in the boot or from here yesterday?"

He thought for a moment. "No, I refilled the water when you were stretching, after the estate affair."

I cursed. "This was put here on purpose. That thing is a water Vilous."

"A what?"

"It drinks and uses water to survive, but it leaches a poison. They're extremely rare, very valuable."

"And deadly, if the way I was feeling is anything to go by."

"Extremely."

"So who did this?"

"I could only think of someone who wanted your mission to fail. I was warned it was highly political, the information you are passing on."

"It might seem that way to some people, but it's not. It's nothing but new trading routes, ways to get better access before and after breeding season. Easier for everyone to harvest the Hismaw and for us to re-sell it to others on Puatera."

"So its value is more because it's countrywide?"

"I guess so." Alex put the bottle outside the cab, looking around. "Do we have enough water to get to Port Troli?"

I shook my head. "No. When the heat rises today, we'll need at least that. Then we have all day tomorrow to travel before we get to any of the nearest water holes."

"No other backups?"

57

I leaned on the Hog. "There's only one choice." I sighed.

"What... that sounds rather dangerous."

"It is. It means we've got to go into the other cave systems. There's a waterhole deep below us."

"There's a catch, right?"

"There's a hell of a catch. Unless we're quick, the Tromoal will be back."

CHAPTER 7

I placed my goggles over my eyes. They had enough of an upgrade for me to see in the dark. Alex didn't have any, so he was on his own. If we used flashlights and discovered something untoward, then they'd have the upper hand on us, and that would totally freak him out. I prayed we had enough skins to fill. The one with the poison inside would be tainted, it wasn't viable anymore. I didn't think I could take a hit like he had. I knew I didn't have any major healing potions left.

The ground ahead of us was so damp it was like the tide had recently gone out.

I went through all the twists and turns in my mind. I remembered pausing at two small intersections to finally think which way was correct. While I was deep in thought, Alex never spoke. He just followed me, as close as humanly possible without actually touching me.

I could hear the slight water trickle ahead. I wanted to hurry this up. Flashes of the past invaded my mind, my soul. The water, the cavern, the loot... then the Tromoal. I'd been terrified, and I'd run only to meet a couple of youngsters outside the cave. That's when my life changed forever. I'd tried to retreat but I couldn't. Then all I could do was defend myself, but I couldn't.

Rounding the next corner, I finally noticed the stream. It was nice to see. I hoped things would be fine from now on.

No sooner had we got to the side of the water's edge, and he started to drink. "That thirsty?"

He nodded. "I didn't want to be any trouble and ruin the supply we had."

"If you're thirsty, drink," I said. "There's no point trying to halt what will come. We're lucky." He obliged, and I added. "Fill what you can, drink what you need to, and then we'll soon be on our way again."

Alex moved to fill the flasks and canisters he had while I did the same. That's when I noticed he'd seen the other caving system. "What's down there?"

"That's where the Tromoal usually start to lay their eggs. It's a huge open cavern exposed only in summer. The water level otherwise fills the whole system."

"You're kidding. It's only exposed once a year?"

I nodded. "That's why they come here, some mineral they get from the rock formations, something they then put back with the Hismaw."

"You've seen it?"

I smiled. "A long time ago, yes."

"Seems like loot heaven to me." I remembered all the stuff lying around the caving system. "Why do you think most visitors come out here and die?" He nodded, eyes gleaming. "But the drag-Tromoal aren't back yet. Can I take a look?"

I wanted to curb his curiosity. There was no good ending here. It had been a while since I'd actually been in there myself, so what harm could there be?

"We can look in but nothing else, right?"

I watched as his eyes lit up. He nodded eagerly, much too eager. Leaving the water canisters, we edged in towards where the water level faded away, and the entrance to the main caving system came into view.

Alex was ahead of me this time, and when he stepped through, I heard him gasp. Then he asked, "Can I use your goggles, just for a moment?"

If I'd had a spare pair, I would have gladly given them to him. I tugged mine from my face, passing them over. I waited for him to give me the go-ahead then followed him inside.

"I've never seen anything this amazing before. There's stuff everywhere!"

"What kind of stuff?"

"Gems, armour, magical loot, everything and anything. Players would kill for this location!"

"Yeah." The more excited he got, though, the more my nerves twitched. I danced from one foot to the other. "Or the players were killed for... you know we should go, right?" I tugged his arm, but he didn't budge. So I yanked instead.

"Wait!" he scolded me. "What's that?"

I couldn't see what he was looking at, but I followed his gaze, then he passed me the goggles. "Right at the far edge of the room."

I put them back on, focusing to where he'd pointed. "Oh no."

"What is it?"

I tugged his arm and said, "We're leaving. Keep close behind me."

"Maddie, what is it?"

"They're already laying. That's the first batch of eggs. Four of them in total."

"They are Tromoal eggs?"

"High-end eggs... move. *Now!*" I started to run, my breath catching in my throat.

We couldn't stick around at all. That clutch was... Alex was moving way too slow behind me. We picked up the water.

"They're not going back yet. What's the problem?"

I slowed down as we made our way back to the Hog. "Sorry, it's just been a long time, but that was the matriarch's clutch. She would never leave them."

"What?"

61

"If she's laid eggs, she's in this cave system, somewhere!"

I reached the final opening and was about to run through when I heard it... the low grumble of something ahead of us made me reach back, stopping him.

"Is that what I think it is?" I heard Alex whisper behind me.

I shooed him back. "You have to stay here."

He obeyed. Crouching down, I slowly edged forward enough so I could see the Hog. There squatting over it, like the humongous creature I knew she was, was the matriarch. Her scales, larger than my head, overlapped each other for the ultimate protection. Where they met, there was a hint of the colour beneath. Intricate silver veins ran through them and pulsed with her life force. I wanted to go forth and touch them, to feel her, but the fact she would rip me to shreds, just like before, stopped me.

I watched cautiously, crouching as low as I could go. She didn't do anything to the Hog. She just moved over it sniffing the air. Then she stomped over towards the entrance, stretched her wings, and just like that, she was gone.

I couldn't breathe, though. My brain and my body needed the oxygen, but I couldn't do it. Alex moved behind me, grabbing my arm. "Maddie, she's gone. Let's get back to the Hog and go."

"We can't go just yet. She's not gone far. If we move, she'll be back sooner than you know it." I looked at him, and the light from the front of the cave just made me able to see how scared he really was. "We have to wait it out. There's no option."

He reluctantly leaned back on the wall, crossing his arms.

"She... I've never seen anything like that before, ever. Why didn't she smash the Hog to pieces?" I paced the area before him, my instinct was to run, but my head won for now.

I really had no answer to my own questions. Alex also didn't have any. "I thought there might be something, maybe outside? Maybe she was hungry or could smell the critter in the water tank?" I could just make out the features of his frown.

After I thought we had waited long enough, I moved with Alex to the front of the Hog. There was nothing different in his makeup. I'd not changed anything in the last few years at all, and there had been Tromoal attacks on me many a time. Then I saw it—the ring glinting on the dashboard.

I put the new water supplies in the back and pulled out one of my silver flasks, taking a nice hit of my pain potions. My problem was I needed more. Was it a weak solution? No, just tolerance, no doubt.

I pushed my thoughts aside, moving to our rest area. We packed up the hog to move it. It wouldn't be far so it shouldn't take long. Getting in the driver's seat, I noticed my ring on the dash again. I picked it up and put it back on my finger. It would be safer on me, I was sure.

Finally, when we were set up once more, I sat cross-legged and placed my head against the cool metal of the Hog, closing my eyes. It was tough, but I really was trying to stop things from hurting, my hip, my head.

"Can I take a better look?"

I stared at him. "What do you mean?"

"Your hip. I know a little about anatomy. Maybe I can help."

I laughed at him. "The best healers in the village and cities couldn't tell me anything. What makes you think you will know anything about my body?"

"You asked me to trust you earlier. To do everything and anything you asked of me. Trust me. I think I have something to help."

"You're not just trying to get my pants off then?"

Alex blushed. He was so easy to wind up that I laughed at him. "I'll trust you, but it's not pretty."

Alex moved back to the Hog, opening the box he brought with him. He rummaged inside, and then pulled out something I'd not seen, an envelope. He brought it over to me and motioned towards my hip. "Please."

I checked my Health status.

HEALTH – 70%

TROMOAL POISON – MINUS FIFTEEN POINTS TO
HEALTH EVERY THIRTY-SIX HOURS.

It was easier for me to stand, unzipping my pants once more. This time, it felt weird because Alex moved in much closer to me. He tugged them down. I knew the scarring was ugly. Three puncture wounds to my thigh, hip and belly. I was told the Tromoal that got me was young because of the spacing of the teeth, but it didn't feel that young when it was tossing me about.

I couldn't watch what he was looking at or going to do. When he touched my skin and ran a finger down from my belly to my thigh, I shivered. I'd not expected my body to respond quite so quickly. The truth was I was totally turned on by this.

Alex did something else. He took my hand in his, squeezing hard so that I would look. "I can see the bones shattered, here and here." He touched the areas where I experienced pain. Then he placed his other finger to my hip bone. "Most of the damage is deep inside, though, where all the muscles and sinews connect from the upper body to the lower. You were mostly ripped in half on this side. I'm surprised there's still connecting tissue. That's why there's so much pain."

"So, what do you think you can do that no one else could?" Finally, I looked at him, seeing the concern on his face, his hand still gently squeezing mine.

"I was going to let Jenni have this in case the potions didn't work. The last resort. But she'd have to find another player to use it on her."

I observed him. "I don't..."

Alex opened the envelope and pulled out what was inside. I could only barely make out the edge of the star-shaped paper.

He placed his lips on the paper, whispered words I had never heard. A language maybe? "*Treonn, mo sipplex*, Maddie." He folded the star, and then folded it again, popping it into his mouth. The green in his eyes started to change, the red flecks growing.

"You're more than human?" I asked. "What are you, a mage?"

He shook his head and then leaned in as he gripped hold of my trousers to pull me closer. He then placed his lips on my hip.

I was about to pull back, to try to move, but found my body wouldn't obey. There was a red glow about the whole of his head now. I could feel his breath against me. Then there was a spark. Something ignited inside me. Pain. I stifled a scream by clamping a hand over my mouth, slapping him on top of his head, but he didn't let go. The pain started to subside, but shocking me more than that was his grip had changed, and he moved to my ass. "Hey," I managed to get out, but then a sting of heat spread from his fingers through to my hip, then out the other side. As if he was drawing the pain from me into him. Whatever this was, it was the weirdest thing I'd ever seen or experienced.

Then, he let go and moved back from me to spit out the folded paper star. It wasn't white anymore but red—red with black spots.

Alex sank back, his eyes as blood red as the paper and my scarred flesh. I tugged my trousers up, feeling self-conscious as his eyes never left my partly naked flesh.

I kneeled in front of him. There was still an intense pain in my side, but it did feel different. "What did you do?"

"It was a hope and a prayer that maybe in a couple of days you'll start to feel different. I nudged your destroyed muscles and cells into re-growth."

"Your eyes, though?"

"They'll stay like that for a while, depends on the injury I tried to heal. I had two stars, that was all. A rare find from completing a dungeon quest last month."

"I don't know what it will do, but thank you for trying. Can you see at all?"

He shook his head as I moved my hand in front of his face. He didn't even blink. Oh crap. "I hope it wears off fast. We might need your eyes in a few hours."

I helped him to sit better, tugging the blanket around him. "But this is a good time for rest, so close your eyes." I pulled my own blanket over me, moving to curl up. I then felt him shift and move beside me. "Not being pervy now?"

He laughed. "No, I just need some comfort, something to hold." The feel of his strong arm around me didn't scare me. I allowed him to move closer because I wanted him too.

"Okay, but remember." I held up the ring finger for him to see. Even though he couldn't.

"He's one lucky guy."

That was a guess, right? That he saw me do it. I wanted to agree, but there was something that didn't, that really didn't. Guilt flooded my veins as I moved to entwine our fingers.

I felt how close he was to me, but said nothing.

"Maddie," he whispered, his breath tickling my ear.

"What?" I didn't mean to sound so rude, I just couldn't help it. I had all this confliction inside me.

"Do you love him?"

I searched inside for that answer, but there really wasn't one. "It's complicated."

"More complicated because I'm here?"

My mouth opened, saying the word, "Yes," before I knew it.

"I didn't mean to upset things. You know that, right?"

I squeezed his hand a little. "I know. I'm not sure I have the time to tell you everything."

I felt him move in closer. "I don't know if I have time, either. But I'm here now."

I didn't know what he meant. I really didn't want to go through everything I was thinking or feeling. "Sleep," I said. "We both need it."

I couldn't see any of his disappointment in the fact I wouldn't talk, but I sensed it. How I knew or felt it was vague to me.

Within a moment, I felt his breathing change, and he was asleep. I was able to rest my eyes and drift off for a while.

CHAPTER 8

*I*t was the smell of hot coffee that brought me around. I wondered where he had gotten the beans. Maybe that box of his had a lot more in it than healing magic.

I stood, easing the blanket around me, trying to tame my long, knotted hair. There were no big mirrors out here in the desert, just the Hog's rear view and side mirrors. I most likely looked awful. But I spun the still knotted mess around and tried to tie it in my usual ponytail.

Alex glanced my way, holding out the coffee, so I took it.

It smelled divine. I took a sip before I asked, "Where did you get this?" It had been so long since I'd tasted such heaven in a cup.

"I have my sources. Did you sleep okay?"

I stretched my hip and back, checking my stats.

TROMOAL POISON – MINUS FIVE POINTS TO HEALTH
EVERY THIRTY-SIX HOURS.

It was better than the minus fifteen yesterday.

There was still some degree of pain, so I guess whatever he did wasn't working. I sighed inwardly and tried not to over think it. Long shot at best. I mean how many broken people had he actually tried to put back together, even if it had been the most beautiful thing I'd ever experienced.

"We need to get going after this." I blew on the hot black liquid, enjoying the flavour as it exploded on my taste buds. I savoured it and stared into his amazing green eyes.

He held up his hand. "I'm sorry. I shouldn't have asked you those questions. I would hate to hurt anything you've got going here. This is your world. I'm just a visitor."

Bellowing sounds of Tromoal drifted through the caving system, I glanced to the Hog. "We need to move now. I don't think it will be long before they're moving in here as well."

He packed the few items we'd used to sleep in. I drained my coffee cup then got into the Hog.

Alex looked focused. "We're almost there, right? A few hours driving at most?"

I nodded and started the engine. "We'll be there soon enough. Don't panic." Backing out of the cave into the dimming light of the day, I wished the journey was longer.

This next part of the day seemed the easy part. To drive the last forty miles or so of the plain. To be so close to Port Troli had my head spinning. But why was I anxious?

Alex had a quest to do when I dropped him off. Getting him there safe and sound was my job. I would be paid the rest of my money, and I could return home to figure out what the hell Dail and I were gonna do about the hungry Tromoal.

I waited till the moon started to rise, and I could see the glint in Alex's eyes. Sheer determination filled us both. We weren't that far out from the city. No matter how much I wanted the quest over, I didn't want it to end. Not really.

"What will you do after you get the healing potions to Jenni and her sister?" I probed, wondering on his answers, his real thoughts.

"I'm delivering the treaty to the council and the members of the guild. The mayor of Trox City wants to negotiate some aspects."

"You think it's really about the treaty?"

"I can only hope. There's no other way we can do it, without war. Everyone wants something different."

I thought back to the Runner who stopped me at the Inn. I couldn't believe this was a way out.

"Alex, is there a backup plan?"

He shrugged. "I don't think so."

"So this is it? For both of us. What happens if it goes wrong? I mean majorly."

He tensed and squirmed in his seat. "You're thinking about war between the two cities."

"Yes," How could he not understand? That frustrated the hell out of me. "I have people I care about in both. I need to be sure they'll be okay."

"I don't think there is any *okay* with war."

I totally understood him there. I didn't think there was a way out.

"You'll go where you are needed next." I sighed. "Is there anything else I can do to help?"

When I saw him shrug, I felt pain. Something deep inside me hurt. Why? Why did I want him to still need me?

"Alex..." My words trailed off. He took my hand in his, cradled it to his chest, and I choked. I didn't speak again, though. What I wanted to say, what I needed to say, there were no words for it, for us.

Oh... no. I thought it. I actually wanted him as more than a friend— a charge, a lover. I knew I never loved Dail the same way and that made this all the harder.

Not realising it, I twisted and turned Dail's ring around and around. Alex stopped me. I linked his fingers with mine once more and moved to place his hand on my leg. An intimate move from me.

"There's so much I need to tell you," he said, lowering his head. "I just don't know where to start."

"It's the same for me... But Dail... I just... I need to tell him, I can't."

"Maddie, I'm..." We both saw the large black dot ahead. The clouds darkened, sheets of rain pounded the sands. I noticed lightning strike the ground and felt the rumble as it did so.

"Alex," I ordered, there was no time for talking. "Take the wheel you'll need to drive."

It wasn't easy to swap while moving, but I managed to slip out from the driver's seat with him in my place. I made it to the back seat, pushing myself up and out of the roof slit and climbed into the back.

The guns were locked, loaded, and ready in moments. I pulled the goggles over my eyes, watching the clouds for any signs. I almost sensed there would be Tromoal up there. Where there be storms, there be hunting grounds for monsters as they searched for food.

I didn't know what kind of food they might be trying, but I hoped it wasn't people food.

"What's got you so worried?" Alex shouted.

My eyes never left the horizon. I scanned slowly as I answered him, "If the Tromoal didn't find their food from the estate, there's only a couple of other places they know where large amounts of stock are kept. The port is one of them."

"Fish?"

"Food of any kind. There's lots of trade going on just outside the port. Those with goods they want on the boats, and those who are bringing in fresh hauls from the ocean and islands."

"What speed do you want?"

"Just keep your foot down." I glanced down at him, the zoom picking up every worry line on his face. "If the Tromoal are up there, we'll need to out manoeuvre them."

Alex pulled a scarf over his face. With the back of the Hog exposed and me standing over it, there was too much sand flying in. It wasn't pleasant to keep at bay, so I did exactly the same, making sure I was zoomed in on the sky and ready for anything.

The shriek came first, then the beating of wings. I looked up, spun the full three-sixty degrees that I could, and spotted them. I shouted to Alex. "Whatever happens, don't take your foot off that accelerator. Got it?"

"Got it," he called back.

I double checked that the gun was ready. I didn't want to shoot any creature, but I had to defend us. The bows were robust and could penetrate Tromoal hide and is why they weren't cheap. I also had them enhanced. The tip, if I wanted it to, could ignite inside the beast, a small explosion which, if in the right place, would rip the animal apart. I didn't want to kill anything. I just wanted to escape, alive, and with no injuries for Alex or for me.

Then I spotted her. The matriarch with several others of her kind, they swooped in low. Then they spotted us. *Fuck.*

"Alex, trust me. Keep your foot to the floor."

The Tromoal descended. The matriarch had us in her sights. Would she kill us? No doubt whatsoever as we were in her territory? If I'd ever had any luck at all, I needed it now.

The shrieks and the dust clouds they left in their wake were massive. I tried not to panic, but sweat dripped down my back, and I zoomed out slightly just so I could work out how long we had.

"One minute," I shouted. "Hold on!"

The sky exploded around us. Several of the huge beasts dropped in ahead, the ground shaking beneath us with their massive weight.

Alex didn't baulk. He kept his foot flat on the accelerator.

That's when the matriarch landed right in front of us, her teeth bared, and her lungs full.

Alex wasn't doing anything but driving. He couldn't. And I couldn't fire the gun. My fingers froze over the trigger. I didn't want to hurt her, and that was stupid.

The matriarch's spark lit up the darkness. When the flames she had inside her spurted forth, Alex reacted badly. Trying to avoid them, he turned the wheel too quick. I knew what was coming before he did. The Hog flipped.

I countered as best I could, allowing myself to go soft. No matter what was going to happen now, it was over. There was several angry Tromoal and us.

As my body connected with the ground, I felt several pain-staking moments, and then nothing.

Blackness.

Light nowhere to be seen. The darkness consumed me.

A voice.

I couldn't make it out. I didn't know if it was male or female.

There was also an echo.

I tried to focus. Were my eyes closed or was it just so dark I couldn't see anything?

"Wake, two legs."

I was trying. Who was that?

Tiny specks of light filtered through my eyes. I opened them. More light.

I froze.

Above me was the giant head of the matriarch. Beady eyes watching me. I tried to fling my hands up to protect myself, but my left arm wouldn't move. Pain ripped through me.

"You're injured."

HEALTH – 30%

No kidding. I wanted to laugh, but what was the point? I was going to be eaten. I couldn't feel my fingers either. But I found the ring, turning it. The energy activated the ring making me feel better, the glowing pink iridescent light twinkling underneath the large head about to eat me.

HEALTH – 45%

"I knew it," the voice said. "I sensed her ring earlier."

"What?" I tried to move some more, but the head moved closer, and the blue-red eyes fixed on me.

"Do not move, yet."

I stopped myself.

"Where's Alex?" I shouted.

"Your friend is unconscious inside your vehicle. It flipped over and then back to its rightful side. He's still very sick, but he's sleeping for now."

"Sick? You mean injured? What? I have to help him."

When I tried to move again and couldn't, I stopped struggling.

"You cannot help him with his sickness. It is not of this world."

"Who are you?" I managed to stutter. I tried to stem my shaking, but the breath from the amazing creature was hot. Too hot.

"I am Riezella, Matriarch of the Tromoal. Who are you?"

"Desert Runner." I swallowed, twisting the ring around my finger. My arm had started to feel better, but there was pain all over. "Maddie Vies, what is this? How can I hear you?"

The female's eyes twinkled as she moved ever so slightly to place her head on the ground beside me. One giant eye trained on me. "The ring you own is mighty, it once belonged to a Queen."

"A Queen." I'd known only what the shopkeeper had told me when she tried to buy it from me, nothing more.

"We have quite the quandary, Maddie."

"What do you mean?"

"Such a naïve small creature. You know nothing of this world. You don't even remember me, do you?"

I attempted to get my brain to work, but the more I tried, the less I could actually recall. It was as if everything was fading away from me.

HEALTH – 30%

It was still dropping. "Am I dying?"

The large eye blinked at me. Its watery surface had a thousand places I wanted to look, all reflecting an image—an image of me.

"Yes, you have severe internal injuries."

"I don't want to die."

"That is precisely what you said to me many years ago."

I struggled. What? There was no way.... "You're the same Tromoal who broke me in half?"

"Yes. I would have eaten you then if there hadn't been something different about you. Now that we meet again, I know there are many reasons why you're alive today, and who you are."

I felt weakness creeping inside me once more. "What did you do to me?"

HEALTH – 20%

"So many questions, but you have little time. If you wish to live, you must do something for me."

"I can live?"

"There are conditions, but yes."

"Then help me..." I knew I sounded squeaky, desperate. I managed to glance over my boots, towards the Hog to where Alex lay.

I needed to know the conditions, but I didn't have the time. I felt my life as it ebbed quickly, even with the ring, even with all the good intentions in the world. There was nothing I could do to protect those I cared for more.

I stared at my health bar once more.

HEALTH – 15%

"I'll accept anything," I cried. "Just help me."

The Tromoal's eye moved back, so her huge toothy grin spread. I could see the blackness of her tongue. She didn't smell so nice either. I guess Tromoal-sized breath mints weren't a thing?

It looked like she was about to swallow me whole. "I mean anything but eat me!" I shouted at her.

There was a chuckle. "You must place your ring hand on my nose."

I struggled to move high enough up to do so, but then I felt something. I tried to spin around, but I couldn't see. There was a push, and I felt like I was floating. Had she picked me up? Was I actually off the ground?

I didn't look. Instead, I concentrated on doing exactly as she asked. I placed my hand on her nose.

A flash of white light exploded around us. Blinding me... "Now what?"

"Repeat exactly as I say this, but insert your name instead of mine."

Worry flooded through me, and yet I was curious to what she was intending.

"I, Riezella, Matriarch of the Fifth Clan from Trofoth, am now duty bound to Dessert Runner Maddie Vies. We are joined as one, will live as one."

The words... What did they mean? I had no choice, right?

I looked over towards the Hog once more, and my heart ached. For Alex, for me, for everyone on Puatera. "I, Maddie, Desert Runner of Maicreol am now duty bound to Riezella, Matriarch of the Fifth Clan from Trofoth. We are joined as one, will live as one."

This time, when light exploded around me, there was also something different. Energy, beautiful, freeing energy.

HEALTH – 95%

I hadn't had that high a health bar in years. No pain either. I seemed to gain strength—and something else. I felt dozens of entities within my mind.

"What is this?"

Riezella's voice resounded inside my mind this time as I had no idea where my physical body was, nor could I see.

"You are sensing the others... they're your family now."

I could hear them and feel them. There were hundreds—seven hundred and two males and one thousand eighteen females. So many more than we thought. There were also several other tiny voices...

"They're our young awaiting hatching."

"They speak to me already?" I had no idea... I felt overwhelmed but suddenly complete.

"We've much to discuss. But your friend and the quest you are on is important to you, yes?"

"Yes, I have to... I want to talk more, though."

"Then you shall return soon, but for now, go. We leave you. We must search for food."

I felt a sudden drop, my feet touching the ground. When the light subsided, several gusts of wind pin-wheeled me around. When I got my orientation back, I sprinted for the Hog.

CHAPTER 9

"*A*lex!" I shouted as I ran. There was no reply... I wrenched open the door. The side window was smashed in, all the stuff in the back everywhere, glass and bottles of water spilt.

A gash dripped blood from the side of his forehead. I reached out to touch him gently. "Alex, can you hear me at all?"

There was a slight moan, and he squirmed. I let out a breath, kissing the side of his cheek. "That's it. Come back to me... Here." I pulled the strap from around his middle, and he moaned once more. "I need to get you in the passenger seat. Do you think you can move?"

He didn't respond but managed to help me slide him out of the seat. When he tried to stand, he wobbled, almost pulling me over with him.

I did the best I could, taking my time in getting him around the Hog to the other side. I had to move several bits of rubbish out of the way before he could sit. Then I handed him a healing vial and some water. "Drink both. You need them."

Chug, brrr, chug.

The engine growled angrily. Dammit. The Hog wouldn't start. I said one silent prayer and then tried again. There was very little life left in him—I doubted it had much to give, but with a splutter and a huge bellow of smoke, the engine roared to life.

I slowly backed up from the crater that had almost been Alex's deathbed. We pushed on forward to Port Troli. We weren't that far now, maybe an hour. The mountain terrain had been a great lead-in. Although not the easiest path, it had proved at least an interesting one.

I twisted the ring around my finger and wondered what the hell had happened. Was it a dream? Had I been knocked out that badly I'd hallucinated it all?

There were several giggles inside my mind though, and I stifled my own. "Sorry," I tried to say back. I wasn't sure if they heard all my rambling questions or thoughts.

Riezella's voice came to me again. *No, they do not. But I do. Do not fret, Maddie. We'll be here for your return.*

I turned my attention back to Alex as he glugged the last of the water. "What happened?" he asked. "Where did the Tromoal go?"

"I don't know," I lied. There was no way I could tell him that there'd been some weird binding ritual. I had no idea what it meant for me. For us?

God dang! There was no us. Who was I kidding?

"Your ring..." he said. "It's glowing still."

And yeah, it was. There was a soft pink glow that hummed around it. Alex paused then he looked away. I couldn't find a reason to try to make him glance back at me. Or to do anything that might heal this. As far as he knew, I was still going to marry Dail, though that was the furthest thing from my mind.

Then I felt something. Uggh. That familiar ache in my hip. The pain was there, and then there was more pain. Whatever I'd just been through had zapped all the healing magic Alex had used on me. The one thing he wanted to give me, a pain-free life.

I tried to hide things, and I'd do it well until we parted company.

The glass-etched road of the plains melted into the soil once more, and then there was something else. Water. It had rained recently, and a lot of it by the looks of the state of the ground. The Hog would struggle if we stayed on this path, so I turned a little and moved to a sturdier setting.

The silence in the cab was horrible. I didn't know what to say or do. I wanted to stop the Hog and confess all, to do anything to keep this man at my side, but the words and the pedal to the metal seemed to be stuck.

The usual city market signs appeared to be burned out. My instinct rose. They'd recently been attacked. Of course, they had. The Tromoal hoard had been this way. As I looked around, I could see this was the aftermath of their raid. There were upended carts, small animals and chickens running loose. Then there were the bodies. Burned, ice burned. There was no end to this destruction.

Had I sided with devils?

No, I couldn't think like that. They were my family now, no matter what they were. They weren't cruel. They just needed what they needed. Food. A place to stay and a place to have their young. The fact the estate had taken upon themselves to supply them for so many years and for Hanson to abuse it... I was mortified.

Destruction lay all around us, I tried my best to keep going.

"Stop."

I had no idea why he wanted me to stop, we were in the middle of the market. He exited the Hog though, like there was a bomb under his ass. I followed and ran with him towards a stall.

It looked like he knew something. "What is it?"

"This was Jenni's," he said. I noticed the sheer horror on his face, how he'd paled.

I looked around, seeing nothing but the devastation of what had happened earlier that day. I had no answers, no warm offering to comfort him.

"Where do they live? In the city?"

He shrugged. "I don't know exactly. They've probably moved around a bit. Not staying in the same place was better for them. I don't have time to go hunting for them."

I opened my mouth then stopped myself. I didn't want to be stuck in the city any longer, either. But I couldn't help myself. "Give me their last known location. I'll drop you off as designated, and I'll take the potions to her."

Alex glanced at me, then around the market. The burning smell, a mix of rotting flesh and foods hit me in the face with the prevailing winds. I gagged.

"Come on, let me get you where you need to be, then I'll go look." Alex turned back to the Hog, and I followed. "This will work out okay. You can get the info needed to your friends." I tried to act like I knew all about this. The politics of cities, however, scared me. So much and so many people at stake on the whim of some deranged man, chaos. "And then you can meet up with Jenni and her sister later."

He forced a smile. "Onwards then."

I drove past the carts and the bodies. There was nothing we could do for them. The Port clean-up was obviously not a priority due to the fact there weren't many guards here. I wondered what they were all thinking now that the Tromoal had been to visit. I really had to help get that sorted as soon as I could, diverting food as much as possible towards the lands. Not just because it was the right thing to do, but because they were my family now. I had to help them.

Alex gave me the address I needed to take him. It wasn't far, and an awkward silence still sat between us. I really didn't like it.

When I pulled up to the doorway, there were two guards, just like when I'd picked him up. They just wore different uniforms.

I turned off the engine, and the guards glanced our way but didn't move.

Alex flicked my map reader up, keying in two addresses for the girls. "Try them both for me."

"I will. I promise I won't give up on this."

Alex glanced at me and red spread up his neck. "I might not see you again," he said, "but thank you for everything you've done for me."

I wanted to say so much, the words burning the tip of my tongue. Instead, I reached forward, pulling him to me in a hug. "No, thank you."

And he got out.

My insides screamed to go after him, but my body froze, my actions uncertain.

I watched as he nodded to the guards, and they escorted him inside.

I looked at the ring on my finger.

A voice came to me. *Maddie, are you all right? What's happening?*

It wasn't the matriarch. I didn't know who it was, but the voice was rich, male.

"I... I don't know," I replied.

We're here for you, no matter what you need. I am Dalfol.

I looked inside myself and then admitted, "I just let the one true love of my life walk away from me. How do I move on from that?"

Everyone says time heals all, but we know that it does not. If you're so strongly inclined, then you should break the fear that binds you and risk something you've not before.

"You can see that?"

We see everything that was and will be.

Wow, I really did have a lot to learn about the Tromoal.

As do we about you, the voice replied. *If I can help ease this pain, please come and seek me out.*

The little fog that surrounded me when he was there faded, and I focused on the dash of the Hog.

I needed to move. The first location that Alex programmed in was blinking at me. About five minutes away at most. So pulling away from where he had gone, I headed off on his mission. To find Jenni and get her the potions she needed.

The city streets grew more and more crowded, people milling about, but their faces told their stories. They were scared, hurt, worried. A couple glanced my way, and then two guys tried to stop the Hog. I revved the engine and aimed at them. It wasn't long before they moved out of the way. No one messed with a Runner.

I didn't recall being over in this section of the city much. The streets themselves started to grow smaller. I would soon have to give up driving and walk. That never bothered me usually. Now, with the darkness and the fact the city was almost un-marshalled, my stomach knotted.

I found a semi-decent place to leave the Hog, grabbing a small bag to put Alex's box inside, making sure I had a fair number of weapons and my potions. I plucked the reader from the display so I could use it to find the location.

The reader beeped slightly, and I followed its direction, keeping my head low and my stance unapproachable. No one would tackle me here, I was sure.

Yet just ahead of me stood three figures. I was heading their way. And it seemed to be the location I needed. The closer I got, the more attention to detail I took in without openly staring at them. I assessed their stance, their displayed weaponry. They were heavily armed, and they knew it.

One of the taller ones caught my eye and didn't back down. So I took him to be the leader of the trio. I stepped in closer, my hand instinctively lay on the hilt of my dagger.

"No need to be jumpy, miss," he said. "What brings you over to this side of town?"

"Looking for a sick girl... her and her sister. They used to live here. I was checking up on how they're doing."

"That's mighty kind of you," one of the others said with a sneer. I didn't like the look of him as he bounced from one foot to the other.

The taller one placed a hand on his shoulder, which instantly calmed the guy down. "None of that, Trei."

"Do you know of these girls?" I was short and to the point. I didn't want to waste time if this wasn't the right place for them.

He nodded, and I breathed an inward sigh of relief. "We took the house from them about six months ago. They were moving on."

Oh no, there goes that lovely feeling.

"However," he grinned, "I took a shine to the little one, Jenni, and we persuaded them to stay."

"They're here?" It seemed too good to be true.

"Inside." He indicated the house.

I wasn't falling for that one. No way. "Could you call her out?"

The guy's demeanour changed in a heartbeat. Gone was the friendly grin, overtaken by someone slightly deranged.

The second guy, who hadn't spoken or done anything, was the one to lunge for me. Grabbing for my backpack at the same time, I slid out of it and whacked him in the face. "Don't you know what these mean?" I said pointing to the badge on my shoulder.

"Never seen them before."

"Shame. All the better when I kick your asses then." I pulled my daggers from their hilts and waited for their move.

The second guy drew a sword. Crap. I really didn't want to do this. These guys looked like they were highly trained.

Glancing at the taller man, he nodded and moved in to strike. It would have been easier to parry with someone holding daggers like me, but I had dealt with swords before... just had to get used to dodging and, unfortunately, get in closer to actually get a strike.

He wasn't expecting me to be so good. I did exactly what I knew I had to do. I managed to get in under one of his swings, close enough to take a chunk out of his arm.

"Marcus," he yelled.

The tall guy, Marcus, cocked his head and the attacker stepped back. I half expected Marcus himself to come at me, but, instead, the door in front of me opened, and a young girl stepped outside.

CHAPTER 10

"*M*arcus, what's all the damned noise about?"

That was Jenni, I was sure of it. So they were telling the truth.

"Hey, kid, you know, just trying to have a little fun."

I slid the daggers back and stood with my arms crossed. "You do know who I am, after all?"

"Hard not to hear the rumble of a vehicle way out here," the young girl said as she approached me with the three guys looming over her. "You're a Runner, and you're here for something big, or you wouldn't be in the slums of our city."

I pointed to my backpack. "Yes, I am. Alex sent me."

The girl's face changed, and she ushered the big guys back. "Alex! Why? What would bring him back to the city?" Then she turned to Marcus. "Wake Melee. We may need to move after all."

I was sure confusion graced my entire face. When she turned back to me, she raised her lovely eyes to look at me fully. She studied me for quite some time before she spoke again. There was a great sadness in her voice. "He found the cure, didn't he?"

I followed Jenni into the building that was their home. The

rundown outside didn't give anything away in their neighbourhood, but inside, I was pleasantly surprised. When Melee was carried in by Marcus, I swallowed my frustration. Melee was the younger of the two and was obviously sick, her wasting body so small. You couldn't guess her age by looking at her. I moved to them, my heart in my throat.

"Hi," she said, trying to smile.

"Hey." I watched as Marcus moved to sit with her wrapped around him. I tried not to let the pure emotion of the scene get to me. He looked like a doting father, not the thug I just mistook him for. The other two guys milled about the room. When I glanced further, I noticed they were starting dinner.

Jenni motioned for me to sit. Placing the bag on the table, I brought out the box and gave it to her. Jenni opened it with great care, tears in her eyes as she read the note from Alex, and then she slipped out the potions. She moved to where one of the guys watched a pot on the stove and instructed him on how to make it. I didn't know much about this kind of advanced gift. The magic Alex used on me was different to how this one would work. I tried to understand the instructions but gave up halfway through. Instead, I watched as they were prepared.

Melee squirmed in Marcus's arms, and I noticed his concern. "Is she in a lot of pain?"

Marcus nodded. "Constantly. There's nothing we've ever been able to buy or give her to take it away."

I felt sorry for her, so young. Yet she was loved by all the people here, and Alex. "I should go," I said, trying to allow myself some room for thinking. It felt wrong for me to be here.

"Please stay, just a while. You can have dinner with us."

I shook my head. "I have to get back across the desert again before the breeding season really does kick off."

I realised she didn't know about the estate or the Tromoal, but their stall had been attacked earlier, so she knew something.

"The world is changing," she said. "I feel that." I noticed her eyes changed colour as she spoke to me. "There's also something about you that I really like. Alex wouldn't have trusted you with these potions otherwise."

"The Tromoal might come back to the port. If there's anywhere else you could hide out, I'd suggest moving there."

"Maybe, when she's feeling better." Jenni looked to her sister. "Do you know what happened? Why they came for us?"

"Yes, Hanson's estate was poisoned. Their food and stocks were down so much that the workers abandoned it. Hanson committed suicide with his entire family."

"Then, yes, we will move as soon as we can." Jenni's face fell as she watched the guys help Melee with the potions. "I believe the Tromoal will return because of the high food supply. The city defences aren't good enough to protect us. Nor will they want to give up so much to keep the Tromoal at bay."

"They'd best be doing so until we have a solid working plan available to supply them with their usual foods."

Jenni pulled something from her pocket, passing it to me. It was a slip of paper with an address. "If you wish to see us again, do come. You'd be honoured at our table anytime."

"Thank you."

"No." Jenni smiled. "I can't thank you enough for this, for bringing this to us. I'm sorry Marcus took some of the day's frustration out on you."

"Don't be. It was nice to think I might have stood a chance against these three brutes."

I moved to leave, standing with her in the doorway as Melee was given the potions. "Let Alex know how she's doing if you can?"

She smiled, but it was a sad one. I couldn't understand why. "What's wrong?"

"You don't know he's sick, do you?"

Sick? I felt the colour drain from my body. I leaned on the door, not opening it.

"You understand he's a visitor, though?"

"Yes, we talked a little about things."

"Well, in his world, he's sick. He understood Melee's illness because of his own."

The matriarch had said something similar. I wobbled slightly. "How sick?"

Jenni opened the door for me as I suddenly needed the fresh air. I tried to stop myself, but panic for him flooded through me.

Jenni answered, but her voice was low. "He talked about this being his last adventure."

I had to go, *now*. "I need to find him." I rushed off, grabbing my backpack. I vaguely remembered where the Hog was and I ran for it. Ran until my breath came so ragged I had to stop or fall over.

Why hadn't he said anything? Or maybe he had tried. I knew there was something he wanted to tell me, but then we'd seen the devastation of the city...

I wished we'd had more time. I had to find him. Now!

The Hog roared to life. I turned around in the street as best I could while tears stung my eyes.

I found my way back to the place I'd dropped Alex off by sheer luck. The guards weren't stationed outside anymore, and I moved to knock. Maybe they'd still be here. It was hopeful at best.

Silence echoed throughout the street, the only sound my heart beating in my chest.

I tried the door handle to find it open.

With a deep breath, I pushed the door open. It looked like any typical room and any ordinary house.

No one was home, though. Two cups and a few empty plates sat on the table. I scanned for any clues.

Nothing.

There was nothing here that said where or when they had moved on. Or where they went...

I picked up a bottle of ale I found in the cupboard, pulled out a glass, and filled it to the brim. The day was getting on, I'd nowhere to stay, and I needed something to take this pain away.

There was a ping. A message from Dail popped into my view. I really didn't want anything from him right now. But I clicked it open and read. *Maddie, we've located enough food sources from the lands to last a good few days, been rallying the North, but there's been no word from the south. Can you check the Port's suppliers? See what's going on?*

I slugged back some of the ale and nearly spat it out. Ugh, disgusting.

I typed back. - *We arrived safely. Alex has gone. The Port's already been attacked. I'll see what I can do in the morning, and I'll let you know when I start my return journey.*

I took another swig. The ale had a horrid taste, so I stood, leaving the building. Any hopes of ever finding out what happened to Alex drifted away. The only thoughts left were that of my future.

The Hog rumbled to life even if I felt there was nothing left worth living for. I made my way across the port, closer to the docks where I knew an inn was and food with my name written all over it.

A ping came through, and I saw the note on my credits.

QUEST COMPLETED
PAYMENT MADE – 39,000 CREDITS

I'd been paid in full, and there was a nice bonus to boot. That meant Alex had gotten the information across to the right people, his mission complete. Did that mean he'd left? Gone back just like Leon had all those years ago? Leon had been my first real love. It devastated me when he vanished. No rhyme or reason. When he left me, I bounced about from one relationship to the other, and then met Dresel. That had been interesting but also ended badly.

I wished I could stay away from men altogether, but programming.... If I ever met these game designers, I would kick their asses. Then get them to rewrite me.

I parked the Hog. The door to the bar creaked as I opened it, and I headed to a corner booth. The waitress was soon over. I ordered the finest bottle of whiskey they had and a glass along with two plates of their roasted meat, veggies and a dessert. I was going to stuff my face and drown my sorrows. Tomorrow was another day. I'd worry about that then.

The familiar aura drifted over my psyche as Dalfol's silvery voice entered my mind. *What's the problem, Maddie? Do I need to retrieve you from your location?*

I choked back on the whiskey, shocked he'd even think of that.

Are you like my keeper? I asked internally. Hoping the question wouldn't offend him.

No, but I am the one assigned to your well-being and thoughts. It seems you're struggling with a lot. I can help.

How can you help me? Alex has gone back to his own world, by the sounds of it to die. And I can't contact or help him. The food supply is short for you guys, so you're at risk. If you continue to attack the cities, they'll fight back. There will be many lives lost. I'm stuck between you and the people I love, with no way out.

There is always a way out, Maddie.

I laughed and attracted some unwanted attention from the far side of the bar. Yeah, I looked like a crazy person, laughing and talking to myself.

I waved at the staring patrons who tucked themselves back in and carried on a conversation. Probably about me.

How is there always a way out?

The answers are complicated, and I feel the grip of inebriation. You must rest, come back to us. There is hope for all. With you at our side, my matriarch is not worried for our young.

She might not be, but I am. I don't like death at any level. She's already had her clutch.

You've seen that, so you know several of our females have already decided to return without birthing.

I slammed my fist on the table, again getting strange looks. *We need them here. I can't let them leave. Without your numbers and the young, there won't be enough Hismaw to sell, the world will be taken by...*

The creatures that live here... why is that so bad?

I thought about it. Yes, why was it bad? The surrounding cities, their lands and situations would change. The creatures kept at bay by the Hismaw would have greater roaming distances. It would put a slight stop on the growth of us. I realised it wasn't so bad. The arguments over land, the imminent threats of war. They'd stop. They would need to protect their own lands, and not worry about ours.

I see we do have a lot to discuss. I will eat and sleep this off. Join you in the desert at noon.

And Alex? His name ripped through me.

Maybe I'd marry Dail after all. The pain would subside. I just had to block it out once more. Forget. I could do that.

I picked up the whisky tumbler, filled it, and then downed it.

Yes, I would forget. I had a new goal now.

Family.

The End

If you enjoyed this book, please consider leaving a review, they help keep writers motivated! :)

DESERT BORN

PUATERA ONLINE BOOK 2

CHAPTER 1

*M*y eyes opened to the whir of the overhead fan. The smell of my own sweat and antics of the night before assaulted my nostrils and turned my stomach.

Thump, thump.

Man, what was I drinking?

The memories of the past couple of days filtered through the alcoholic fog, numbing everything, but the bile wanting to rise up my throat was strong.

I swallowed as I reached over to the side cabinet and pulled out a bottle of cool water. It instantly eased my throat but did nothing to treat the threatening rise of my hangover.

What was I thinking? To numb the pain, the heartache of losing Alex?

It was temporary at best. Ugh, I groaned. This was the pits!

I pushed myself up, licking my lips and feeling the knots in my hair. A shower and clean clothes would help me recover. I would wipe away the night and the thoughts.

Stumbling to the bathroom, I turned on the shower, letting the steam billow up into the extractor.

I paused for only a moment, and my stomach heaved. I turned quick before I missed the bowl and parted with the contents of my stomach. Nothing worse than being so drunk to make you sick. It usually never got to me, but last night had. Alex had.

I stripped off my underwear and double checked all my clothes were in the right 'dry cleaning slot.' By the time I got out the shower, they'd be cleaned and dried. Always good to stop in a decent inn with cleaning facilities. I stepped into the blasting heat, happy to wash away everything from the scorching desert plains. Even as I'd bent over the toilet, I hadn't noticed there was no pain from my hip. There, in the shower, where the water usually stung the still healing wounds, I ran my hand over smooth skin. There were no pinpricks or any scarring.

I blinked as my eyes ran down my thigh—nothing.

Did Alex's magic work? I was dumbfounded.

I stood for quite some time wondering about everything, then continued to wash off. Conditioner eased the knots from my sand-blasted and sun-scorched hair. No matter how much I looked after it, a few days in the desert drained the moisture and turned it brittle. I always kept a bottle of excellent damage control oil in the Hog. I might be a badass to most people, but I still had pride in myself.

I dried myself by allowing the fan to cool off the water. Eyes were drawn down to my naked body again as I admired the new skin there. How could it wipe away all that hurt and pain? I doubted how long it would stay this way. Would it suddenly revert to being sore if I took on damage from another source? I shook my head wishing there was coffee waiting for me as well as the freshly washed and warm clothes.

The room spun a little, and I focussed on the fan once more before pushing myself up to get dressed and go down to the inn's bar for something to quell the alcoholic poisoning my body had just been through.

The smell of freshly cooked food drifted towards me, and I tried my best to look like I was hungry and not feeling sick. I sat at the bar and waited till someone spotted me.

"You look like you could do with some strong coffee, my dear." I heard the voice from behind me and turned to see a tall, lithe man, in slacks and a shirt heading my way with a fresh pot in his hand.

"That's for sure." When he poured me a mug, I added my thanks and sipped the fine liquid, suddenly feeling much better. "This is enhanced?"

He grinned, the greying hairs in his beard moving with the smile. "What kind of inn would I be if I let my patrons wake up with a killer hangover and didn't offer them a decent remedy the next day?"

I felt normality returning to my fogged brain. "That's very kind of you. I think I drank enough last night to put a dwarf to shame."

"That you did, my dear." His eyes twinkled, but then they turned sad. "You must have had your reasons."

I watched him pull up a chair. He sat close to me. He pinged the small bell at the side of the bar, and a lady poked her head out. "Breakfast is coming right up, Dem."

"Make that two." Dem motioned towards me with a wave of his hand.

I listened to Dem's tales of the previous day. The people, who had been injured and those talking about the Tromoal attack. The food came and went, satisfying the hunger inside and settled me right up for a day of preparing to head back to the Runners Village.

I didn't clarify anything for him or tell any of my stories. They were for me alone. Besides, what good would it have done to spread panic amongst them, knowing the truth wasn't for the lower-end citizens of any city. The government heads would be sorting all this out and rallying with Trox City and the others to pacify those who were potential killers.

I thanked them for the good stay, made sure I left the room as clean as I could and went to find the Hog. I had a vague idea where I'd left it from the day before, but it was almost as though those memories had been blocked. Probably survival instinct to keep out the memories I didn't want to keep reliving. Alex.

I noted the Hog up ahead of me, and I grinned. No matter how much trouble I got myself into, he had my adrenaline running, and then there was nothing but freedom on my mind. I needed the breeze in my hair, the open road.

That was when I saw the pair of boots sticking out from under the back wheel.

I froze.

Boots I recognised.

Dropping my backpack, I sprinted as fast as I could, rounding the side of the Hog moving into emergency action. I leaned over Alex, feeling for his carotid artery. He was alive but severely battered and broken.

I palmed the Hog open and grabbed for any healing potion or mix I had left. There was one bottle, and it wasn't a strong mix. I looked around for someone else to help. Anyone. Alex needed a healer and fast.

I knelt before him, cradled his head as I felt his pulse again, finding it was there, thready, weak. Dripping the mixture into his mouth, I did the same as I had two nights ago, massaging his throat, trying to get the liquid into him without it going into his air pipe. He swallowed slowly, choking a little, and then was unconscious again.

There was no clue to the damage he'd taken or what had happened. I couldn't see any of his visitor stats. Struggling to lift him, I eased him into the back of the Hog where I packed the blankets around him. I hoped he would hang on. There was a healer I trusted if she'd not been wiped out with the Tromoal visit. A chance I had to take. I was also risking the amount of fuel I would have to get back to the town.

The Hog didn't know what hit him, and neither did the streets of Port Troli, as I sped through like a demon had possessed me while people swore after me and animals scattered.

Hitting a bump, I heard a soft moan. At least Alex was still alive. I had some hope with that.

The city limits faded, and a soft tree line appeared. We were far from our original destination now, heading for someone who helped me once, way back when I was first injured by the Tromoal. Shalice was a Spirit Elf and very powerful. The locals avoided her because of her affinity to take life as much as she gave it. If you get on her wrong side by killing some of the animals she held dear, you would soon know about it.

Life and the land around this part of the port belonged to her. Some say she was evil, but I knew better. She loved wildlife was all. She chose to stay with the animal side of the world rather than the civilised. I can't say I blamed her. At this moment in time, the animal world had much more appeal to me too.

Years ago, Shalice's home had been the only training facility for healers. On the bumpy drive up, I remembered all the people I'd met. I slowed the Hog right down trying not to bounce Alex about any more than I had to. I didn't know how many broken bones he had or how much pain he was in.

Rounding the corner, I could see the house, built into the sides of two large trees, billowing out in many directions. Crisp, clean.

Shalice waited for me, dressed in her medical whites. No matter how she knew I was coming, or how angry she was with me, I was glad she was ready.

"What happened?" she asked as I opened the door to greet her with a small bow.

"A friend, he's badly beaten."

"Roastol," she shouted. "We need you." Moving to the Hog, she glanced inside. "Not just a friend. A visitor?" She raised an eyebrow at me, and I couldn't meet her eyes. I was pushing her boundaries in helping me, and I knew it. She didn't falter, though. As a huge guy strode over to the Hog, I moved out of his way. Carefully, Roastol picked Alex up and then began to move him as gently as possible to the inside of the house.

I followed, my head low. What this would cost me, I had no idea.

Roastol moved through Shalice's wooden home with ease, his huge frame bending the boards. I glanced around as we followed behind him. The once elite and sterile home had dust bunnies? I had questions for Shalice, but not now.

Roastol found a side room, and he placed Alex onto the table. The white sterility and scent of cleaning fluids assaulted my nose and eyes, but it was the best place for us. The equipment in here, clean, glinting. A large open window allowed in the one power Shalice regularly used —the sun. I watched as she carefully eased Alex's jacket aside, then proceeded to get a large pair of scissors. She glanced at me pointing to another pair. "Help me cut everything off. I need to see him unencumbered."

I took the scissors and followed what she did, cutting from his trouser legs upwards and then through the thicker material at his waist.

His exposed skin was black and blue, welts and cuts everywhere.

"Do you have any idea what happened to him?"

I struggled to keep my focus without tearing up. "No, he was supposed to finish a job, get paid, and return home. I've no clue. I'm sorry."

The shirt was easier to cut, and when it parted, I could see the large bruising developing around his right ribs. Broken for sure. I swallowed back my tears and asked plainly, "Will he live?"

Shalice's amber eyes met mine, and she replied with, "I do not know. You will need to give me some time."

I nodded and was about to leave, but she reached for my hand. "I will need your help here. This is not something I can do alone. The spirits ask that I take from another."

Her use of the word take made my mind crawl. "Take what?"

But her eyes narrowed. "You know the what, my dear."

I let out a laugh. So, this was the deal. Alex paid dearly for my hip to heal, and to help him, I knew I'd have to accept it back. That lifetime of pain.

"Do it," I said, placing a finger to his cheek. "What's a life of pain for someone you care for?"

With a nod, she smiled. "It is nothing, so please, let us concentrate. Do not talk while I work. Just keep your hands placed from his head to his chest."

I did that, but the cold feeling he gave off worried me. Almost like the other day.

"Do you see his life bar?" Shalice began to draw a circle around us in a mixture of powders.

I tried to focus on him. I'd seen his name tag before, so maybe if I looked deep enough, I could see more.

A slight ping and there it was.

ALEX DUBOIS – HEALTH 7%

"It's at seven percent." I gasped.

"Then I have serious work to do. Please focus."

I tried to, I really did, but the thoughts flashing through me were desperate. I would have given anything to help him, even my life. I realised that I didn't know much about him or his world. I cared more for him than I did for myself. Was that love? Real love. I mean I knew I loved Dail at some level, but would I have died for him?

The short answer was no.

The room around me started to glow, pinks, blues, and greens. I heard Shalice whispering in her elven language, little that I understood of it. She moved to me, glancing at the ring on my hand. "Very interesting," and her eyes met mine. "Your friend has more of a chance at surviving with you at his side."

And then I heard something else. Dalfol.

Shalice, of the Elven Spirit dynasty. We hear your plea. Please, let me confer with Maddie. Alone.

Dalfol? What is this? I thought back to him.

Your friend, Shalice belongs to the spiritual lords of the forests. She is, however, asking the lords of the skies to help Alex.

She's asking you? What can you do to help him?

Not I, you.

I shook my head. *I don't understand. I can't help him.*

I felt Shalice place her hand on my shoulder. "Maddie," she whispered in my ear. "You are the only one who can."

I felt Dalfol draw back. I knew no magic on this level. I wasn't a sorceress. I panicked, removing my hands from him.

His health dipped all the more.

ALEX DUBOIS – HEALTH – 5%

The more I thought about it, the less time Alex had.

ALEX DUBOIS – HEALTH – 3%

Maddie, the crisp cool voice of Riezella came forwards. *Trust in us. Trust in yourself.*

I placed my hands to their original positions and focussed hard.

It is the transference of life that you're asking for. It is only fair you are the one to do so. Riezella said. *Think of what he truly means to you and why you want him to live. Feel your energy, then let it go.*

I did think of what he meant to me, and I spoke the words clearly for everyone to hear. "I love him. I'd do anything for him. My energy is his. My life his."

The room seemed to fizzle, pop, the voices and feeling of the Tromoal clan around me grew in intensity.

That's right, Maddie, Riezella whispered. *Draw not only from yourself.*

Pain ripped through my leg as I knew it would. I didn't lose focus, the burning growing hotter and hotter. Alex's health bar flickered...

"Come on!" I screamed.

Then it moved, just slightly but it did.

ALEX DUBOIS – HEALTH – 5%

This was going to take some considerable effort. I sucked in a breath, cracked my neck so the bones popped, and put in all the determination I could, till blackness started to swirl around me.

I heard Shalice. "Maddie, stop. You'll kill yourself."

Hands grabbed onto me, pulling me away from Alex, and the room vanished.

CHAPTER 2

I had no idea if what I had done would help Alex at all. By the time Shalice pulled me away from him, sheer exhaustion must have been written all over my face. I wobbled, and Roastol picked me up to take me to another room where he put me in a comfortable chair.

Thoughts whirled about in my mind. I couldn't process any of them. Shalice brought me some elixir. I thanked her and sipped it, the fruity flavour reminding me of other times, as my foggy brain started to come around.

Shalice joined me a while later, with a steaming mug of tea. She offered me some, but I declined since her tea always gave me a headache. Probably because it was meant to help, and any liquids I consumed for my pain relief were meant to numb everything inside me. I knew this, because I knew her, just like she knew I was coming. I believed when I was here the last time, when she'd done her best to heal me, we had this connection. I also thought she was one of the only other sentient people on this world, though we'd never talked about it.

She said nothing, just watched the woodland of her surrounding home and waited. I was glad for her company and the fact that she kept quiet.

"You're struggling here," I eventually said. "You need help."

Her smooth facial features took on one crinkle. "I am. I can't hide that from you."

"When this is all sorted out," I managed to lock eyes with her, "I'll make sure to send people your way. They'll help."

"This may take some time to sort out," she spoke, softly. "Maddie, do you realise what you did in there?"

I shrugged. I had a vague idea, but not to the true meaning of how it was possible or the why.

"Let me tell you a story. Many years ago, there was a rumour that the Lord of the Tromoal would return, and with him would be his Lady. Originally, the Tromoal came here with the purpose of keeping their broods safe from fighting clans. They came with a powerful sorceress. Lady—"

"Lady Mysiol. Yes, I heard some of her story a few days ago."

"So you understand some of the power you have in that ring."

I wanted to say I didn't, but I did. I knew what it meant to Dail, though I'd no idea how he'd uncovered the ring. Another story I would love to hear.

"The ring was said to rest with her body. Not only that but in a place protected by all the Tromoal bones of the past. The ring is sacred to them because she died protecting them against an evil Visitor."

"There's evil all around the world." I nodded.

"Yes, this Visitor wanted control over the Tromoal. Not content to have taken one of their eggs, he came back to take control of them all. And he needed her for that. Rumours say the two of them died together in some hidden caving system. Possibly out there in the plains."

It would have been in the plains. I had no doubt about where it was, either. "I think Alex and I saw it earlier today when I first saw the Matriarch."

Shalice raised an eyebrow. Now she wanted to hear my story.

"We were going to be attacked, and when she landed, Alex flipped the Hog, and I was almost eaten." I laughed remembering.

"But she didn't eat you, did she?"

"No." I crossed my legs and ran a hand down my thigh, the dull pain throbbing away once more. "She didn't after she noticed the ring."

"And you what? What did you do?"

I regarded her with a great thought. "You already know what I did because you've just seen me do the one thing you couldn't. Bring a man back from the brink of death."

Shalice smiled, but there was sorrow there, tugging at the moisture in her eyes. "It seems our world is changing. The sky has a new Lady in charge... with you and Alex beside the Tromoal. I think there will be many a transformation coming."

I didn't know what she meant, but her words didn't soothe me. "The Tromoal are going to starve. If we don't secure them enough food, they will die. The young will create the last batch of Hismaw we will ever see, and the animals of the night will rule. Maybe those are the changes you see coming?"

Shalice didn't answer, just twirled her mug around. "I will get some food prepared for dinner. There's a guest room I will settle you in after you're fed and watered properly. You will sleep well tonight, my dear."

It was the way she said it, I understood what she meant. No doubt the food or the drinks I had would be laced with something nice and soothing.

"May I take a shower or bath?"

"There's a hot spring, just out to the left of the back tree line. No one will disturb you there."

I watched her finish her drink, and take the mugs with her as she left. Now finally feeling a little better, and more capable of standing without falling over. I moved to exit the home. I was nearly at Alex's room when I saw Shalice leave a bundle of my clothes, presumably from the Hog, and a towel for me at the door. I paused no more, pushing Alex's door ajar and stepping inside.

Memories flooded through me of the day Dail had been injured, the smell of burnt flesh as the healers worked on him. The feelings I went through then were nothing like they were now. I was worried for Dail, but it wasn't enough. I realised now I loved him only as a friend. He would have given me anything, of course, but it wouldn't have satisfied me. I'd always be off looking for the next big adventure, and it would have meant I would eventually leave town and him far behind. Those big adventures were calling for me. Alex included.

I saw Roastol move to the edge of his seat, unsure what to think of me. "Just checking on him. I won't do anything else." He settled in his seat again and went back to reading a book.

Approaching Alex, I noticed his matted hair had grey streaks spreading through it. Had the injuries aged him or was this magic? I picked up a stray strand and tucked it behind an ear. His stubbly chin looked pinker, not as bruised.

Focussing in, I managed to see how he was doing.

ALEX DUBOIS - HEALTH – 60%

That was much better, but why wasn't he awake? I didn't understand.

I lay a hand on his chest and felt the rise and fall as he breathed. It wasn't as laboured anymore and was a good steady pace. I leaned over and kissed the side of his cheek, whispering, "I'll be back soon."

Making my way out of the house and down to the spring, I stripped and got in, the water refreshing and warm to my skin.

I dipped under and washed my hair with the wonderful potion Shalice gave me. It was a treat as it softened my locks after the day's antics. I needed this as much as I needed a good night's sleep.

Drying off, I heard a whirring of wings in the distance. Dalfol. I sensed him close by.

Yes, he said, *it is I.*

What's wrong?

I am here to make sure the creatures of the night do not bother you. There are many heading into the forest from deep in the woods. Do not fear. Nothing will get near you, but you need rest. The Matriarch has a lot to discuss with you tomorrow.

What if Alex can't travel yet?

He will be fine to travel, though Riezella is worried his presence alters our future.

Alex is coming with me. I felt panic rise in my throat in case they rejected him, knowing I actually needed him.

I will speak to her, make sure she understands. She felt exactly as we all did when you performed the summoning of energy to bring him from the edge of death.

I sighed, the cooling of the night air making me shiver. The sun was disappearing behind the mottled clouds. I dressed in clean clothes quickly.

Thank you. Eat and sleep. I'll make sure we're with you and on the road again by mid-day tomorrow.

I felt his contentment as I moved to walk away. However, I wanted to go and really say hello. After hearing in my head, I needed a face to put to his voice.

So I approached through the tree line. Slow and sure. The fact was, even knowing what he was to me, family, I was terrified as he towered above me in his full glory.

Dalfol was a grey Tromoal with a yellow underbelly and orange sides. As the moon settled around us, he glinted with silver flashes as his scales moved. He spread his wings out, seeming to settle a little more, but when he moved them, great gushes of wind swept my damp hair around my face. I brushed it out of the way to see him all the more.

You are very curious. I like that about you.

You're not curious about me? I reached out, and he hovered closer with his nose in front of me. He smelled of the river and fresh chewed grasses, not rotting meat or death like I would have thought.

Yes, I am. As are the rest of our clan. You bring with you a new sense of adventure, but they're worried for their unborn.

I nodded and ran my fingers down the side of his cheek, in a kind of scratch. I laughed when he leaned into me and almost knocked me over.

I do not know my own strength. Apologies.

No need. I moved back to scratch him again. *You're amazing.* The sheer size and intense magic energy he emitted fogged my brain. *Everything about you is power, beauty, so much more.*

As I scratched and moved further up his chin to his cheek, a low belly rumble vibrated through me. *You sound like you're purring.*

I am content to let you scratch my scales. He carried on with the belly rumble. *It is something only the closest of species can do for us.*

I stopped what I was doing. *I'm sorry. I don't mean to....*

I don't mean quite like that. His low rumble exploded around me in a laugh, and I had to cover my ears. *I am here as one of the Matriarch's guards. Now, I also protect you. That is even more of an honour for me.*

I don't know what I'm doing. I sighed.

Go, for now. He pushed me gently away. *You need rest.*

I stumbled back to Shalice's home where she fed me, and we talked small talk about the local animals. The fact that a Tromoal was nestled inside the tree line, keeping guard didn't bother her, but it bothered her companion. He seemed to be on edge all night.

By the time she brought me a mug of tea, I laughed, knowing I had needed it, but my headache would need soothing with something else tomorrow. I would have gotten under a blanket and fallen asleep anyhow, but I honoured her by drinking the tea and watching the night sky twinkle.

Soon, my tired body was stripped and on the bed, probably snoring before I knew it.

Pitch black greeted me when I woke sometime in the early hours of the morning.

Alex is awake, Maddie.

I heard the door creak. Having not really heard Dalfol's words. Someone was in the room? My room.

I reached under the pillow to where I usually put my daggers, but I realised I'd been extremely tired. I had just undressed. Whoever this was, I wasn't going down without a fight.

As a shadow crossed the light from the window, I could only make out it was a large male. As he got nearer, I prepared to pounce, the glint of a mirror catching the silvery light, illuminating a startled face.

"Alex!" I spat. "What the hell are you doing?"

"I was looking for you. I had no idea where we were. I've been creeping around this crazy house for five minutes until I saw your boots at the door."

I reached up, grabbing his arm, tugging him into an awkward hug. "Thank God you're all right."

I breathed in his scent, filled with sweat and blood, but I didn't pull away. I squeezed him gently until he finally hugged me back.

When I felt like letting him go, he chuckled. "Thanks, I needed that."

I patted the side of the blanket when I noticed he just hovered there. "Sit," I commanded.

He edged closer to me and plopped down. His own clothes in tatters so now all he wore were slacks that Shalice had probably dressed him with. Even in the dim light, I could see the muscles etched into his physique. I ached to touch him more, restraining myself the hardest damned thing I'd ever done.

"What happened?" I finally asked.

"You mean apart from the fact that I almost died?"

I nodded and moved to turn the night light on so I could see him properly.

"It seemed the people I was taking the information to weren't legitimate. They wanted it for the wrong reasons. They were going to use it to launch a war on the City of Trox after breeding season. I destroyed the info. I wouldn't let them have it."

"You risked your life to save the city?"

"I don't know about save it, but I didn't want innocent people to get hurt."

I leaned back into the pillows. "Do you remember coming here?"

He shook his head, scratching the stubble on his chin. "No, nothing."

I let out a breath, hoping he wouldn't recall anything of the ritual or me saving his life. "Maybe it's best you don't remember almost dying."

"Maddie, there's stuff I want to tell you." He sighed.

"I already know. You're sick."

I saw the sorrow in his eyes. "I joined the beta program to test Puatera Online because I was sick. It would help with the mounting bills and give me some dignity in the last few months of my life."

I felt bile rising up the back of my throat. I didn't want to listen, but I could see he wanted, no, needed to tell me.

"I started off weak, but I became stronger here. Where I could barely walk back home, I could walk and run here."

I hated the thought of him in some place, sick, dying.

"Do you know how long you have?"

He shook his head. "I could slip away at any given moment."

I reached for his hand and gripped it tight, leaning my head on his shoulder.

"I didn't want to lead you on," he whispered. "I wanted you to know my time is short."

I tried to stop the tears, but I couldn't. They were silent. It was all I allowed myself. I was sure he felt my sobs, though, as he lifted me up and wrapped an arm around me and then kissed my cheek.

"Shh," he whispered. His gentle kisses moving along my jawline until, eventually, his lips met mine. Everything around me blurred into just being with him, an emotion so raw, I didn't want this to end.

CHAPTER 3

S halice wanted to make sure we had food and fluids in us for the day, but all I wanted to do was get Alex outside and towards the grove of trees where I knew Dalfol was still hidden.

Had Shalice known he was there? She never said anything when I finally went to leave with Alex in tow.

I knew and alerted Dalfol to what I was doing, but Alex didn't have a clue. I wanted him to meet the Tromoal in all his glory. To see, feel and live as he wanted to. It meant being scared as well. Knowing only the basic system mechanics he'd told me, where everything newly discovered as a player felt amazing, I hoped everything he'd see and feel now would give him the joy he needed.

"Where are we going?" Alex complained. "Ya know my ribs still hurt."

I laughed but kept walking out to the tree line, the low rumbling sound vibrating the ground.

Alex heard Dalfol's rumble and moved around before he realised there was something large up ahead. He stopped dead in his tracks. "What is this?"

"I want you to meet Dalfol, a friend."

The Tromoal moved to intercept our path, placing his giant head in the way. I couldn't help but watch as Alex's face fell. Clearly, his first instinct was to run for cover.

I reached out and grabbed hold of his arm. "No, you don't need to run. Seriously."

I saw the fear in his eyes, then the wonder. "What really happened out there in the desert?"

"If I told you, I might not get to take it back. It would mean I trust you."

He reached for my hand. "After everything I told you last night… trust me, Maddie. I won't do anyone any harm."

So I quickly explained the meeting with the Matriarch and the subsequent circumstances.

He grinned and moved to get closer to Dalfol with his arm outstretched. I wasn't sure if Dalfol would let him near, but the creature started with that infernal vibrating again. Alex placed a hand on his neck, then slid it down to his shoulders. "He's as large as a house!"

I moved to Alex's side and placed my hand on the Tromoal.

"Does this mean we get to traverse the plains without being bothered?"

I shook my head. "I don't know. I guess we have some immunity, but I think if a hungry Tromoal were standing in front of me, I still wouldn't want to risk it."

Alex nodded but leaned in and placed his head against Dalfol.

What is the human doing? Dalfol asked.

I have no idea.

"He smells like water, fresh grass, and lilies," Alex said.

There was something on his mind. I couldn't work out what it was, but I could see the wonderful reaction from Alex as his grin spread from ear to ear and glistening tears moistened his eyes. Alex's happiness then spread through me.

I watched them for a while then rubbed water from my own eyes. *Dalfol, are we safe crossing the plains?*

Dalfol's purring stopped. *There are still many dangers besides us, you know.*

Of course, bandits.

I shall, however, be close by to make sure you aren't in the path of any hunting Tromoal.

That was a good thing.

Alex moved away from Dalfol, still grinning.

"What is it?"

"I always wanted to get close to something so big, something that in my world is nothing but a fantasy. Yet here, it all feels so real. I'm glad I had the opportunity."

I wanted to hug him. To tell him everything would work out, but I couldn't. His sickness and the chance he could be whisked away from me had tears brimming once more.

Dalfol nudged me as I was about to turn, and I fell over. "Hey," I shouted at him. "That's not fair." He started to laugh, the gentle purring when he was happy turned into a ground shaking bellow of air. I laughed with them both as Alex pulled me up. Dalfol was trying to shock me back to reality.

I mentally thanked him.

We got out of his way, and he spread his massive wings and took to the air. The sheer energy blast from them almost had us back on the floor.

Alex whooped, twirling around to watch Dalfol fly away.

We made it back to the Hog, and Alex slid in. I started the engine, and Dalfol led us out of the area. Shalice wasn't good with saying goodbyes, so we left knowing she was tending her animals and looking after those who needed her magic. I was blessed to know her, and she was thankful she'd been able to help me realise my potential.

I drove for a while before Alex said, "Your plan now is to rally everyone together to get the Tromoal more food, yes? Call in players and master this quest?"

"I'd never thought of it that way, but yes, it would be." I noticed a popup flickering out the corner of my vision. I slowed down while I looked at it. Then stopped, dead.

NPC NOTE
SYSTEM ERROR
ERROR LOGGED
SYSTEM REBOOT
MASTER THE QUEST EVENT – FEED THE TROMOAL
DETAILS – TO FOLLOW
ERROR
ERROR
DETAILS – TO FOLLOW
ACCEPT Y/N

What? There were so many errors, I had no idea what was going on —what was I accepting if I did click yes? I'd never had that kind of power before. Sure, I knew I could pass on small quests to players, but to master one? Wow.

I clicked accept anyway. Maybe I'd get more notes later on.

I thought I was just to feed the Tromoal, protect them as a species, but knowing what was going on in the city bothered me, and then I saw it.

EVENT STARTED – CONTROL FOR MAICREOL

Alex watched me. "What's going on?"

I had to deflect this somehow. Not knowing how to tell him the severity of the situation. I started driving again. "The guys who beat you up, do you think they'll try to find you, to get more information out of you?"

Alex struggled with his words. "I think they'll be waiting for me to cross the plains with you. So yes, they'll try anything if they think I survived. They will want to prevent me from going back to the City and revealing their intentions."

"And what are their intentions?"

"War. You said that yourself." So he already suspected where this was going. I let out a breath. "In fact," he added, "I know they poisoned

Hanson's farmlands. Tricked him into thinking it was something else. He salted all his money into a cure, which didn't work. They took him for everything he had, knowing the Tromoal would come in and devastate the North first."

"They didn't, though. They split. The Tromoal aren't stupid. They wanted to hunt to see where the food sources were."

"A good thing. That's the only reason the port hasn't already made their move."

I thought about this for a little while, hoping it wasn't true. Then I turned inwards. *Dalfol, do you know where every Tromoal is?*

I do not, but I know Riezella does.

I think I have a plan. Then to Alex. "This will work out, trust me."

He grinned. "After what you did for me, I more than trust you."

The final landmark of Port Troli's lands drifted by, and with it, the vast plains opened up. Alex kept checking the skies, expecting something to drop out in front of us again.

"You don't need to worry," I said, pain spreading through my hip.

I then noticed my own health bar.

HEALTH – 45%

Reaching for my potion bottle, I took a large swig, the sweet elixir sliding down my throat. There wasn't enough.

"You're in pain?"

That was the one detail I'd failed to mention. "Sorry, yes. Whatever I did to help you, reverted my injury."

Alex passed me one of the other bottles, and I took it from him, popping the lid.

HEALTH – 65%

"I'll drive for a bit if you get tired."

I passed the bottle back after a rather large hit. I could have used the ring's buffer, and I fingered it lightly. That was for emergencies only. "I'll let you know. For now, I'm good." Of course, it was a lie.

I looked out onto the road ahead. It was nice to know the skies were being watched for us.

Dalfol's voice drifted to me. It seemed like he was much further away. *There's an ambush ahead.*

I gripped the steering wheel. Alex realised something was wrong. "Dalfol can talk to you, right?"

"How did you know?"

"It was like a whisper, something passing through me to you. I never heard it before today. Really weird."

"He said there's an ambush ahead."

Alex dropped his head. "I guess they were expecting us to make a run for it."

"They couldn't have known you'd survive."

He reached down, under the seat of the Hog. "No, but they suspected I might have hidden something. Only place I would is in the Hog."

I looked at what he pulled out from the Hog's seating. A data chip. Damn. I'd no idea he'd hidden something in the cab.

"You expected them to double cross you somehow?"

"I had a backup plan if I had to destroy the original."

"What's so important on that disc?"

"Trade routes through and under the plains. One that the City's been using for many years."

I almost stomped on the brake. "There's a route under the cave system?"

"You were the one who said the water receded, right?"

I knew what he was going to say. So I said it for him, "They follow the river bed, genius. Why didn't you use that to get you over to the Port?"

"Because they'd know. It would give the secret away before I knew if they were worthy."

It was a good call, really. I never thought the caving system was that great. "I explored a lot of it, some while the Tromoal were there, but I never saw anything that went deeper than their breeding cave."

"Maybe I'll get to show you. If I can see the Tromoal eggs up close, see the cavern."

It wasn't because he wanted to steal anything. I knew it was for the experience.

"I've got a lot to talk about with the Matriarch. She's said as much. I guess it won't hurt, but it is her decision."

"All right." He grinned.

"Would you tell me more about what's going on at home? Distract me while we drive to meet this ambush. . ."

"My world is usually pretty fun. I had friends, even a girlfriend."

I cringed, but he carried on. "My life was just fine. Then I started to get pain in my knee. I went to the docs. They sent me for some tests."

I saw him shiver with the recollection of the events. "I'm sorry, I shouldn't have asked."

"No," he said, pulling my hand into his. "I have a form of bone cancer. They treated me for a while by taking out the affected bone. I had a knee operation and treatment, but it didn't work. So I lost my leg."

"I had no idea. I'm so sorry."

"The cancer was already deep seeded, spread quickly. I was diagnosed with months left to live. Told to get all my affairs in order. So I tried, and I drank myself into a stupor most nights, blew all my friendships and relationships apart. I was an ass."

"And you thought it would be a good way to spend your last few months?"

"Yes, gaming was exactly the right way to spend the rest of my life."

"So why did you end up in here, in this game, our world? Not another?"

"I saw an advert on a local TV station." I must have looked confused as he explained. "It's like your monitors, but a live show. They were seeking players to join them in their alfa stages."

"Tell me about how this game works?" I asked. I'd gathered certain elements of the how, over the last few years, but I wanted to know more.

He blew out a breath. "This is as simple as I can make it. Every Visitor has three Aspects and six Aptitudes. The Aspects are what you are, and the Aptitudes are what you can do. Every trait a person has can be categorized as Body, Mind, or Soul, any activity a person may engage in can be slotted into one of the six categories: Combat, Endurance, Diplomacy, Faith, Logic, and Subterfuge. While the Aspects are self-explanatory, the Aptitudes are a bit more complicated."

Alex watched me carefully. I nodded to let him know I understood and eased off the Hog's gas, this was interesting and I hazarded a guess. "So, you gained Aptitudes in talking with Dalfol?"

"I did." He pointed ahead, where I could see the horizon and most likely where the ambush would happen.

"Is there a way that I can see what I am. My character?" I questioned, unsure if I should see the inner workings of what made me... me.

"I could show you, but that would be..." his voice trailed off, yet he took my hand in his, adding, "personal, right?"

"What does all this mean for me?"

"It means you're very unique." Alex stared out the window, then pointed. "They're up ahead."

I already knew. Dalfol was keeping me informed while I tried to keep myself focused.

Do you want me to take them out? he asked. I wanted to laugh. No way was this Tromoal getting all the fun. No, I wanted to fight some of my own battles.

Alex then asked the same thing, so I answered them both.

"No, the Tromoal can't take them out. Any of them. If anyone sees them do so, or sends a message to a friend before we destroy them, the Tromoal's cover, my cover and yours are blown. We must keep our friendship a secret. There will be a time and a place for us to strike hard, and that time isn't now."

Alex looked to the back of the Hog. "I guess you need to man the weapons then!"

I smiled, and just like we had before, Alex slipped into the seat, and I headed up and out the back to defend us.

Slipping my goggles on, and covering my face as much as possible, I zoomed in so I could see where the enemy was. The trap was pretty easy to spot, and I instructed Alex to try to avoid it the best way I could. We'd be chased no doubt, but they had to have something up their sleeve if they thought they could catch the Hog.

Then I saw them. With a sigh, I shouted, "Alex, they've got bikes."

They also had a car. I could make out someone standing on the back of it, just like I was. We were outmanned and outgunned.

"Keep that foot on the floor! We're in for a rough ride."

I tried to balance the gun and work out a way I could fire the other hidden weapons. Maybe with some luck, I might be able to take out a bike or two. The truth of the matter was, we needed another way out, and Dalfol wasn't the answer.

As Alex drew closer to them, the bikes sped towards us. Each had a pillion, and their intentions were to try to take me out as much as take the Hog. We couldn't let them do either. I couldn't have a rival gang with two cars. Where did they get it from anyway? Were they associated with the Port? All this seemed highly unlikely.

I noticed something else—a man standing on the back of their car. It was Dail.

How? What? Why? Everything inside my mind exploded as the car's guns turned to aim our way.

Was he just after me to win this war against the city? What the hell was going on? I wanted to scream at him, punch him and do much more than gut him. Love. What was love when he stood there ready to attack us!

I wouldn't let this lie. This was him being a traitor on all levels.

I felt sick, but I focussed all my energies into defending the Hog, Alex, and the Tromoal.

CHAPTER 4

The first bike's firebolt came hurtling towards us, and I was shocked to see the pillion also had a weapon. I pulled my gun around, cranking its energy pack, and was about to fire. I had one chance to hit the pillion, and hopefully, that would derail at least one of the bikes.

I pulled the trigger, and the energy blast shot out slamming into the pillion's shoulder. He fell, and Alex whooped.

The rider didn't come off, though. He whizzed past us and spun around while the second bike's pillion began shooting. The Hog's thick hide took the blasts, but the softer top wouldn't last for long. I could only presume Dail had also told them all the tricks and advantages I had. I screamed.

Spinning the gun back around, I turned to face the second pillion. As he lined up his shot, the Hog's gun blanked and spluttered. No. It couldn't fail. Not now. I slammed my fist onto the battery pack and hoped it would start up again. The energy light flickered, and with a flash, I was able to let off a shot. I missed.

With both our current speeds, I had one more chance. I focussed, sucked in a breath, and fired again. This time it, hit the rider and took them both off in a spectacular explosion of catapulting bike and bodies.

We reached level with the other vehicle, and this time, I noticed Dail was aiming directly at the Hog. He was going to go for the fuel tank.

"Alex!" I yelled. "Hard right!

The Hog complained, but this time, when Alex spun the wheel, we didn't flip. The shot blast from Dail flew past us and didn't hit the tank. The explosion behind us, however, was enough to take out the last rider. Yet the car made its way out, racing to push us off the road into a more dangerous track or to flip us.

I tried my best to keep hold of the gun, the road becoming more and more uneven. I was being bounced around something wicked. "Alex, don't let him run us off."

"I'm trying!"

I took aim this time, and instead of trying to shoot Dail or their tank, I was going to aim for the one place I knew I could stop him, at least for a while. The wheels.

As much as anyone was prepared, there wasn't room for two spares. This double tap shot was something I needed more energy for. Kneeling down, I struggled to pull out the battery pack stuck under the back seat of the Hog. A loud pop and I felt burning pain. My back seared with a fiery blast.

HEALTH – 50%

It had meant to kill, but it hadn't. It caught my left shoulder, almost leaving me with no feeling. I needed that arm to hold on while I aimed for their tyres.

I had to try anyway. The first strike hit, and the tyre popped. The second also hit. I let out a cry of relief although the pain was excruciating. The car behind us was off the road. We'd be safe for now.

Dalfol's voice screamed in my head. *You're injured. Get to the safety within the cave system as soon as you can. The Matriarch will be able to help.*

No, we need to finish this. I pushed back to him as I noticed my health drop all the more.

HEALTH – 45%

Then I ducked down and grabbed something to wrap around my arm. I slid down into the passenger seat.

"Keep driving," I said to Alex. "We need to get to the cave system, and I'll manage until then."

I saw the concern on his face but smiled. I wanted to hug him. He had done great with the driving.

Dalfol directed me, and I passed the info onto Alex. We were coming in from a different spot this time, a section I hadn't even known about, but Dalfol wanted us safe and inside as soon as possible. I knew why. *Can you hide the Hog's tracks, though?* I asked.

Do not worry about those. We'll fly overhead and dust them. They won't have a clue where you've gone.

I wanted to agree with him, but if Dail knew about the underground caving system, he'd also know where we'd go.

That was when I heard the ping. A message waiting from him.

I didn't want to open it. Alex didn't know it was Dail who was chasing us. "Alex, that was my fiancé shooting at us."

"What?"

"That was my fiancé, and now he's sending me messages."

"What does it say?"

"I don't know yet."

"Well, open it."

Dail's message came through clear: *You've no idea what you're doing. You're aligning with a player! A monster, who will have you and everyone you love killed.*

I read it aloud.

"I'm not a monster," Alex said, his brows creasing.

I knew that, but I didn't know what Dail was harping on about.

I tapped out my reply: *I don't know who you are? You almost killed me.*

Dail returned: *I needed the Hog to stop. I needed the chance to talk to you.*

By talk, you mean kill Alex and take the information he has? I asked him.

Yes. The information he should have given us back in the port. Why he didn't, I don't know.

Maybe because he suspected it would all be used for the wrong reasons. Greed! I was getting angrier with each message.

Not just greed, Maddie. You don't understand. We wanted to go in and take the loot that was surrounding the Tromoal eggs.

You have no chance. They'll destroy you. Goodbye!

Alex's shaky voice came to me through my angered argument via our pm system. "What's going on?"

I quickly found the delete point and did the one thing I never thought I'd do again. I erased Dail from my memories.

"I blocked him. They'll be coming to look for us and the entrance to the Tromoal hiding spots. They know it's around here somewhere."

"Yeah, but the Tromoal can defend themselves surely?"

Alex stopped the Hog once deep enough inside the cave. I noticed that after a while, Dalfol's voice echoed back to me.

Follow the cave system as deep as you can. We'll meet you at the bottom junction. There's a spot you can leave the Hog and follow on foot. It widens out a lot and goes deeper.

"This is part of the water system, isn't it?" Alex asked.

I nodded, but I noticed he looked pretty blank for a while. So, I answered clearly. "Yes, it is. This is a huge section of the caves. I think they really need to defend this spot if Dail's going to follow."

I had my doubts, but I spoke to Dalfol. *Don't worry. I want to hope that there's a better way.*

So do I, Dalfol thought.

The caving system was as Dalfol described. It expanded, and we opted to leave the Hog. I took out my backpack, shoved some water, rations, and a few flasks inside. I had no idea how long we might be down here or if the Hog would be safe till we returned, but I wasn't chancing it.

We walked along as the walls seemed to twinkle and emanate a glow to allow us to see ahead.

"Wow, this place is beautiful," Alex said. "I know I've seen parts of it before with you. Just never seen it like this—so alive." We seemed to walk for ages, the cave dipping and then climbing as we took several turns.

I heard and felt the vibrations coming from ahead before Alex asked, "What's going on up there?"

I didn't know, but I wanted to. It sounded like some sort of. . .

Not an argument, Dalfol came back to me, *but a slight disagreement.*

I cringed, and then I smelled the burning acrid smell of Tromoal fire.

Don't be afraid. As soon as you enter this domain, they will stop squabbling.

I breathed in and moved forwards rounding the next corner.

Dalfol bellowed, and I could see him. He was facing off with a pale silver Tromoal, much larger than he was.

The Matriarch, where is she?

Dalfol didn't answer. He seemed to be talking to the one he was fighting with. The other Tromoal looked over to me, and then suddenly stopped its vibrating annoyance and dipped its head. Dalfol lunged, gripping its neck, forcing it to the ground.

I heard part of their conversation.

You will not ever challenge me again! My decision to bring them in was mine to make. She is the lady of the skies; she is our lady. We obey Riezella and her. Understand?

I didn't hear the other side of the conversation, but I was worried he was going to kill the other Tromoal. I ran forwards, and Alex tried to stop me, but he couldn't I was too fast. I moved in quickly my hands up, and Dalfol glared at me before he let the other go. There were sharp teeth marks in its neck, and I wanted to cry.

I realised there was probably some kind of hierarchy that had to be adhered to. They needed to have a dominant and submissive.

The other Tromoal's eyes trained on me, and I felt its regret.

I stepped forward and placed my hand over the wound. It started to heal, the ring on my finger glowed, and then I pulled it back. I heard the voice of the silver Tromoal. *Apologies and thank you for your kindness.*

I looked to Dalfol, not knowing what to say or do. Alex was the one who came up behind me and caught me as I was about to wobble over. "You've got to stop healing things," he said.

"Why?" Then I saw it.

HEALTH – 30%

"I can see your health drop. You're putting yourself at risk."

He handed me some water out of his pack, and I felt the pain throb in my hip once more. I wanted to slug all the elixir I had, but I couldn't.

Riezella is waiting for you. Dalfol motioned to the back of the large cavern.

Can Alex go with me?

Dalfol shook his long neck. *No, you must go to see her alone first. There are some things you need to see, which he cannot.*

There was probably a lot I didn't want to see—or know about—let alone Alex.

So I headed off. "I'll be back as soon as I can. When you're allowed through, I'll give the nod to Dalfol, and he will let you know."

"They won't eat me, will they?"

I laughed. "I sure hope not." Then I moved to leave the cave system I was in.

The cavern dipped and then opened up once more. It revealed a large chamber filled with loot. So many gems, glittering objects made of gold, and then much larger objects, armour maybe? I reached down, picked out a solid red gemstone, its glittering energy pulsating into me.

This cavern was richer than anyone's wildest dreams. I put the gem in my pocket. How far were we actually underground? Was this all full of water at some point? I had so many questions I wanted to ask, so many.

Up ahead, I saw Riezella, her large frame seemed so tiny in this room. There was also something—no, someone—standing before her.

Who was that?

I moved forwards, and the closer I got, the more I could see. This was a woman—a woman in a white flowing dress with sandals whose laces traced up long legs, her glowing red hair shimmering around her frame.

She moved to greet me. "Thank you for coming to visit as you promised. I am the human form of Riezella."

I was totally confused now. "Can you explain this to me some more. I'm not with you?"

The Tromoal seemed to be asleep, and I placed my hand on her flank—no, not just asleep, but stone cold, like she wasn't alive anymore.

That was the weirdest feeling I'd ever come across. The woman smiled. "I've taken this form because I'd like to show you another side of this world. One I think you'd be most interested in."

She held out a hand for me, and I took it. "There's a place where we can go, with a little magic."

She turned, and the whole room lit with red hues. The sparks around the room made me jump, but she held on tightly. I was surprised at her strength, but I shouldn't have been. At the end of the day, she was a Tromoal, right?

Waving a hand in the air, the room before me shimmered, and with a flash, the wall opened up, and I could make out something on the other side. A different world.

"I wanted you to see the place where Alex comes from."

What? My mind whirled. That wasn't possible. "How can I see into his world?"

"The game they think they created is very unique. But," she paused seeming to struggle with the words she picked, "to those of us from another world, this is a way in, a digital space, which we can inhabit or cross. To them, it might be just a game, but they created lots of ways for those of us who know how to manipulate things, to control what they thought *they* did."

"So that's the reason for all the system errors I'm seeing?"

She nodded and waved her hand over the world before me. "You see all of this like I do."

The planet was mind-blowing. Buildings galore, lights, and cars. Oh my... the number of cars driving on their streets. How, I had no idea. I stepped forward, the grass squelching beneath my feet. I could smell damp, thick smoke, engine fumes, and many things I couldn't put a name to. I reached out and touched the side of a manmade wall, dilapidated and falling over, but amazing to run a finger over.

The people here were all just going about their daily lives. They had no clue we were here. "So, I'm not just an NPC?" I questioned.

"You started out as one," Riezella squeezed my hand, "but, no, you are not. What you really are, I must let you remember."

"You know what I am?"

Riezella pointed upwards to a large sign. It pictured my world, and I read: Puatera Online Open Call 29th April 2096. "You're like me," she said. "A crossover of sorts, a soul that's been reborn and integrated into a digital world."

"And Alex knows this?"

"No, he suspects some things. In fact, he suspects many things. He's just not voicing them to you."

"So there's a portal to his world. Where I could visit him for real?"

"I do not know if you're ready. It might be too much for you to handle, and Alex might not want you to see him. That is something for you to consider."

"Because he's sick, right? Here he's handsome, whole, but there he's not."

"Correct."

"I could ask him, talk to him."

"Maddie," her sharp tone stopped my thoughts in their tracks. "The reason I wanted to show you this is because he's not got long."

"You mean in his world?"

"His energy levels are being kept alive by the Clan. When they start to weaken, due to lack of food, they will not support him."

"That's a little harsh."

She lowered her head, turning away from the bustle of the strange planet. "It is the truth."

"Riezella, I love him. What can I do?"

"There is one answer, but I don't think you will like it."

The fact that there was an answer at all had me grasping at it. I wanted anything. Would do anything. She was intriguing me, but I physically shook.

The image shifted, and there was a large familiar cavern before us with four Tromoal eggs.

"The three larger eggs are growing well. There's enough energy inside them to form and bond with their souls. They will become strong individuals."

I could see it then. There was a smaller one. It was so tiny, compared to the others.

"The fourth egg will not survive." She reached out with her other hand, as if to touch it, but didn't. "He was supposed to be my first son, to carry on and have lots of Tromoal of his own, and to birth with his mate, the next Matriarch. But the egg can't call forth his soul."

Realisation sank in. "You want Alex to be the soul for your egg? I can't let him do it..." I gasped out. "I can't watch him become one of you." I tugged my hand away from her, and the vision of the cave vanished.

Riezella locked eyes with me. "You wish for him to have a wonderful life, no?"

Of course, I did, I really did. My heart was screaming at me to tell her 'no.' But my head nodded.

"Then you know what must be done, for him, for us *both*. I wouldn't have offered this if I didn't think you were both strong enough to handle it, and to work through any pain it would cause."

"If he returns home, he will die. This really is his last few months?"

"Not months. If the Tromoal do not get enough food, this will be his last few weeks. Maybe even less."

"Dail hasn't alerted anyone of the dangers, has he?"

Riezella shook her beautiful long hair, her chin dipped.

"If I see him again, I'll kill him myself."

"The next time you see him, you might have to."

I looked back to the caving system where I knew Alex was tucked away with Dalfol and the others. Was he scared? What was he doing?

"He's having the time of his life. Don't worry about him."

"Will you see him?"

"No, I don't want to interfere with his decision when the time comes. If he saw me, he'd be compelled to help, but that decision will have to be his. . ." She held up a hand, "and his alone. You can't interfere. Do not try to persuade him at all. This really must come from him."

"We have to rally the city and the surrounding people. We have to get you enough food to survive and to raise the broods."

"There is not enough time." Riezella's body shook.

I was the one now who stood defiantly. With confidence, I met her shimmering red eyes. "Yes, there is. We'll make time. To survive, we'll do everything we can. Dail and Port Troli will regret their betrayal." I smiled at her. "There's a way for us to move the food without them knowing. We can do all of this, and they'll only see the Tromoal staying fat and happy."

She wasn't convinced, but I had to keep going. "I need to know everything about the caving system."

"I can't tell you that."

"Yes, you can and you will. Alex and I will be the only ones who know. I promise you."

She regarded me with complete silence. I wasn't sure if she would agree, obviously

"I will inform my second and mate what it is we are doing."

"Your mate?" I was the one who grinned this time. "Dalfol?"

"Of course. Did you think I would have anyone else watching over you?"

"Alex will be pleased that at least he's been keept company with the man of the clan."

Riezella moved back towards her Tromoal body. "The silver Tromoal he was fighting with is his sister, Fie. She's never wanted me to be his mate and thought I would bring nothing but trouble to the Clan. I have protected him and our brethren for many years. It's time someone else thinks for us, helps us."

"That job is now mine," I said. "I will think on this somewhat. I've colleagues I can trust, those who aren't associated with Dail. Some I'd lay my life down for."

"You never wondered why you couldn't be with him?"

"I do now." He was a traitor and more, a liar, and I hated that. I now hated him. Maybe I'd get my retribution. Maybe I'd be the one to bring down all his plans.

I hoped Alex would make the right decision for him. I didn't know how he would become one with the youngster or what might happen afterwards. Would he remember anything? Anything of us? I swallowed my pride and moved to go back to them.

I glanced to Riezella and watched as her ghostly appearance vanished into the sleeping Tromoal. The next time I looked, the large beast was awake and staring right at me.

Go, Maddie. I trust you with the whole of our Clan's future.

I breathed in and stepped back through to where Alex and the others were waiting. He sat by a small fire, totally dominated by Dalfol and his sister's body. They were curled around him and sleeping while Alex talked away. I wondered who to until I saw the shadow of someone near him. The Tromoal weren't sleeping. They were in that stasis like Riezella had been. Dalfol was showing his human self to Alex. My heart wept.

CHAPTER 5

I moved to the fire pit and sat by Alex. Dalfol bowed his head to me and vanished.

"You know how amazing he is?" Alex said.

I picked up a stick, noticing the rabbits cooking. They smelled delicious.

"I do. I'm glad he showed you a part of what they can do."

"In my world, as I said, they're called dragons, but these here... they are so much more than that. They have two parts to their nature. An almost human side and the part that is animalistic."

I listened as he explained most of what I'd just seen. His voice was full of excitement and happiness or was it all a ruse?

"What's the plan now? You were gone for a really long time. Dalfol helped me catch these..." He poked dinner. "They've been cooking an hour."

I rubbed my shoulder. I'd lived with pain for so long, it was a habit. Then I realised there was no pain. Had Riezella cured me?

HEALTH – 80%

Alex watched me carefully. "How's your shoulder?"

"Seems fine now, I think Riezella healed me."

"And our plan?"

Dumbfounded, I nodded. "Getting back to the village and the City is a high priority. We need to rally everyone and get food down here to the Tromoal. Without food, this world is lost."

"Then let's eat and make a plan."

I was surprised, but the rabbit tasted amazing. Fed and watered, we worked out the details to move underground to the city. I saw something move out of the corner of my eye. It was Dalfol and his sister. Together, they shuffled into the light.

"We would like to assist you," she said. "I am Fie, and I apologise for my earlier behaviour."

Dalfol punched her with a soft fisted hand and spoke. "It is good to converse for real, Maddie." He grinned, stepped towards me, and took my hand in his. I shook it, and he sat before us. "We've listened to most of your plans. I think they will work out well, but there's only one section of the cave system where you'll be able to corral the cattle without spooking them."

"There's a large farm to the north of the city. We've spotted them already, but moving that number of livestock will not be easy," Fie informed me.

"I think there are a few mages and other folks who will help," I replied. "We've got to keep you fed for the next. . .? How long?"

"My eggs are all laid," Fie said while patting her flat belly. "They will hatch in a day, and they'll be flight ready in two."

"We have less than three days." I glanced back to Alex.

I felt totally selfish looking at him. Could he make the right decision for his future? What if I told him how long he really had left? No, because he'd make the wrong choice then. I was sure of it.

I swallowed. "We'll sleep here tonight, then make our move back to Trox with the Hog."

"We'll not move. Dalfol and I will fly you through."

"I might need transport when we get there."

Dalfol rubbed the side of his face, almost like he might scratch as the Tromoal he was. "Then we will get your Hog to you."

I had no idea how, but I wanted to see that. "It might take a few of us, but we can carry it. Maybe even... my sister is strong enough."

She rolled her eyes. "You get the two of them to the city, and I will sort out that stupid Hog."

I liked these two. They bantered like any family would. Alex reached over and tugged me to him. "We need to rest. This has been one very exciting day."

I agreed and settled back in Alex's arms. Staring at the Tromoal scales around us. I reached out, my bare skin touching cool flesh. Dalfol nodded his goodnight and vanished as did Fie.

I will speak with you first thing. We will then get you to the city as soon as possible. Rest well, my friends. We'll sleep beside you. Do not worry. We won't turn over in the night. He laughed, and I did too.

Alex leaned in, his lips brushed mine. "Thank you for being so amazing," he said.

I pulled him to me and hugged him tightly. I wanted to be with him, to make love to him right here... *nope.* I snuggled against his neck and drifted off to sleep.

I woke with only the pain in my hip as a reminder that things were the same, yet I was still against Alex's chest.

Dalfol's cool scales poked into my back, and I squirmed. "Why don't you guys feel warm? The sheer amount of heat you have inside should be like radiators!"

Dalfol laughed. *We'll take you to the cave entrance on the opposite side of the mountain. My sister is getting that vehicle of yours with a friend.*

"Oh, she actually has friends."

I heard her snort from a distance, and I laughed. Standing to stretch, Alex lost the one thing keeping him warm, and he grunted. "Hey, that's not fair."

"Come on. We need to move," I said and gently kicked his boots.

Alex stood and shook the dust off his trousers. "I have to admit, I'm nervous as hell."

I couldn't agree more. The thought of getting on top of this humongous creature with wings was terrifying. However, I was prepared to do anything to get home, fast. And that meant we needed to fly.

The walk through the rest of the cavern was tough. Even for Dalfol, he almost got stuck twice. *I'm not as small as some of the others.* He sighed as I worked to dislodge some stalactites to help free him. They were not easy things to move. They clung to the ceiling for dear life.

Being stuck underground is my worst nightmare. Dalfol lowered his head and waited for us to finally get him free.

For a creature of the sky, I can only imagine.

The cool air drifted in as we approached the other side of the cavern. The outside light was just poking its head up. A good a time as any to actually get some fresh air.

Dalfol stretched his wings out fully when he could. The glinting of the sun on his massive frame astounded us. When he shook, the ground moved.

Turning to face us, I could swear he was grinning. *Are you coming?*

I moved first, towards his front legs, hoping to use them as leverage to climb up. Alex followed me, and when I needed a push, he gave me one. I reached down to help him.

The back of Dalfol had large sharp spines, so we could each sit between one. "Use your jacket to hold on," I shouted having almost sliced my hand open.

I held on with my new jacket sleeves. I hoped the fabric was strong enough to hold.

Dalfol lowered his wings, and with one powerful leap, he thrust upwards and launched into the air. I let out a scream.

I never thought it would be so cold up here. The sky so blue, clouds above and below us beautiful and fluffy...and freezing. Wisps of the atmosphere whizzed past my face, and I wanted to try to eat them.

Alex reached forward and managed to wrap his arms around me. "This is amazing. Thank you."

I wasn't sure why he was thanking me.

The journey took less than an hour. I thought I heard Fie behind us but couldn't see her. I hoped the Hog wasn't going to land in some field way out in the desert smashed to smithereens. That would put a real dampener on our progress.

I pointed to the City of Trox. *Do you know where to drop us?*

No, I only know of the city. If you wish to go somewhere else, point to where now.

The only landmark I thought I might see from the clouds was the town's main halls. Its large white three-story structure should stand out. Dalfol circled until I pointed further out where he could land discreetly.

Dalfol set himself down with ease, but the ride was bumpy for us. I fell off and landed on my ass, and Alex almost did the same. Dalfol turned to face us, his tongue hanging out.

Behind him, Fie and another Tromoal were carrying the Hog in a hammock, and they managed to land with only a slight bump. They glanced to Dalfol and then left without another word.

I must leave you, too, he said. *I need to hunt.*

I understood. Reaching over, I scratched the side of his face, a low rumble echoing within him. Alex and I walked towards the Hog.

"Where are we going?" Alex asked. "I've never seen this side of the city before."

"This is my town. The main organiser of all the Runners is here, Dresel."

"Oh, your boss?"

"I am the boss of me," I retorted. "No, he's just an organiser. He lands the jobs and gives them to the runners he trusts the most. He does a good job, and we pay him a small fee."

"Whatever works."

I unlocked the Hog, finding him a little worse for wear on the inside, the contents of the back seats strewn all over. "I guess his ride was a rough one."

I pulled out a few things and began to repack it with Alex's help. When we were ready, I started the engine and drove towards town.

It didn't seem like many people were about and this worried me. Usually, there was a lot of hustle and bustle around the stations and the main pub and inns. A couple of guys looked over at us as we drove past, but that was it.

I parked the Hog, and we got out. Dresel's office door was partially open, and I moved to knock.

Dresel shouted, "Come in."

And I pushed it open. He took one look at Alex and me, and then he let out a breath. "Thank god!"

Standing up, he moved towards me and grasped me, holding me tight. I pushed him off. "Dres, what is it?"

"Dail said you were dead."

Alex shot me a glare. "He hoped we were."

"Dres, we need to talk. This needs to be private. Is your office totally secure?"

He frowned, and then shook his head. "Come with me."

I never once thought his office hadn't been a safe place. The talks we'd had, the arguments. Our relationship was, complicated. As I hated him, I also trusted him. Who else would offer me jobs they knew I'd complete?

But if he knew the office was being watched, why did he do business there?

Dresel took us outside to what I thought was a back door to a shed. He removed a piece of wood to reveal a control panel. He palmed the panel and moved to go inside. Once we were in, it seemed to suck the air out. Pitch black, I struggled to see and reached for Alex. He was still there.

Dresel then spoke. "Don't be annoyed, Maddie."

"Annoyed at what?"

A soft light broke the darkness at the far wall. "Walk towards it. We'll take a short trip down. There we can talk."

I did exactly as he directed and found myself in a small box with the two of them. Dresel pushed another panel on the wall, and a voice spoke. "Access granted, Commander Dresel."

"Commander? Since when? What is this? What's going on?"

Alex looked as shocked as I did when the light came on in the box. I had no idea what this was.

"This is a lift, Maddie," Alex replied. "It looks like we're going down under your town."

"Correct," Dresel said and held out a hand for Alex. "I presume you're Alex Dubois?"

They shook hands and their eyes locked. "Do I know you?" Alex asked him.

Dresel turned to me, and something about him changed. I saw a flicker above his head. And I stumbled back and hit my ass on the wall. "You're a visitor?"

"No," he said. "I'm not."

"Then what is this?"

"This is a project I've been working on for a while."

"Ahh, then I think I know." Alex smiled, but I didn't understand their conversation. How could he *know* when I didn't?

Dres waved us to the wall. "Please, come on in."

A doorway opened before us, and Dresel stepped out of the square box. Alex followed and held out a hand for me.

"If you're not a visitor, then what are you?" I could see where his tag should be, but nothing was there.

Alex whispered to me, "I don't see anything. What are you seeing?"

Oh, so he didn't know.

"It's almost like your player tag. The space is there. There's just nothing written in it. Why?"

Dresel moved down a corridor inside this strange place. The walls were white, and a strange smell permeated the air. I shivered but wasn't really cold.

Dresel opened another doorway. "You wanted somewhere to talk. This is the only place I have that I know isn't being tapped by a tech or mage. Please come in, and make yourself at home. I'll get some drinks then you can tell me why Dail says you're dead."

Alex sat on a couch, placing his feet on a footstool. I thought he looked really relaxed considering what we'd just been through. Then I noticed his health bar. I went to him and sat. "Are you feeling okay."

"Tired."

I swallowed. The Tromoal were struggling already with his health. Or maybe it was because we were underground.

Dresel moved to sit, offering up a tray of drinks and some snacks. I didn't understand everything that was going on, but I took the drink. I was thirstier than I'd realised. "Thank you. It's got surois in it?" I noted it had healing properties as my Health increased.

HEALTH – 100%

He nodded. "I always keep some in stock. In case."

I watched him as he sipped his drink, the buzz from having full health washing over me. He met Alex's gaze and then asked me, "So, tell me, why are you dead?"

It didn't take me long to run through the last three day's events. Alex backed me up as often as he could, and Dresel didn't interrupt. He just nodded in all the right places.

When I finished and sat back rubbing my eyes, he picked up a large flat device off the table. Within a second, he'd tapped into the screen.

Several views popped in front of me, and I could see the desert plain, Port Troli and the City of Trox. I didn't understand why he had all of this.

Alex whistled. "You've got quite some tech on hand. Where did you get all this?"

Dresel placed a finger to his lips. "When Dail messaged me you were dead, I came down here, not wanting to believe it. I tracked back and watched this. . ."

A moment later, I saw the Hog blasting across the desert plane with the bikes and another car in tow. The view stopped.

"There's something very amiss here, and we've got a lot of planning to do if this town and city are to survive."

I pointed to the far screen. As I saw something glisten in the darkness of it. "You're watching the Tromoal birthing cavern?"

Alex let out a gasp. One of the eggs at the centre of the cavern rocked, and a crack appeared on the surface.

"Yes, I watch them every year. I was the one who snuck in and placed the cameras around the chamber. I make sure that nothing is amiss and that all the young are healthy." Dresel grinned. "I asked you not to be mad at me, yes?"

I sat forward on the edge of my seat, but all I really wanted to do was grab him by the scruff of the neck and order him to tell me what the hell was going on.

Alex coughed. "I understand, Maddie. Dresel is one of the game's designers."

"The what?" I stared at him, then looked to Alex.

"All this is where I keep an eye on the world," Dresel said. "The whole of the world. I am the one who created Puatera."

"So why do you look out for me then?"

"You're different, the Tromoal are also different. Something changed a few years ago. That day you were attacked, the day you almost died."

Alex pulled me back. "Tell her the truth, Dresel. The day she did die."

"Alex is correct. That day, Maddie, you did die. You were, however, the first NPC..." I scowled at him. "Sorry, you were the first person to re-spawn back here—with memories."

I felt Alex let out a breath beside me. "I knew it," he said, his fists curling—not from anger but excitement. "I knew that was what happened to her."

I shook my head. I couldn't quite believe this. It seemed impossible. The fact that I'd actually died out there in the desert at the hands of

Riezella... she hadn't said that. Or was it still after the fact? I couldn't remember, and I needed to.

I pushed myself back into the chair, placing both hands over my eyes to try to wipe away everything I was feeling. It hurt. My hip hurt, and this hurt my brain a lot.

Dresel looked to Alex. "I'm sorry you got caught up in all this," he said. "Your experience and level in this world should be so much more for what you've been through."

"Levelling up isn't everything. Seeing the things I have, the loot, the Tromoal was... so much more," as I watched as Alex's features changed from wonder to anger, though. "We need to do something now, though, to aid all the people around here. We can't let this world fall apart."

"I don't want to add any more influence than I already have." Dresel sighed. "I guide the game by nurturing quests and players, but I can't alter the paths that are already deep seeded."

Struggling to follow, I asked, "You're not going to help us rally the city to get food for the Tromoal?"

He lowered his head. "I can't. What happens from here on out is something the players and the people must do."

I breathed in. I was going to fail them. I was going to fail them and let them die.

"Fine." I pushed myself up, and grabbing Alex's hand, I moved to leave. "Then we have a lot of work to do. I must speak with the Runners."

Dresel moved to follow us out. "Maddie, I am with you, I just—"

"I understand," I said. "Alex, go on to the box thingy, please. Let me speak with him alone." Alex reluctantly moved away from us, and when he was out of earshot, I followed with, "I also understand why everything went wrong for us."

Dresel lowered his head, heat flushing up his neck.

"Don't be upset," I said softer now. "I never regretted us giving it a go. I just hated the arguments we got into over jobs. You never wanted me out on the more dangerous ones. And now I think I know why..." I paused. "What would happen to me if I died again?"

CHAPTER 6

*D*resel displayed genuine emotion for me as he gazed into my eyes. I wanted to shy away, to pull back. "Dres?"

"When Leon left you, you were devastated. I picked up the pieces. Remember?"

Memories passed through me of our first few romantic encounters. "I do. You brought me back around. Treated me with respect..." I let out a breath. "Tell me. I can take it."

His eyes dimmed, and he looked away when he answered. "I don't think you'll get another chance. Of course, you'll respawn, but you might be the person you were before, without memories. What happened between you and the Tromoal was unique. It wouldn't be played out in the same way."

I swallowed, watching his emotion change again. This time, tears brimmed in his eyes.

"Maddie, the day you re-spawned was the worst day of my life. Do you remember it at all, really?"

I hadn't wanted to, but I looked back. "Bits and pieces from it, but no, not all of it."

"We fought all morning over a job you wanted to do. I knew something was going to happen to you, stupid game programming, and I'd begged you to not take that job. You went anyway. I kept track of you in the lab, and then I watched you die."

"It must have been horrible." I wiped a tear away from the side of his cheek.

"It wasn't just that, though. When you re-spawned, I expected our relationship to have ended. But," I felt him physically shudder, "you re-spawned with your injuries."

I took in the words, not remembering much of the ordeal after the Tromoal attack. I listened, though.

"Not just injuries, which I'd tried to help with immediately. You were screaming at me to help you. Screaming you didn't want to die, that I could help you. You looked around the lab, and it was like you knew everything. You hated me but didn't want me to leave you. Can you imagine how horrific it is to watch someone you love in that amount of pain?"

I could only shake my head. "I'm sorry."

"Don't be. It might have been the death of us... a good thing if I'm honest. But the re-birth of something no one expected."

The pain, I didn't want to remember. Much worse than just my hip. Broken bones, torn muscles, burnt skin. "You drugged me and took me to Shalice?"

"Yes. She did everything she possibly could to heal you. It wasn't pretty, though." Dresel wiped away his own tears, eyes blinking.

I understood more of him now than I ever could. Pulling him to me, I embraced him, feeling the tense muscles of his shoulders relax after a moment. "Thank you for being honest."

"I promise I'll be honest from now on."

I pulled back from the hug to stare into his eyes. "Just keep pointing us in the right direction, if you can."

"I will. But everything that happens from now on is not part of our programming. This is a totally unique event that will change the life of Puatera."

"Let us hope for the better then." I frowned, still not understanding everything. "Oh, do me one thing," I asked. "My programming *to fall in love*. Remove it."

Dresel nodded. "I promise." Moving to the strange box they called a lift, we returned to meet Alex. This lift thing was really weird. I wished we could have more of them in the world, especially to take us down into the Tromoal caves.

Alex walked beside me as we headed back to the Hog. "To the bar it is. We'll pick up the other runners there."

"How many of them are in this town?"

"Enough to make a difference."

Alex grinned. "Good. Meanwhile, a drink or two would go down well."

The short trip to the bar was quiet. The horses and Ebolos were grazing in buckets as usual outside, and Alex exited the Hog first. I recognised a couple of the horses and knew which of their riders would be inside. A few rivals, but more importantly, one of Dail's close friends, Josh. I wanted to see who he was aligned with since he was still in town.

I pushed the door open, and we strode inside, going straight to the bar where three guys were standing with pints in their hands. They stopped laughing when they saw me.

"To what do we owe the pleasure, Madz?"

Josh was Dail's friend. Yet he never asked me where I'd been? Why I wasn't dead? He didn't know about it.

I motioned the barkeeper over. "A bottle of whisky and several glasses, please."

He seemed reluctant at first, but when I stared him down, he complied. All three sets of eyes were on me. "First, I'd like you to meet my partner Alex. Alex, this is Josh, Brey, and Mrish." Alex greeted them all. But they looked reluctant to shake his hand. Josh placed his pint down, and I poured them all a drink. "I want to hire you all and those who you'd trust with your lives."

"You couldn't afford to pay us for any job like that!" Mrish laughed.

I reached into my pocket and pulled out the gem I'd taken from the Tromoal cave system. Alex gave me daggers. "Sneaky!"

Mrish took the gem, and I saw his eyes light up. "Where did you get this?"

"You won't get to know that, but you will receive more than your share of the wealth. If you listen to me and gather your men, we'll meet at the edge of town before sunset. Drink, then get sobered up. You've a long ride ahead."

Josh took the gem back handing it to me, then chased the other two off. "Go gather the men. I'll be there in an hour." Josh then also looked at the piece. "I trust you, Madz, but this has me worried. Where's Dail?"

I looked him in the eyes. "Dail's a traitor to the Runners, to everything we believe in."

He raised an eyebrow then nodded slowly. "Always thought he was on the shady side. What's really going on? If I have to persuade the others, I need to know."

"Hanson's estate lies in ruins, his family all dead. The Tromoal have no food, Josh. We need to get it to the desert plains as quickly as we can. They're hunting at present, and it's not going well."

Josh picked up a shot glass and downed the liquid. "I know where there are a few wild herds far out beyond where the Tromoal can smell them. The mayor's private herds are kept way up north. If we get to them, I think we can bring them down to the top of the plains."

I smiled. "We'll do anything we can to help."

"If I give you the coordinates to another camp, we might be able to corral both herds at the same time. How much food do they actually need?"

I had no idea. The sheer size of the Tromoal couldn't be used to gauge it. "Hanson's farms were massive, right? But he didn't breed stock just for them to eat. I don't really know. Just enough to get them through the next couple of days. A thousand, maybe less."

Josh turned to the barkeep. "If any Runners come in, who know me —Vic, Andy, Abel, let them know where we're meeting."

The barkeep agreed, and Josh finished off his pint and then another shot. "I think this might be the last bit of ale I get for a while."

I picked mine up and so did Alex. "Dutch courage," he said.

Walking out of the bar, I felt different. Maybe we had some hope. Alex tugged my arm. "You trust this Josh?"

"He's never let me down in the past, even though he was a friend of Dail's."

"You don't think he'll double cross you?"

Of course, it crossed my mind. After all, there was nothing to stop any of them. But I think they'll see the bigger picture. The fact was, the Tromoal and lack of Hismaw would affect us all. "We can only wait and see," I said. "I've got to try. I must have faith in the people around me."

When we rounded the corner, there was a gathering of about forty men and women. All eyes turned to me, and Josh indicated for us both to move to the front.

Josh shouted out to them, "Maddie's brought us a job. A big one." He hoped everyone could hear. They remained silent. "It's not just a job, though, but a matter of life and death. For us, and for our part of the country. The Tromoal have no food. Hanson's estate fell, and his workers abandoned him. We must reach the farmlands far north and bring down the cattle and raised sheep, pigs, and ebolos. Anything we can do to support the Tromoal through their breeding season. Without them, we'll have no Hismaw. Without that harvest, the creatures of the night will win. Our towns will no longer be safe."

There was a lot of whispering amongst them all, and then it went quiet. All eyes were on me.

I wasn't good at public speaking, but the words tumbled out. "I'm asking the most of you. I'm asking you to lay down your lives for our future. I don't know the outcome. I can only hope that we save the Tromoal to give us a better chance. There's a lot at stake, but you'll be rewarded, I promise you. I've never lied to any of you, and I won't start now."

No one spoke, though, and I wanted them to. It was as if they just needed a poke.

I stood and waited, and they did the same.

One of the ladies, Sarah, stepped forward, her long hair plaited behind her back. She wore traditional riding boots, jodhpurs and a jacket stitched with beautiful red and blue highlights. "We're all wondering the same things and wanting the best for us." She bowed her head. "Maddie, you've been amongst the élite for a long time. If you have something we need to do, we'll do it."

Internally, I grinned with pride. I wanted the admiration of them all, but I needed their loyalty more than anything. It seemed I had both.

Josh moved to my side, and spoke, "We're looking for three teams. There are farmlands I know we can tackle, and use, without it upsetting the stock for the cities, at least for a while. There are other ways we can grow or catch food I am sure. What's more important right now is that we keep the Tromoal here. Without food, there's no guarantee they'll stay."

I hadn't even thought of that, but then there were several large clutches of eggs—I'd seen them.

Riezella's voice drifted to me on the winds. *Maddie, I'm sorry, but I've already sent many of our Clan home. There's not enough food to go around.*

I looked to Alex, and I knew—when his health dipped, it was because the Tromoal had left the lands.

Riezella, we'll do this. Please, don't send any more away.

I hoped, with all my heart, she wouldn't. *I will do my best for all,* came the reply.

Quickly, I opened my interface and sent out a quest invitation.

OPEN CALL – TO ALL OF MAICREOL
QUEST – FEED THE TROMOAL
REWARD – HIDDEN TREASURES
BONUS – SAVING THE TROMOAL, YOU'LL EARN NOT
ONLY THEIR RESPECT BUT THE RIGHT TO SEEK AUDI-

ENCE WITH THE LADY OF THE SKIES. GENERAL
REQUESTS WILL BE CONSIDERED WITHIN REASON

I looked out to the crowd as I saw each person receive the notification. "The Tromoal are already leaving, but I know that some won't
go. I've already seen their eggs."

They gasped, and Sarah asked, "How did you see them?"

I looked to Alex. Yeah, that was a bit of a moot point. So I held up
the gem from the caves. It glinted red in the sunlight. "This is from
their cave system. There's not many who ever make it there, no visitor
ever returned. I did because Alex and I were lucky to get there when
they weren't. Trust me, they won't go, not all of them. But if we want to
keep their young alive, and for the Hismaw to form, we need cattle and
food."

"My Lady," Sarah lowered her head.

They knew. I looked around to them all, and they did the same. All
of them.... Sarah moved to stand beside Josh, Alex, and myself. "I
accept. My team will take whichever farm you think is easiest for us.
We're on horseback, though."

Several of the guys nodded in agreement, and an older gentleman
stepped forwards too. "I can take a team out with the Ebolos. They
move quickly, and through tougher grounds than the horses, we'll take
another sector."

That left just a few others, and of course, me and the Hog. "We
really need one more set, someone who can travel the furthest." I was
hoping there would be someone other than me to do that part of the
journey.

That's when I heard the pop-pop sounds of an engine, and a motor-
cycle rode in, stopping before me. The man on the bike, built well, and
with a long dark beard said, "Heard there's a job that needs doing, you
paying well?"

I clung to the gem, noticing his visitor tag –

CHIP MROTH – HEALTH 100%

He glanced at it. "If you can pay us in goods like that, we're in."

I hadn't seen this man around before but knew Dresel had a few bikers on his teams. "The name's Chip." He grinned, then spat out a wad of tobacco. "I'll invite the others over. You can invite the whole party on your quest then."

Josh didn't look so happy, but I wasn't turning down someone with as quick a transport as us. Even if I didn't know them, they would give us an edge. Besides, weren't normal visitors expendable? They'd respawn and come back to fight another day. I might not.

Get away, stupid humans.

I sensed Dalfol's unease. Was he struggling with something?

Josh coughed, bringing my focus back to Chip. "Then we've a plan. Josh can coordinate everyone." I motioned to Chip, and we moved over to a different side of the grounds. "Is there anyone else in your party?"

Chip glanced to Alex, and they shared a mutual note of respect. "Nice to see another player involved," he said. "What's the bonus for you?"

I didn't have a clue what he meant, but I wanted to keep them happy. Alex didn't look so pleased, either. "I'm just helping out. This isn't a quest for me."

Chip looked my way, and his grin widened. "After a little local, I dig it."

"We'll take the furthest farm. We need to get those cattle moving as quickly as possible. The fact you have a bike—"

"Bikes," he said. "There are six of us."

I swallowed. "Where are the others?"

"They're dealing with a small problem on the outside of town."

"Problem?" My heart flipped.

Darned pesky humans... I'll kill you if you don't leave! Dalfol bellowed in my head.

"Oh no." Both Alex and I shared a glance. "Dalfol!"

Alex reached out, grabbing hold of Chip. A knife to his throat. It was a split second event, and I had to stop him from putting the operation at risk. "Alex, take a breath."

Alex held my stare. "If they're hurting Dalfol, you have to stop them."

I locked eyes with Chip. "They're tormenting a Tromoal, back them off."

Chip gawked at me as if I were crazy. "No way. They've never been that close before."

"They're trying to capture him?"

Chip was going to nod till he realised the knife would cut him. "Yes, they are. What does it matter?"

"It matters. Call them off. Get them here. Now!"

Chip's face paled as Alex pushed the blade into his throat. A trickle of blood started to pool where the knife met skin. "Now!" he demanded.

CHAPTER 7

I watched on as the concentration on Chip's face changed, and within a moment, he looked to me. "It's done. But lady, you better have one hell of an explanation for this."

Josh had seen some of the altercation but hadn't intervened. The others had moved on already.

I heard the rumble of engines, and a few moments later, five more bikes came into view. The players dismounted. A woman in all black leathers slowly walked over, her tight clad figure showing her curvaceous body. She noted Chip with his throat bleeding. "Can't help but get yourself in trouble, can ya?"

Chip looked away embarrassed. The woman stopped before me, taking one look at Alex, and then Josh. She wasn't fazed at all, her attention solely on me. She was smart.

I checked out her tag:

CANDICE MASTERS – LEADER SAVAGE ANGELS –
HEALTH 100%

I found the name for her party interesting. They did look savage, that's for sure. But I felt drawn to her. I wanted to get to know her and the others, to know more about this game and the way things worked for them, especially after what Riezella had shown me.

"Maddie, I believe." She held out a hand to shake mine. "I'm Candice, a pleasure to meet you."

"Pleasure's mine. Nice bikes. They'll sure come in handy for this job."

"So it seems." She looked to Alex. "You can drop the knife now. Little ole Chip here will behave."

I was not surprised she was in charge. Watching her, I didn't like the way she looked over Alex. With a nod, she smiled at him. "Could do with someone of your stature, Alex. Would you like to join our party?"

"No," he was quick to respond. "Thank you for the offer, though."

"Your loss, but then again, I see you're doing well for yourself. Chip should have known better than to be argumentative with someone of your stature."

Her words confused me, most of their game talk did. The way they played the world around me, I found it fascinating. Then again I only knew how strong I was because of Alex. He'd told me most players wouldn't mess with me.

"Pleased to be here." Candice grinned, and a second later, she also accepted my general quest call.

The others in her party gathered around, and Candice introduced them with a nod in each of their direction. "You may or may not have noticed their tags, but Chip and Mark are our tanks. Rose and Mandy do the damage while Steve and myself take up any slack."

I saw the slight glow to her eyes, realising she might well have been a mage. Good to know even if I struggled with the grasp of how they *played*.

Josh coughed. "I don't have a vehicle to keep up with you guys. But if there's room for me, I'd like to come with you."

Six bikes, one Hog, and two hands. I didn't know what kind of retaliation we might come up against taking the cattle, but at least, with this number of people, we stood a chance.

"That's fine. Are we ready to leave?" I asked around the group. "Anyone need anything specific. If so, we'll trawl the village until we find it."

Candice looked about to the others. "As long as you've got water, food, and weapons."

Josh nodded. "I have a warehouse. Let's stop there before we leave the town."

I wanted to agree with him, but arming these bikers was worrying me. Candice placed a hand on my arm. "I see worry," she said, and I noted a spark in her eyes. "Don't be. We've accepted this quest. We'll do everything we can to get the job done, which includes laying our lives on the line."

I swallowed. Josh was the only one who didn't understand the meaning about their lives. "I hope that it doesn't come down to that, but if you lose anyone, is their re-spawn nearby?"

Candice let go of me and raised an eyebrow at Alex. "No, it's in Port Troli."

"Then we've one more stop first. We'll tie you to the village if that's acceptable?"

Candice nodded. "That's very thoughtful, thank you."

Alex smiled. "Where is *your* re-spawn point?"

"You were there earlier," I said and pointed towards Dresel's office. "The shed."

His eyes lit up. "I should have known."

"Maybe, but we'll make sure you're all aligned there."

Convincing Dresel to do that would be tough, but I'd do it. Somehow, if these people were going to die for us, they'd need to be somewhere safe at least near to us to come back. It was only fair.

Candice moved to her bike. I followed her, admiring the mechanics. "I'd really love to talk more." I touched the tank, and its engine sparked at me.

She smiled. "Seems he likes you, but I think you already have an affinity with the mechanics in this world. Yes, we must talk more, but on the road. Time's a wasting."

Candice started her engine, and I listened to the purr of the beast. I moved to walk away while the others mounted their bikes. This was quite the expedition for us, and yet I knew we had the most dangerous trip. The Northern farmlands were protected by the mayor's men. Maybe they'd defend it with their lives, I hoped not. This was the only option for all of us. They might not see it like that, and all three teams were up against a big problem.

I heard a whisper. *Maddie, thank you. The mechanical creatures were a little too fast for me to watch them all.*

I opened the side of the Hog, and Alex got in while I moved a few bits so Josh had some room. *No problem. I think they mean well, but they were just after some easy points in their gaming system.*

I will follow you as much as I can without being spotted.

Don't put yourself at risk. Return to Riezella. You can't afford the expended energy.

Dalfol knew I was right. *Come back to us safe.*

I let him go, and moving around to the front of the bikes, I led them out of town and towards Dresel's hut.

He was waiting, and he took all seven inside, leaving Josh and me. I walked around their bikes admiring the paintwork and their enhanced weaponry.

"You think there's going to be a lot of firepower up there, don't you?"

I nodded. "I didn't pick this job because it was gonna be easy. This short trip for us will be tough. Probably tougher than any I've ever had."

"Even crossing the plains in breeding season?"

I frowned and let out a sigh. "Mm, there's a few things you don't know that I don't want to share yet with you or the others. Just know that Alex and I can do this, and we've got everyone in this as top priority. We'll protect you any way we can."

"You've got me worried, Madz, but I do trust you."

"Why me over Dail? Really?"

He ran a hand through his hair. "We had an argument a couple of years back if I'm honest. He was going to ask you to marry him, and I told him you'd say no, that you weren't that kind of chick."

But he didn't he know that Dail had asked me again? I laughed at his words. "But he asked anyway, and I said no, so you were right."

"I had a thing for Dail a few years back."

"Oh." I hadn't known that. Was he trustworthy then?

"He didn't like me much after I told him my feelings," Josh freely admitted. "Used me on a few jobs then went his own way."

"I'm sorry."

"Don't be. He turned out to be an ass. I don't know what I saw in him."

I shook my head. "You and me both. We had a good thing while it was going, but when he got clingy and wanted me to retire off the road and marry him, the only thing that tempted me was he promised me a life of doing something else that I loved. When he didn't even know what else that was, I backed off. I couldn't imagine not being on the road."

"I know that." Josh smiled at me. "But after the injuries and the healing time, he didn't want you at risk."

Even Dresel didn't want me at risk, but I'd pushed him and pushed him until he started to give me the more entertaining and lucrative jobs.

I heard a couple of clinks, the door to the hut opened, and Candice nodded at me. "One more stop, and we're all set?"

"Yes, Josh's home is far outside of town. We'll head there and get whatever you think we'll need."

"The boys are eager to see." She grinned, and then looked to Josh. "Do you think you and Alex could take a ride on the bikes to follow us? I'd like a little talk with Maddie on the way there, in private."

Josh nodded. "Never been on a bike, but of course. Just tell them to go easy with me."

Alex watched me, but he agreed because I didn't protest. Seeing the two of them get on those bikes was exciting. Another thing that might help him see life in a different way.

I palmed the Hog open, and Candice slid into the seat beside me. She checked out the internal dashboard and systems with a nod and a wink. "Some serious upgrades here. Even I don't think we could do some of this stuff to the bikes."

"It took me a while, but I saved and earned my way through them. I also learned how to do some things myself."

"Good call. You never know when you might have to be the one to fix it all."

"Exactly."

I let the bikes lead us this time, without Josh next to me for directions.

"So, what is the reason for the chat?" I wasn't sure if I really wanted to know.

"Alex. What's the deal? I've not seen anyone with his skill set before. But his health is extremely low. You seem to know about our game. I'm curious to what you think of it all, of him."

Was she just curious about him or was it a bit of everything? "He's ill back in your world. That illness seems to have started to carry over here."

"He's dying." Her brow furrowed as she nodded. "I understand now why he didn't want to join the party. If he did, he might have lowered our chances. He's a nice guy."

"Yes," I said keeping my eyes on the road ahead.

"There's one more thing... you called us off the Tromoal? I mean I get they're important to the world, but it seemed much more personal. Is there something I should know?"

If I couldn't tell anyone else, then I wasn't going to now, so I held back. "No. Without them, we're going to face some very bad situations. The truth is some have already left. The less chance of their young surviving means we're all in trouble."

"And Dresel?"

"Just an NPC like me. He passes out quests, assigns jobs for us as Runners. Nothing more."

Candice's expression was cold, but I could see her inner self working. She didn't believe me. Then she tapped on the screen. "The boys have stopped. Must mean they've arrived. We should catch them up."

I turned down the path I'd seen them follow and pulled up behind the bikes. They were already inside of the building. When we found them, they were selecting weapons off a pile. I was shocked. Josh had been holding out. This was more than one hell of a haul.

"Josh? What were you storing all this for?"

"I don't know. I like collecting things. Seemed a good idea at the time."

I looked about the vast room. There were swords of all shapes and sizes, armour, shields. Then things got a little more exotic, guns, and their different types. Harpoons to magical plasma blasters. Sand holsters. One of the more antagonistic shotguns in our world. Some of this stuff was more than just a haul. "Josh, this is getting ready for war. Don't lie to me."

He frowned. "Yeah, I guess I was preparing for that. I knew it would come to us fighting the Port. Just didn't know the when. To be honest, Dail kept mentioning a few things—things I didn't like. So I kept it all hidden from him and others, hoping one day I'd be the one to help save the day."

"You think the time is now, though? Looking at this lot."

"Yes, I do, and after we've got the cattle down here, we need to maintain everything."

There was another nightmare about to unfold. But I didn't want the peaceful life. I was a Runner.

I pulled out some of the newer charges for the Hog. The square tips to the harpoons were magically enhanced. I liked that. I could do something with them. I wasn't the strongest of magical users, but with a boost, they'd likely find their targets much easier. I pulled out a dozen and stacked them at the side of the room.

Candice also pulled out a few items. "I think Josh is a hoarder." She laughed. Then with a whirl, she turned to the guys. "Boys, lock and load. We've an hour's ride into unknown territory. Then we need to get the goodies from the locals and pull them back here. The ride back will be slower. Never herded a group of cattle before, but I think we can pull it off if treat the bikes as horses and we corral them. Maddie, Josh, and Alex will bring up the rear."

The plan was solid, but the outcome might be a whole lot different.

"Let's go then," I said and moved to grab the harpoons.

The plains had been long and arduous, but the way to the north was tough, bumpy, and filled with the Mayor's men.

The first set we encountered, I thought we'd come unstuck with them.

The road, however, wasn't bad, but the time with Alex and Josh was. Josh asked too many questions. He didn't understand some of the things I tried to explain about Visitors. Alex took over, and I watched as Josh's face changed with understanding.

ALEX DUBOIS – HEALTH – 72%

I noted how Alex's health dropped a few more points while we drove North. Maybe this was because of the distance from the Tromoal. I hoped not. We had many more miles to go. If his health continued to drop, we might not get him there alive.

ALEX DUBOIS – HEALTH – 68%

He noticed I was looking his way. "I can't continue." He let out a sigh. "You'll have to leave me."

"What?" Josh put his hand on my shoulder. "Why?"

"I can't leave you."

"Yes, you have to pull over."

I eased off the gas but saw his health still dropping.

ALEX DUBOIS – HEALTH – 60%

I stopped the Hog, and three of the bikes stopped with me. Within a minute, Candice and Chip were back with us. When she pulled her helmet off, she only took one look at Alex and motioned to Chip. "You two are gonna stay here. You can make sure the land stays clear. We need the path out with nothing in our way."

Chip was confused, but he also didn't argue with Candice.

"We'll be fine," Chip said to me.

Alex agreed. "We can look after the road. No one will stop this train from coming home."

I moved to kiss him, and the other guys whistled in our direction. One shouted for us to 'get a room.'

I'd never felt so much before, but even a kiss like this was more than I'd ever experienced with any other person. Alex made me want to stay alive, and more than that, I wanted him to live.

"We'll be back soon, two hours, tops. As long as there's no real retaliation."

He didn't know so he just hugged me. "I'll not kill him," he motioned to Chip and Candice.

"I hope not," she said, "because if you do, then I'll come hunting you!" There was a playfulness to her this time though.

CHAPTER 8

The closer to the farmlands we got, the more my nerves frayed. I let Josh stay on the bike ahead since he wanted to scout for us, with one of the gals. He seemed to be enjoying riding to and fro, so I let him. That left Candice and me in the Hog. I took a swig from my flask, which she noticed but didn't speak about. Most of the runners knew of my ailments, but none of the visitors did. Or at least, I didn't think they did.

Candice managed to slip out the top of the Hog and started to load weapons. She was adept at doing this, using everything her skill set allowed.

Focussing in, I reached for my goggles and used the zoom. I slowed the Hog thinking I could see a twinkle of lights ahead. Candice must have sensed this, maybe seen them too.

"We've got company up ahead," I shouted.

Candice tapped once on the Hog's roof. Her speak for 'got it.'

I thought maybe they'd let us approach. Maybe things would be okay. We'd talk, negotiate, and it would work out fine.

But then there was a spit, spat, and one of the bikes was hit with a huge explosion. I swerved and managed to miss where a large crater appeared.

"Five up ahead," she shouted. "Looks like they're heavily armed, too."

"No kidding. Do you think the guys can take a couple of them out? We're not even near the main herds yet?"

Candice went quiet, and I finally understood what was going on. Two of the bikes sped up ahead, leaving two with us. Josh deftly swung around to face me and tapped the side of his head.

I focussed and brought up my interface, managing to find his. When there was a click showing a connection I typed out, "We need you in the rear. I've a feeling we're going to get some behind us. Candice can watch ahead. You make sure we're not flanked."

"On it," came Steve's response.

His bike spun around, and they started to tail off. If we were picked up by someone else, there would be hell to pay.

I slowed down just a touch more and let the two lead bikes find their marks. As a huge gunfight ensued, I pushed down on the throttle. Maybe this would go another way, but it didn't look like it. One of the guys was knocked off, and he ran towards the offending enemy, two swords glinting in the dimming light.

Candice tapped again on the roof. I put the pedal to the floor. If this was turning to a full-on hand-to-hand fight, we needed to back them up.

The Hog blasted past one of the bikes lying at the side of the road, smouldering. I hoped it would be all right. The two guys were now fighting off four others.

Candice looked at me. "I'm better picking them off here. I'm a healer too." Her energy sparked in her hands, and I winked. That meant I was going in. One more chug for the pain. I downed the last of the flask and threw the Hog into a spin, creating a huge dust cloud that choked off the four enemy attackers—and our own, of course, but at least we had an advantage.

I jumped out of the Hog, daggers ready, and flew at the first person

I saw. This turned out to be a guy, large build, and yet I found myself easily able to tackle him. They weren't very well trained. Which was good. I quickly managed to disarm him and put him out for the count without slitting his throat or killing him.

Candice had done exactly what she said, sending healing magic blasts to her guys to boost their injuries. Then she popped off the plasma blasts and hit one of the other guys in the chest. Now the remaining two men held up their hands to surrender. It wasn't really what we were after, but if it worked.

I stepped towards one. "We're not here to kill. We're taking the cattle, that's all. Your boss will be compensated fairly. But they are coming with us. Get it?"

He looked at me. "What? We were told you wanted the estate.

"No, there's a food shortage for the Tromoal. Don't you check your messages?"

One of them shook his head. "We got word there were several inbound enemies."

"Just take us to the head of the farm. We'll deal with everything else."

He stared at me until I pointed the dagger in his face. "Move, now!"

Reluctantly he did. The other guy followed. And we moved inside some incredibly large gates. "The bikes and Hog all right outside?"

"Josh will watch them and our backs."

"Good." The last thing we needed was no escape.

The men led us into a small dark corridor. There we walked through, and it took us out into a lighter side of the mountain range. We seemed to be high up and in the valley. The inside was huge. Up ahead was beautiful greenery, and then I heard them—hundreds of tiny feet and different levels of braying, and other things I'd never heard before.

This land was massive, the animals here free, happy. I turned to Candice. "I had no idea this was here."

"Nor I. There's enough animal stock here for years... more than years. The Tromoal would live for a long time in there."

"No, we're just after enough to get them over this hurdle. Then we'll get someone else into the estates and manage the lands there for following years."

"Got this all worked out, haven't ya?" she said with a grin.

I hadn't, but there was no reason to take more than was needed. Internally, I asked Dalfol. *How many do we need?*

Three hundred head. A hundred extra if possible.

So I informed the others. "We need four hundred headcount. That's all, no more. Just see whoever you need to in order to get it organised. We leave the grounds as the sun rises, with a day to get them to the Plains."

"You want to take them all the way to the plains in a day?" the smaller of the two guys asked.

"That's what I said."

"It's impossible."

I pointed the dagger at him this time. "No, it's not, and it won't be. We'll do more than get them there in a day. We'll get them all there in one piece."

"There are traulers out in the day. If you want to move them, it has to be now. Tonight."

I looked to Candice. "What's a trauler?" she asked.

I frowned. I'd heard the term once. "I thought they were myths."

He shook his head, and answered, "Creatures of the day to keep away strangers and other monsters." He shivered. They must be horrid creatures themselves to ward away other monsters. "If you take four-hundred out of here, there will be a hundred left by the end of the day."

I swallowed. "We can't move them at night. We don't know the area. They'd get away from us easy in the dark. We're on bikes, not horses or Ebolos."

The smaller man stepped towards my dagger and placed a hand on it. "Miss Vies, if I may ask why and tell the others. Maybe we would be willing to help you."

I stared at him. "Why would you want to help me?"

"I can see you're with a good group with working vehicles. Not many have them I'm told, only the best runners do."

"Ahh, so you know who I am?"

"Maddie, yes, we know who you are. As long as you're paying these guys, you can sort us out, right?"

"You mean the boss."

"I mean all of us. We've been on low enough pay as it is, hoarding these for all the wrong reasons. Maybe it was about time the world knew they were all here, to be distributed about somewhat. There's a great bloodline I think would really benefit the outside population."

"Oh, that is interesting," Candice said. "We have something to talk about in the future."

I was puzzled, but I didn't push her. I just wondered why she was so interested in animal breeding—money or was there something else. I looked to the guys about her, and yeah, I knew why. Maybe they wanted somewhere to call a base, to call home. The breeding of good stock would sort that out. She looked at me. "We're taking five-hundred and some breeding stock. And you'll compensate all of these men, yes?"

I didn't argue.

Several other workers came running out from one of the buildings. They spoke to the two men with us and then ran off.

The smaller man held out his hand for me. "I'm Karl, one of the foremen. This is Brost. We'll round up one of the far herds. They're more than a good age for feeding and carrying on the bloodline."

"That sounds like a plan. I think Candice and her men would like that and maybe someone to stay on and help them manage afterwards."

Candice threw me a dirty look, but I ignored her and motioned to the land. "There's so much here. Why is it so overstocked?"

"The mayor thought there was going to be a war for many years, and it didn't happen. Then he thought it would be soon, and again, sooner than before. Seemed all we were doing was herding animals to breed and keep, it was getting more and more expensive to keep them. But we managed."

"You've done a great job. Will he know there's so many missing?"

"I doubt it. We've kept the books clear of some of the finer animals anyway. We had a small competition going over the last ten years or more about who could breed the finer Ebolos."

I almost fell over. "You're breeding Ebolos, too? Don't they need special conditions to raise their young?"

"They do, but we managed to replicate it, and we've been getting a nice herd together of those, too."

Candice's eyes lit up. "May I go with him to look around the lands, see their other facilities?"

I didn't see why not, but that meant I would be left with no one to back me up. I wasn't scared, though. Or maybe I should be. It was the buzz from the fight and the potions I think.

I watched as Candice and her two guys followed the others out into the lands, and I waited. I could see there was a lot of activity, and going to find myself a nice vantage point inside one of the buildings, I'd be able to see much more.

I walked to the main building. Trying the door, it opened. I went inside, up a couple of flights of stairs, and out onto a balcony. There I had an amazing view.

The land itself went on for miles and split into five sections of animals. There was some amazing amount of work here, something that not only took ten years but many more. It showed a lot, and I was proud of these workers. Even if the mayor hadn't been to see them or acknowledge what they'd accomplished, I would.

I think we'd be back for more stock in the summer. When it was better to move them and not at night. Trying to get five hundred cows out and down a hundred and eighty miles to the town wasn't my idea of fun.

But within an hour, it seemed there was a herd moving down from one of the fields. I watched as several hands worked them. Ebolos moved in and out with them, and like only a trained group could, they moved as one. How I ever thought we would be able to move the herd on our own, I had no idea.

I heard something click behind me. I turned to see a young man, maybe about twelve. He was thin and scraggly. "What are you doing up here?" I asked, but he just turned and ran away. I followed as he went back inside the house where I found a young girl.

"Who are you?" She was the one to ask, though.

"I'm just here to take some cattle. Why are you hiding here?"

"My mum died," they said together. Her eyes filled with tears, the older boy pulling her to him.

"I'm sorry about your mum," I said. Suddenly concerned for these two, who was looking after them? "I'm Maddie. I'm just trying to figure out what this place is. Looks nice."

The fact the two children shared a look of horror, their already pale faces turning even whiter.

"You're scared. Can you tell me, what you do know of this place?"

"It's a huge genetic experiment," he replied. "They breeding out certain things in their stock."

"Bit complicated a thing for you to understand, but what do you mean?" I moved to sit before them, wincing as my hip groaned at me.

"I listen and watch what they're doing. There are differences in the way the cattle behave. What they eat, what they do to each other." He actually physically shivered, he was so terrified.

I touched the girl's hand. "What have they been eating?"

The girl pointed to herself and her brother. . . I froze.

"The cattle have been eating humans?"

When he nodded, I rubbed the side of my head. Where had they been able to get these people? How could the mayor sanction this? Did that mean the cattle they wanted to give us were tainted? What was the plan for afterwards? What would happen if the Tromoal ate bad food?

"Is there somewhere I can see for myself? Find out what we're really looking at? Are they cattle monsters or what?"

"You don't really want to see." The kid sighed. But, yes I did, I not only wanted to, but I needed to see.

I followed the kids out into the hallway accessible through and then deeper down into the main house. The dank smell coming from them and the walls stung my nostrils. The girl reached out and grasped my hand. I wanted to pick her up, so she wasn't walking barefoot on the splintered, dirty floor in the wretched house.

The young boy pushed the door open, and we slid inside the walls of the building where there were small peeps to look through. I now had a much better sense of why this place went into the mountainside and was lit from internal lights.

Several voices ahead got me really worried, but they were inside the rooms in the building. The boy stopped and pointed to the highest hole to him. I had to lower my head to see through it, but I was looking in a white room with several pieces of equipment. I could see weird screens with glass boxes containing terrible un-thought of creatures. Suspended in animation somewhere. There was an Ebolos, crossed with it—a monster. The creatures he was scared of in the day were theirs—they were a defence. To protect the farm.

Then I saw something else, and my heart stopped. There was a Tromoal egg. The final glass box pride of place on the wall had the most precious commodity in the world inside it.

I had to get it. I had to rescue that egg. I remembered Riezella telling me an egg was stolen many years ago. I shivered.

I pointed to the room, to the kids and then the egg. I bent down as much as I could in the small space, and I whispered to the little girl, "I will speak to them, and I will rescue that egg. Do you know where it is?"

Her eyes opened wide, and then tears. She nodded. Her brother was shaking his head and tugging my arm. "You can't."

"Yes, yes, I can. And I will."

CHAPTER 9

*T*he young girl led the way down into the depths.

A voice echoed in my head. *Maddie, where are you? What is going on? You're angry. Why?*

Don't take this the wrong way, I spoke to him, *but remember that missing egg?*

I heard him choke. And then he spoke clearly. *Maddie, what are you saying?*

There's a Tromoal egg. It looks like it's in some kind of suspended animation. I need to know whose it is, Dalfol.

He didn't answer me straightaway. He seemed to freeze inside my mind.

There's never been an egg go missing. Not for many, many years.

So it was the one Riezella had spoken of. A shiver ran down my spine. *Then you know who this is?*

There was no answer.

I wanted to get a message to Candice. I contacted Josh.

"Tell Candice's party member to contact her. The message is this. 'All hell is going to break loose. This place an abomination. The cattle aren't coming with us.'"

Josh's response was simply, "What?"

There was no time for me to answer. The girl was nodding ahead. I peeked through a hole to get my bearings. The room had one door and a guard.

How could I get out of the internal walls? The girl tugged my hand and then pointed at the ceiling. A small hole to squeeze through, crawl over and drop on the guard.

Could it be that simple to get inside and take something that was so precious?

I'd find out soon enough.

I pulled myself up and kicked my way into the roof space. Across the hallway, I could see through the slats in the roof to know what he was reading. Porn, of course.

I prepared myself to jump through with maximum impact and surprise him.

I sucked in a breath and then counted.

Three.

Two.

One.

The guard tried to jump up from underneath me, but I stuck my blade in his throat. He gurgled once, and blood gushed forwards when I pulled it out. I wiped it on my trousers and slid it back in its sheath. Then I opened the door.

I stepped inside and carefully closed it. The box had the beautifully coloured egg inside. I'd not been this close to one before. I had seen them before, but wow, this one glistened. The sides were golden and black crystal, shining in the light of the outside corridor. I held up a hand, my ring hand, and the ring started to hum, and I felt something, a presence in the room with me. This was so strange. Then there was a voice.

Hello... is someone there?

I'm here. Do you know where you are?

No, I just woke up. It's cold.

It won't be cold much longer. I promise.

Maddie, who is that? Who is with you?

I could sense the terror inside Dalfol. So I turned my focus to his voice. *I don't know, but it's a young male, and he's scared. Could he be from another clan?*

There wasn't an answer from him, but I moved closer to the egg. There wasn't a crack in it, the surface glittering in the light.

I noticed a camera was in a position to view the egg. I had to grab the egg and make a run for it and hope to get away before anyone missed it.

The roof creaked. Looking up, I noticed the boy, a slow glowing bright light emitting from his hands as he whispered, "Turn the camera forty degrees right."

I wanted to question everything this young man knew, but I complied. He dropped to the floor, beside the glass box. He worked quickly, but then stopped. "You'll have to carry it. I can't." His hands were still glowing. He was some kind of mage, but I'd no idea on type.

I reached inside the box and lifted the egg out. It wasn't light. About the size of the kid's sister. I held it against my sore hip and said to the boy, "If you get us out of here, you can come with us."

The kid nodded, and we turned to the door, his sister motioning us on.

I followed, hoping I wouldn't drop this darned egg. It really was heavy. We managed to get quite far, almost to the front of the house and out the door, before the alarms went off. The whole place erupted into a frenzy of activity. Lights, everything.

Josh's voice came over quickly. "I don't know what the hell you did in there, Maddie, but get the hell out! Candice and the others are under attack."

"What do you mean? From who? The workers?"

"No, the cattle. They have no intention of letting them come with us. They're trying to eat her!"

I shouted to the kids, "Run! We've gotta hustle now! Get us to the gate!"

The youngsters sprinted, and I followed, just as a main light shone off the top of my head. It lit up the path, which was much better for me as I could actually see where I was going now. I grinned and ran faster. Overtaking the kids, I could see the Hog, and I sucked in breath after breath to try to get there.

They both stopped behind me as I palmed the panel and the doors opened. "Get in!" I watched as they hopped in, and then I heard something else entirely. Footsteps—no, not footsteps. The pounding of many hooves. Had they just let the herd out? Where were Candice and the others?

Then I saw her. She was running full pelt towards me shouting, "Get that piece of shit started!"

She was running for the gate, which was closing. I guessed they didn't want to let the zombie bovine out the main doors after all. At least, not yet.

I climbed in, resting the egg as well as I could on my lap, and started the engine. By the time she got to the door, I could see the mess of animals behind her. The herd was chomping and gnashing. She leapt inside the hog, slamming the door, and I spun us around and headed out as fast as I could.

"Where are the others?"

"Dead."

"I'm sorry."

She looked to the kids behind me, then at what I was cradling, while driving. "Is that what I think it is?"

"Tromoal egg, yes."

"And you thought it was a good idea to steal it?"

I shrugged. "I like to think I rescued it."

"They're going to come after us. You know that, right?"

I nodded and patted the egg. "I have no doubt whatsoever. Let's see if we can get back to Chip and Alex first, though. They shouldn't be able to catch us."

The herd had been stopped, but that didn't mean they couldn't get the bikes. We had to hope they couldn't.

"The bikes?" I asked.

She shook her head. "Like your Hog."

I let out a sigh. "Good."

We had more than a chance then. They wouldn't catch up.

The egg rattled, and I could feel the creature moving inside. Every instinct running through my body wanted me to protect him, nurture him, love him—and I would.

CHAPTER 10

I drove for as long as I could and let the chattering and whispering from the kids settle my nerves. Candice handed me some potions after she saw me wince. She offered to take the egg from my lap. It did kind of get in the way, but I wasn't letting this out of my sight for anything—or out of my grasp.

We met with Chip and Alex, and they rode ahead. I could see Alex glancing back now and then, and eventually, we stopped so he could get back in with me. We couldn't talk much with the kids in the back, though. In the end, I noticed they were all asleep. I sighed. Josh was manning our guns again, and I took solace in that fact someone other than me was alert and watching. The riders in front and back stuck to us like glue. It felt like we were a real team, and I liked this. As much as I had loved working alone up to now, this was good, too.

Routing through my mental voices, I found the one I needed. Riezella.

Dalfol told me all he can. We're going to meet you at the edge of the village.

If you're seen, there will be more than talk, I replied, but it was already too late.

Yes, it is. It's time your friends understood. There's also a marching army gathering at the edge of the plains. We've too much to deal with already with the shortage of food without trying to keep them at bay.

You're allowing them through.

It's not that we have a choice, Maddie. I don't think you realise how weak we are.

I did. I could sense it within her.

How many are left?

There are less than a hundred of us, but there are three hundred eggs.

If we had only gotten the cattle! If there hadn't been some horrible science experiment. Ugh! I slammed my fist on the side of the door and woke the passengers. "Sorry," I muttered.

"How much further are we from the village?" Alex asked.

"About thirty minutes," I said. "Not long."

"Want me to drive?" Alex placed a hand on my arm.

So I could do what? Cuddle the damned egg till it hatched? I thought moving it again wouldn't be a good idea. The fact was since I'd grabbed it, the egg had gone quiet, very quiet.

"I just need to get us there," I said. Looking down so he could see I was talking about the egg. "He's too quiet. I think something is wrong."

Alex placed a hand on the egg, and instantly, there was life. The egg moved, cracked. I almost swerved as I wanted to jerk the wheel, but managed not to.

"I guess he likes you." I smiled, but the nerves inside me were worrying. Then I noticed Alex's health bar was back up.

ALEX DUBOIS – 80%

"You feeling all right?" I watched his reactions.

"Yeah, why?"

If I voiced my concerns, would it give them more tangibility?

"Let's get to the village. You guys can rest properly, and we'll call a meeting first thing."

No sooner had the vehicles approached the town could we see

something was going down. Alex shouted up to Josh, "What do you see?"

Josh poked his head back in the cab. "A lot of movement. I think one of the teams is back early with their cattle."

Waves of relief washed over me. It wasn't some kind of attack then.

It was a mad dash of people running about everywhere, though.

I pulled the Hog to a stop at the outskirts, and Dresel ran straight for us. I managed to slide out from under the egg and give Alex a knowing nod. He covered it up.

"What's been going on?" he asked, his face white.

"Why?"

"There's Tromoal sitting outside our ground lines... no one dared approach them. The cattle are terrified."

I felt sorry for them. Yeah, brought to slaughter. Not nice. I motioned to Josh, who hopped down from the back of the Hog, and I started to shout, "They are here just to talk. Please get the cattle to their fields. Get them some Dros Grass. It will calm them down. Then get everyone else moved inside. This is not the time to do anything but listen and keep calm."

There were a few grumbles, and I noticed Abel rallying them all, his large frame standing out amongst most people. I grinned when I saw one of the only other Runners I fully trusted. Sarah.

"Dres, let me deal with the Tromoal. Get the kids somewhere safe for me."

He looked to the back of the Hog and then nodded. But he didn't move. "You'll let me know what's going on fully after, right?"

I didn't answer, just waited while the kids hopped out and followed him into the village.

Alex turned to me. "We taking the egg with us?"

I nodded and moved to take hold of it. That's when I heard the little voice once more.

Are we done bouncing about now?

I smiled inwardly. *Do you not like being moved?*

No, came the reply. *I'm tired and cramped and I want to get out.*

Can you take me somewhere safe while I negotiate getting outside of this egg some more?

Gently picking up the egg, covered in a blanket, I motioned to Alex. "I need to take him to my home, somewhere I think is safe for him to hatch. Will you stay with him?"

Alex nodded but moved to my side. "I'll take him. You go talk to the Matriarch first."

I didn't want to let the egg go, but I added, "Don't let anyone near you, at all, hear me?"

I could hear Riezella and some of the others, and their bellows and pawing at the ground weren't doing the village any favours.

I walked out, stretching my hip as I did so, the muscles and sinews around my lower leg were twisted, bent and ached. Hurt much more than I wanted them to, and I wished I'd managed to save Alex and keep my healed body.

Riezella and her flanking guards, Dalfol and his sister, were bickering amongst themselves as per usual. I instantly smiled as I walked on over, their sheer size able to crush me in an instant. I put a hand on my hip and shouted at them, "Going to keep on screaming at each other or are we going to talk?"

Riezella's beautiful eyes turned my way, and her body quivered. *Maddie, I am glad you're here.* The stunning creature moved to my side, but her eyes didn't waver. They dimmed, and I followed the haze as her humanised body formed. Slim, flowing white dress, and red hair. Beautiful.

"It is good to see you again," she said. "I'm hoping you might take me to see the egg."

She had probably seen my exchange with Alex. "He's not going to be an egg for much longer. I think within the hour, he'll have hatched."

"He?" She looked puzzled, but she moved me to one side, and a hazy blue shield grew around us. I reached out to touch it, but she didn't falter the power to it.

"Maddie, I do not know who you found or how long he's been inside the egg. There could be dire retributions if we do not find out."

"I was right to think he was from a rival clan?"

"Maybe he is, but there's been no chatter amongst the world to say an egg was stolen for many years. I don't know where or when he's come from."

Was he really the missing egg from a thousand years ago? "I can take you to him like this," I indicated her body, "but I won't allow the others to come. Is that okay?"

She nodded. "They would not leave my body unguarded anyway. They must protect me while I project outwards. I accept this condition. Please, let us go and find out this mystery."

Riezella walked by my side as she observed the movement around the village. "They've done well to get so much of the herds down from neighbouring towns and cities. That will help alleviate the problem, but I must warn you that I am going to send Dalfol and his sister back in the next day before she's ready to lay. She can absorb the young on her flight back. She will not be too weak then. She's past her time here."

I stopped walking. "But doesn't that mean. . ."

"No, it doesn't mean that her young will die. It just means it wasn't their time yet, as it wasn't for some of the others. They will get a chance, thanks to my decision to send them home and your help in securing us enough food for these eggs."

"The eggs. What about you?"

"I will not survive this transition, Maddie."

Shivers ran across every pore of my body. "What?"

"I thought you knew. This is my time to pass on leadership. I choose you."

The thought was more than a slap in the face. "I can't lead the Tromoal. I have a home, here."

She smiled at me. "You have nothing here, and you know that, as I know it. What you do have is a future filled with great adventures."

Though the idea of more adventures really was a pull, I would be leaving the Hog, the land, the only things I'd known.

"You're telling me I'd have command of all the Tromoal in your clan?"

Riezella bowed her head. "We are more than a thousand strong, but this blow will knock the clan back for a while. It will take some steady planning, and work to come back from this. Maybe not next year even."

"No, they must return every year," I exclaimed.

"Then you have a lot to do as their new leader."

"I have a lot to do right now," I said, and we carried on walking to my humble abode. I knocked on the door and went inside with Riezella behind me. Alex was in the kitchen making a drink. He turned to me and noted the lady at my side. "Alex, this is Riezella, Matriarch."

Alex dropped his head and put the kettle down, looking to me. "Good to finally meet you."

"There's much we should discuss, Alex. If you'd let me." She held out a hand to him, and he took it, but confusion crossed his brow. He looked more like a lost child than an adult. No matter the worry that filled me, I knew she had his best interests at heart. Or did she?

I left them to it as they sat at my small table. I wanted to visit the egg, to see if anything had happened. I had an inkling that it had.

I pushed open my bedroom door to see it on the bed, still wrapped in the blanket. I moved to the side and turned on a light. It glinted off the black crystals of the egg.

I placed my hand on the surface, responding to every tiny bump and crack. Then I felt it, a push, and the egg shattered at the top. I peered inside and noticed one blue eye looking back at me. It blinked, then moved, and I heard a tap at the shell. I wanted to help but knew this was somehow something he had to do himself. To make them strong, all creatures had to crack their own eggs and escape, or they'd die trying. I didn't want him to die, so I sat and waited.

His frustration was evident as I heard the constant growling from within. When the shell finally gave way, a hole appeared, followed by a foul smell. "Gee, gonna have to get you a bath."

The blinking eyes moved, and then his head appeared, followed shortly by two legs. This baby Tromoal's skin shimmered and glistened. I was tempted to reach out and to help. But I waited until his back and wings emerged. They were almost translucent. I could see the veins as they pulsed his life energy around him.

"Sakril." I lowered my head.

I placed a finger to his nose, and he nudged me. *Thank you for my name, Mother.*

"Mother." I sighed. "Not quite! But I do hope to maybe find her. Do you have any connections to anyone inside your mind?"

I held out an arm, thinking he might cross over from the egg to me and he did. Heavy indeed, the size of a medium dog with wings. He stretched them out, and his tiny daggered teeth dripped with liquid. Was that venom?

I stood, feeling the pull on my hip with the extra weight, and said, "Fancy a bath?"

The Tromoal's eyes continued to blink at me, and I moved out of the room into my small bathroom. The bath wasn't very large, but it was fed by a local spring as were a few from around here.

I let the water from the faucet drip into the tub, and Sakril hopped off my arm to bathe under it like you'd see a bird in a water bath. It was cute to watch.

I heard raised voices from the other room and wanted to go and investigate the why. I hesitated at leaving Sakril on his own. He glanced at the door, though, and I nodded. I headed out to the corridor to see what was going on.

Alex paced the small kitchen space with his head in his hands. He looked to me, pain evident and he asked simply, "You knew what she was going to ask of me. What that might mean?"

I didn't have to answer it. He knew I had. I moved closer to him, wanting to wrap my arms around him, but it was obvious he didn't need me right now. His anger permeated the room in waves. He turned his back to me, staring out the one small window that I had.

Riezella pushed her chair back and rose. "The young one is awake. May I go and see him?"

I shot her a glare. "No, he's in the bath. You move when I say so."

I cringed realising who I was talking to, the giant creature who had almost, well, actually, had killed me.

Riezella didn't say anything. "Then I will leave you two to talk. Just know this. You don't have long to answer. I will need it before the sun sets today."

I waited for her to leave, and then I moved to Alex's side, touching his shoulder.

He wrapped his arms around me, pulling me in tight for a kiss so wonderful that the world around me melted into blissful oblivion.

CHAPTER 11

$\mathcal{A}$ growling sound brought my attention back to the real world. Sakril. I pushed Alex away, even though I wanted more.

He stopped me from returning to the bathroom with a tug. "I am going to say *yes* to move my soul to her egg," he said, but the furrows in his brow told me of his worry.

"To be reborn in a way no one ever has before. I want to wish you well." I lowered my head. I couldn't see his pain or his hope. He tried to grab me, but I moved out of his way and went for Sakril. He still played under the tap. Alex and I laughed.

"So tiny," Alex said, moving to sit at the side of the tub. Sakril hissed at him. "Tiny, yet ferocious."

"Well, at least he smells better."

Alex sighed and reached out to pet the Tromoal. He, however, wasn't having any of it and squirmed away. "I thought he liked you before."

Alex stood and shrugged. "This seems a different kind of like, like how he wants to eat me."

I couldn't help but laugh. "Maybe he is hungry." I noticed Alex's health bar had dropped once more. "Yeah, let's get him some food and take him out to meet the others."

"You think that's wise for him to meet the Matriarch at this young age?"

I didn't know or understand any of their world, but it couldn't hurt. "This little one had been taken, and we need to find out how and why."

"It is worth a try."

Alex tried to pick Sakril up, but he blew a puff of smoke in his face. I lifted up my arm, tapping it. The little Tromoal jumped right out of the bath and onto my arm. His wings were already taking on a different colour.

Alex frowned. "Show off."

"No aptitude available for Tromoal taming?"

"No, and doubt I could even dream of acquiring one."

That was good. No one should ever be able to train these wonderful creatures.

I approached Riezella and Dalfol with the young Tromoal on my arm. He squirmed a lot but didn't fall off.

Riezella turned towards us, her wide glinting eyes narrowed, focussing on the youngster, and she froze.

You recognise him?

Riezella lowered her head, got to the ground and began that low keening. My whole body shivered, and Alex held me.

"What the hell is the noise they're making?" Alex asked.

Dalfol and Fie also lowered their bodies and started with the same noise. The young Tromoal squirmed, then his wings flapped, and he belched his first blast of ice into the night.

Maddie, this Tromoal is not just a member of another clan—he is the King of all Clans.

"Huh, what?" I said aloud.

You have done us the highest favour. He was taken from us almost a thousand years ago. His egg was laid here with our Lady of the Skies. The wars and upcoming battles will be tough. We must return him to the homeland now. We cannot wait for the hatching.

I was about to stammer out the 'what' again when Sakril jumped from my arm and landed on Riezella's nose.

She chuckled, her whole body shaking the ground, but she didn't move. She allowed him to perch there, like a bee on the nose of a dog. The strangest thing I'd ever seen. Then I heard what Riezella said to Dalfol. I'd never heard their direct talk before. Was it because we were so close? Or was my strength to listen growing? *Gather the clan. We must leave despite the consequences.*

I stood forward and placed a hand on her nose, near Sakril.

There will be no consequences. I turned to Alex. "If the only way we can protect the Hatchlings is to go to war, then we will. Those incoming warriors from the Port will not get to them."

"My youngest cannot be moved, or there will be no place for Alex."

Alex stepped forwards, and he placed his hand on Riezella's nose. "Do not fear, Matriarch of the Clan, I am ready. I will accept the gift of life that you chose for me."

I watched his eyes twinkle as he spoke. "Maddie wouldn't let anything happen to the clutch or to me. Take me to the cave, let the passing of my soul to your empty vessel mean that I will be truly Desert Born."

"Don't fear, Maddie," Alex leaned in and whispered, "I have a great love for this world and for all that you've shown me."

Tears dripped down my cheeks, and he brushed them aside.

Let us not waste any more time, Riezella said as she lifted her great head indicating we were to return to the cave now, without talking to the others.

No, I need more time, I tried to say, but Alex had already climbed up onto her shoulder. I followed.

Quickly, I reached into my mind and found Josh.

"The Tromoal are leaving, all of them. Gather as many as you can and come down to the farthest point with the cattle and animals. We have but a few hours, they need to eat before they leave or they will die."

Josh responded, "On it. Be there ASAP. Talk after."

187

I reached out to take Alex's hand to join him on the Matriarch's back. She was so much larger than Dalfol and his sister, but Alex pulled me to him and wrapped his arms around me. The sting of the rushing air caused more tears, but it wasn't the real reason I cried.

Alex held me, never once letting go. Sakril put his head on my knees, his tiny vibrating hum trying to settle my fears. I placed my hand on top of his spikes trying not to get nipped and silently thanked him.

Once at the cave system, Riezella, Dalfol, and Fie moved quickly inside. There were wings everywhere, bellows of fire and ice into the sky in celebration and commiseration. They knew they had to leave, but some of the females weren't happy at all. Their bodies were low to the ground, a rumble passing through them, and all of us. I not only sensed everything from them, their fear, their pain, but we could all see it.

Alex took hold of my hand, and he followed the Tromoal inside their cave systems.

How many are there? I asked.

There are two hundred and forty-seven eggs, Riezella said. *One hundred and seventeen females. They are hurting as much as their parents are, and they don't understand the need for us to leave.*

Fie bowed her head and looked towards me. *It is a must that we go, though, right?*

Riezella grimaced, looking towards the smallest egg of the bunch. Hers and Dalfol's.

She seemed to still, and then her essence formed. The swirling mist around us created a dust cloud. I tried to shy away from looking. I couldn't. Her form seemed more solid like she really needed to be here. I watched, the taste of sand on my tongue, until I could make out her figure, her hair. She moved to Alex and took hold of his hands. *"I must take you to the centre of the eggs, this will take some time, but I wouldn't have suggested it if I didn't think it possible."*

Alex glanced at me, and I could do nothing but hold his gaze. I wouldn't be the one to let him see my pain. I knew the risks. He might live a few more days without them. Now he would live as a Tromoal.

Free, flying. I hated it, but I also loved the idea. It might have been programming to start with. It was much more now. It could be much more. I had to believe.

"Give me one minute to say goodbye to Maddie, please."

I felt the others move away from us, and he pulled me to him. I wouldn't cry now. This wasn't how I wanted him to remember me.

"We will see each other again," he said. "I know we will."

I tried to smile. Alex kissed me. I allowed all my feelings, hope, pain, fear to vanish, and I just enjoyed his taste and touch.

"This isn't the end for us."

When he walked away, I watched carefully as Dalfol's and Riezella's ghostly forms went with him. So did Sakril, which I was surprised about. Maybe he was going to somehow help with the transference. I had wanted to be there, but I also felt that maybe this kind of magic was too high level for me. I shouldn't know how it was done, what they needed to do to complete it. So I could only watch from a distance.

Dalfol's human form pulled what looked like a satchel from thin air, he took out a silver pan. There he started to pour the contents around Alex and Riezella in a circular motion. I covered my mouth when Alex began to remove his clothes, his pale skin bright against the cavern's blackness. Riezella pointed for him to sit, and he did so crossing his legs.

The energy around the cavern sparked, red fire mixing with all the colours of the rainbow.

Fie was the one who stayed with me. She placed her large head by my side, a look in her eyes that showed her concern for me.

I'd not once thought of the pain in my hip, but I leaned against her cool scales and rested my head on hers. *Do you think it will be painful for him?*

She didn't answer, and we continued to watch.

The area now rich in energy, hummed, the ground vibrating with it. A silver mist gathered, swirling in like it was being pulled from everywhere, even the different dimensions Riezella talked about. The ground lit in beautiful sandy golden colours, and the walls turned their dark energies also to the mix.

Riezella moved around Alex as he stared towards a central white light. That light started out small, then grew the more she spoke. Her words turned into chanting, and I didn't understand any of it. It was Dalfol that took over from her chanting, turning her words into a wondrous song, one this time that I understood.

Then I heard her words to Alex.

For this universe is one, to understand her, you become one. Where souls and energy meet, there's a space to cross over, cross over you must. The energy you are, can become desert-born, need it, feel it. Where there's strength, there is energy. Where there is hope, life. Feel your life, feel it moving, free.

Her movement around him grew faster. The light appearing before Alex, and I knew his soul had become much brighter.

Know where you wish to go. Focus, Alex.

The twirling and mesmerizing dance stretched on for what seemed like hours.

Sakril then joined them, flying around and around, gaining speed like he was the one actually doing this transformation. His energy sparked brighter than all. He swooped in, sucking in the ball of white energy.

Alex's body twitched and then stopped.

Sakril continued to fly around the circle until the energy around them was so intense, I couldn't watch much longer.

Then, with tremendous speed, he dived towards the egg. Stopping a fraction of a millimetre before it. He puffed out that white energy, and it vanished inside.

Was that his spirit? Sakril then sucked in once more, opening up his needle-sharp mouth to bellow fire at the egg.

A bright light flashed.

So bright I had to shield my eyes. I couldn't see any of them anymore. I panicked.

What's going on, Fie?

But when the light faded, and I opened my eyes, there was no twirling colours. Riezella and Dalfol's humanised forms had gone, and so had Alex. There was nothing there anymore.

I rushed forward to where the eggs were. The smallest of them now seemed to have a faint glow about it, but other than that, there was no other difference.

I screamed, and I didn't stop. The pain deep within would never be dissipated.

Sakril was the one who appeared to me, his small cute form landing before me. *Come,* his voice said to me. *There is no time to mourn what you do not know you've lost yet.*

I stood to obey the command of a leader, as small as he was. I knew what he was. As Lady of the Skies, he was technically my Master, but he didn't act like it. He acted like someone who genuinely cared and who wanted the best for me.

The cattle are here, and the Clan is feasting. Thanks to your Runners.

I looked at him as he hovered effortlessly by my side as I walked back to the edge of the water.

Once outside the caves, I could see the huge turmoil from the cattle and Tromoal as they devoured them. The sounds of crunching bones and beating wings loud enough for me to want to cover my ears and eyes from the devastation.

Yet, inside, I heard the glee, the happiness from the Tromoal. I shivered, trying my best not to throw up.

Josh stood watching with horror on his face. He saw me and moved towards me. With him were Candice and her crowd with the bikes not far behind as well as Abel's men, the horses, and Ebolos.

Dresel's voice came from behind me. "That's some feat these guys just performed for you."

I smiled at him. "Amazing. How did you do it?"

"We did what you said. We used Dros Grass." Candice stood forwards and grinned. "We then glamoured the animals into thinking this was a field full of their favourite foods. They came here with what they thought were empty bellies and got what they wanted most in life —food and sex. They wouldn't have suffered when they died, too high. Even though it looks horrific, believe me, it was as painless as possible."

I really was glad of this. No animal should suffer for the good of others.

"Thank you, all of you."

The Matriarch screeched up above, and all heads from the Tromoal turned.

The ground itself seemed to quiver as they started to lift into the sky. There they circled and waited until everyone was ready.

The Matriarch then landed before me. She placed her head to the ground, and Sakril joined again landing on her nose. I heard her inner muffled *'dawg gone flea,'* and I laughed.

"I am saying this for all humans and species alike," Sakril said aloud. It seemed all at once he could speak a thousand tongues. Every one of the parties drew close to us to listen in.

"Turn to Maddie for guidance. Protect our eggs, for the clutch will hatch next year. There's a war coming, but not just from the Port. It is a war between good and evil on Puatera. It's been coming since the day I was stolen from my mother. Hear this. We will return. We will bring back the forces to wipe this world clean of everything in our wake if you do not succeed."

I placed my hand on my chest. "Sakril, you have my word. We will not let you or the Clan down. Go, go home and come back to fight. We will be waiting. As will your children."

Sakril lowered his head to me, then with one quick flash of power and energy, he was gone with the matriarch behind him.

Do not let us down, he reiterated, *but more so, do not let yourself down, Maddie. You're stronger than you believe.*

I swallowed, watching as the darkened skies with a thousand wings shifted towards home. The tremors as the last remaining Tromoal joined their brethren to leave us rocked my soul. Bellows of sorrow and joy filled my ears. Their mothers were scared to leave, but yet so hopeful for their future. The beating of their wings faded as did the voices inside my mind. The sun finally started to brighten our horizon, and my thoughts turned to the future.

The End

If you enjoyed this book, please consider leaving a review, they help keep writers motivated! :)

DESERT STORM

PUATERA ONLINE BOOK 3

CHAPTER 1

"Turn to Maddie for guidance. Protect our eggs, for the clutch will hatch next year. There's a war coming, but not just from the Port. It is a war between good and evil on Puatera. It's been coming since the day I was stolen from my mother. Hear this. We will return. We will bring back the forces to wipe this world clean of everything in our wake if you do not succeed." Sakril's warning reverberated in my head.

If Sakril had said anything else but for them to look to me, I think everyone would have looked elsewhere, and maybe I wouldn't have a couple hundred sets of beady eyes staring my way.

Seriously, I couldn't breathe. I wanted to turn and run away from them, from everything. A deep fear for our wellbeing settled in the pit of my stomach and wasn't going to budge.

How did leaders of cities and more manage to quell that fear?

Candice moved to my side and looked out at the many faces. "They're waiting for you. Say something."

I stared, not mustering up any words at all.

Blood stained the sands, and the stench of death drifted much further than the planes around us. The animals who lost their lives here, I didn't want them to have died for nothing. I sucked in a breath, pushed myself up tall, and moved to address the crowd.

"There are a lot of things we're going to need. People, resources, first things first, though. We need to clean up, then get a working camp up and running. Food supplies are next. The water we have."

Candice motioned around her to the people left waiting for me to speak, she grinned and whispered to me. "You were born for leadership."

I snorted. "No way. I was born to be a Runner."

"Then you know exactly how they're feeling right now."

Of course, she was correct, I did know. So that is how I began to let my words out. "You're terrified. I know, and I feel it. Our future has changed a thousand fold. We're not just Runners anymore or Visitors. We have become guardians. I know some of the eggs can be moved, but there is one which cannot. That egg must be protected as the heir of the Clan.

One man approached me, his face confused. "We're going to get paid, right?"

"There are many riches we have access to, but this isn't about just getting paid. This is about doing what's right for all of us. For all of Puatera."

He stared at me. "We're here for the money, not to risk our lives again." The crowd around him booed and hissed. Yes, a few nodded their heads in agreement. I couldn't win everyone over. To try that would be stupid.

"Then you're free to leave. I can't force you. I won't." I really didn't want them to go, but as I waited and watched, it seemed the majority didn't want to go. I could see it on their faces, the worry, the hesitation as they bounced from one foot to the other. I addressed the crowd with only hopes I could persuade them. "Anyone who wishes to leave can do so. I will not force you to participate. This is a long-haul job. I am risking my life here. We're risking more than our lives here."

Candice pointed as a few of the attendees started to move on. I can't say I really blamed them. I just wished more of them would stay. They seemed to all be going.

Then it stopped.

I had in front of me a large enough crowd to help me.

Josh was the one to look at me this time. "We can always get more soldiers, more people to stand with us."

"I know. The three teams we had to help get the cattle are here, and I could easily organise them to start up a protection and working ring."

I admit that without Alex I felt lost, but no matter the 'love' I felt or having lost it, those beady eyes staring at me had hope blazing in their souls.

I looked at the long-haired rider from before. "Thank you for sticking around. If you would like to head the transport expedition, I think getting supplies here is a must."

"On it. We've a couple of caravans we can use, wagons too. The horses can pull them easily enough."

Then a large man stepped forward. I'd also seen him around. I then noticed the players tag. Abel Rimmer—Visitor. It was why he seemed familiar. He was a regular at the Runners Vine.

It was his eyes that sucked me in. Deep, blue, but there was something odd—he wasn't completely human. He was something else, something strong and feline. It confused me. "I can organise more men, soldiers. Players if you'd allow them here."

We both looked to Candice. "An open call? For an event?"

When Abel nodded, I wasn't sure what or why that was important to them, but it was. "This warrants it, yes."

They were on the same page. I just didn't want either of them taking over.

"We need a large party for this," she said to him. I wasn't ready to start or even think about a guild, but it was necessary to protect this land and the eggs. So maybe that was what we needed to do.

"Still in alpha stages," he replied. "But I think it would work out okay." Worth a shot.

"There are gold and things we can sell in the caves, right?" Candice asked.

I nodded. "I know there are. Just don't know how much it's all worth. Millions to you guys, artefacts, things stolen along the years. The way things are supposed to be found wouldn't happen here. There are probably items no one should see yet. We also need to protect those."

"A big task for any real player to do and not be tempted to loot and then sell." Abel moved closer to Candice. "You trust your team?"

She nodded. "I've been playing with these guys for ten years. They're close friends and wouldn't ruin the play just for loot."

"Good, because this is one hell of a test for the gaming system and the betas."

"What about Maddie?"

He looked at me, and I just stared back as he contemplated his next words. "Maddie has to become a guild leader?"

Candice coughed. "She's an NPC though."

"Yes. Just not like any NPC we've come across before."

I placed a hand on Candice's arm. She looked at me. "I'm a freak of an NPC, just as much as the Tromoal are freaks of the game's design. They shouldn't be here, but they are."

"So maybe a guild leader she can become then."

"What kind of things would be required of me?"

"I don't know. It's all new to us. Generally, a leader would have access to all player's stats, can work with their skills, and make decisions for the better of the whole team."

"Sounds complicated."

Abel and Candice nodded. "For those who play games a lot, it's not hard to understand. But you've never been in a game so it might be a shock to you to get there. I think you're more than smart enough."

I chuckled. "I hope so."

"Then that's settled. Sarah's organising the horses and ebolos to get back to the village to start the supply runs, and then we'll get the paperwork going."

Candice hesitated, but I saw the glint in her eye. "Might we have a look in the cave system? The main cave where the loot is kept."

"It's very important only a few have access," I said. "You don't talk about it to the others, and you don't let them know any more information than needed."

Candice frowned, but she nodded. "I agree. Just Chip and me for now."

I frowned. Really? She chose him?

Candice laughed loudly and leaned in. "I know he looks and sounds like a lump most of the time, but he's loyal as hell. Think he's got a crush on me."

Now I was the one laughing as I looked towards the big guy who stood by his bike. I couldn't help but catch his tortured looks towards her. I think she was right. He really was sweet on her.

Candice waved him over. "Help the others get the area sorted and cleaned up as much as possible. We'll be camping here for a few nights. The others can work out guards and patrols with those who have stayed. You, me, Abel and Maddie are going back into the caving systems."

I saw how much his eyes lit up, but when he glanced at me, he nodded. "We've already started to work out cleaning crews. Not every Tromoal could eat clean, so there are debris and blood that needs to be washed away just so the area doesn't start to turn rank on us."

"Thanks," I said. "Takes a lot of the pressure off."

He glanced at Candice and added. "Gotta admit, though... this is the weirdest game I've played, where an NPC takes over the *world*."

Candice let out a giggle. "It's different, but I like it."

Standing between the three players, I glanced to Josh who smiled at me then lowered his head. Did I command such respect? Glancing back to the caves, I knew I did. "Josh, watch the entrance. I'm taking a few of us inside."

"Yes, ma'am." With a mock salute, he turned and walked away. I didn't understand why, I wasn't in any kind of military, but it did get a laugh from me.

"Anything weird down there?" Chip asked. "Monsters?"

I cringed. The Tromoal used to keep the eggs safe there. I'd never even thought about that side of things. "I have no idea."

"Maybe we should all go?" Candice asked glancing back to the rest of her team.

I thought about it for a few moments. It wasn't worth risking our lives. "Okay, I agree. Be good to have you with me."

Chip was the one who coughed this time. "Maddie, this is the most exciting thing we've ever done. Don't believe otherwise. We're here for you. Just like when we went to the Mayor's estate, we're not afraid to die for the right reasons. We just have to believe what we're doing makes a difference."

I stared into his blue-green eyes and noted the scar on the top of his forehead. "It will make a difference. It will shape the world of Puatera for many years. The outcome here will stick. There is no reset on this one for us." He looked confused, so I moved closer to him. "This program we're in is evolving. The creator himself, Dresel, stays in the Alstead Village. Where you set your respawn point to. Even he knows something's going on. Stick with me, and we'll all find out the truth."

Chip's grin spread even more. "Gaming gone rogue. Best thing ever."

Candice rolled her eyes at me, moving away to go get the others from her crew. I noticed the exchange with a few nods and shakes of the head. When they moved to return to us, the rest of the people milling around were starting on their jobs. I was glad they were so willing. This place would be a bustling fortitude for us all soon enough.

Candice stopped before me. The party all looked at me. Candice spoke. "You've met Steve, Rose, Amanda, and Mark before, but I hope now we'll get to know each other better."

Steve stepped forward first. "An honour, Maddie." He was the one who looked at me with bright yellow yet very shy eyes. He wasn't human by any means, but I couldn't work out what kind of species he'd followed after. I wanted to ask him, to at least understand where he got his mana and magic status from. But the others excitedly talked about the inside of the cave, so I went with the flow and led them in.

I hadn't had a chance to go back to see the eggs. There were the main four where Riezella and Sakril had just performed the ritual with Alex, but the other eggs were further back. I wondered if once I'd made it inside the system again, would their voices breakthrough? Since the Tromoal left, there had been nothing. No inclination I had a new family. As the lady of the skies, I wasn't doing much of a job when I couldn't even hear them anymore.

The trip to the main cave wasn't hard. A few twists and turns and then a lot of walking downhill. It was easy to see why the water would run this way when the autumn came, and the rain filled up the caverns.

I stopped, finally getting a murmur of something inside my head. Was it talking? Was it actually the Tromoal I was hearing?

I listened in closely to see if I could identify anyone in particular. In all honesty, I was looking for Alex. I needed to hear his voice, to know his actual transformation to the digital world and the body of the Tromoal had worked.

There was nothing specific; just different tones and squeals. The closer I got to the cave, the more I wanted to soothe them, to talk to them all.

When we rounded the corner, I moved a few steps ahead. "Do you mind if I go this alone?" I said to Candice. When she questioned me with a stern look, I answered, "I need to make sure there's nothing strange before you see them. I'm not hiding anything, I promise."

She nodded. "I understand if you don't want us all in there, but please let Steve have your back. He won't do anything to disturb what you wish to do, but he's a good defender and healer if anything goes wrong."

I didn't want to agree, but I lowered my head and then motioned for Steve to follow me inside.

The cave had a damp, egregious, and certainly, an eerie feel to it as the edge of the water shimmered at the far side of the cavern. I walked carefully over to where the first patch of eggs glittered. There I knelt down and laid a hand on the brightest one of the bunch. Steve didn't do anything. He did as Candice had promised and stood behind me watching the other side of the cavern. I was surprised he never once mentioned a number of gems and loot or even acknowledged they were there.

I felt the warm leathery egg behind my hand. The Tromoal inside felt my presence and pushed itself against the inner wall of the shell, attempting to feel comfort from my warmth.

"Steve," I said. "I need you to do something for me."

He glanced down and then knelt by my side. "What do you need?"

"Place your hand on the silver one, and tell me what you feel?"

He smiled, doing as I asked. I waited while his eyes dimmed, focusing on the egg. "A growing warmth, a male presence, concern." He looked back at me, eyes furrowing into a heartfelt frown. "These guys are terrified." I noticed the change in his emotion then. "Maddie, we have to help them all *now*. Please let me get the others." A single tear melted down the side of his face, and I reached out to wipe it away.

"I'm sorry I had to ask, but yes, go get the others. I think we have a rather large task to do before we can look around at the loot."

His eyes glinted at the words, but he nodded, removing his hand from the egg.

Running off, I watched as a yellowing aura followed him. Then I turned back to the egg. I placed my other hand on the surface, feeling the tiny bumps and indentations of its colourful surface. "Hang in there, little one," I said. "I'm here."

That's when I felt the tiny *thump, thump* of its heart and the ragged emotional trauma of separation. "Do not fear. Though your parents are far away, use me as your conduit to them."

I couldn't really express the emotions that crossed between us then —the heartache, of course—because she was also scared like her clutch mate, her brother. Reaching across to the silver egg, I placed my hand on him, waiting for the warmth to gather near. There I felt him and allowed the energy of them both to cross through me. I re-connected them.

Almost as if by instinct, I crisscrossed the energy over the tops of the eggs. In turn, this allowed the several strands of energies to mix at one central point. It felt like my job was done as they were re-introduced to each other as a family. When their parents left them, it broke their internal connections, leaving them alone and scared. Now, this small clutch was joined back together, and they could support each other.

I glanced up, seeing Steve re-enter with Candice and the others in tow. They glanced around the cave in awe, but they also noted me and what was swirling around me.

Candice approached with caution. "What's going on in here?"

"The Tromoal are alone, trapped inside their eggs, the connections to their parents gone as they're too far away. If I show you how to reconnect them with their clutch partners, will you try? We must repeat this process until all of them are re-connected. Without this, they'll go insane, and their lives will be lost."

CHAPTER 2

*T*he others joined us as we stood around, and I found it hard to look them in the eyes. I think it was mostly because Steve had told them what was going on. I didn't like having to instruct them.

I moved over to another clutch, instructing Steve to what the process was. He then translated it in their terms so they could easily understand what I meant. That was really something to listen to. He talked about using his internal mana to actually work with the energy inside the eggs, linking them.

I watched him copy me, making sure the souls inside the eggs felt more comfortable. I watched as the others attempted their first tries.

I thought these guys and gals were amazing fighters, and now I'd seen an entirely different side of them. The other two guys, including Chip, had tears in their eyes as they waited for me to make sure what they'd done got a thumbs-up.

Candice stopped me. "Can you get word to Josh? Ask him to send in refreshments. It will help with mana regeneration."

In agreement, I nodded toward Abel, asking him to do so. I think he was the only other person I could trust to actually come inside with a horse or Ebolos loaded with equipment.

I smiled at Candice and nodded. "He'll get it sorted so don't worry."

She looked around the cave. "Good. We've quite the job here to make sure all the clutches are linked again."

I couldn't agree more. The task was pretty huge. Including all the eggs around us, there were more than eighty clutches. If we spent an average of twenty minutes with each one, it was indeed going to take some time.

I turned my attention to the clutch at the centre of the cave. It called to me even though I had others needing my attention. I motioned to Candice. "You've got this. Carry on, and I'll call a break in an hour or so."

Of course, I wouldn't stop anyone from taking a break. These tasks were emotionally and physically draining. The youngsters' emotions were overwhelming, and that worried me. Were these humans able to take this kind of mental punishment?

Stepping towards Riezella's clutch, I sucked in a breath. I hoped I'd be able to feel something different or new about Alex's egg. From the outside, it looked like the others as it shimmered and glowed with a hint of white energy.

I stepped inside the nest's protective edges and kneeled before them. Placing my hand on the surface of the egg, it felt cold. There was no warmth inside. Panic rushed through me. Was it dead? I worried his transference hadn't worked. Then I felt it, a tiny heartbeat. The egg seemed to shiver, and then I felt the heat growing inside. I made a tiny squeal as I covered my mouth with the other hand.

I wanted to talk to him. To touch his mind, but I needed to wait. This had to come from him.

Then I heard a low gruff voice. *Anyone there?*

I waited to see if I recognised it, but I didn't. It felt different. New. It might be Alex, but it also wasn't Alex.

"I'm here," I said, trying to stem my heartache from feeding into his mind. "Don't fret."

Where did they go? All the others?

"They're still here. They're with you, with us. But I need to re-connect you together. Can you hold on?"

I placed my hand on one of the other eggs, another male, and woke him too. With some twisting and turning, I called forth my energy and connected theirs back together. Then I worked to connect the other two. When all four were communicating, I was about to back away when something tugged at my mind carefully. *Maddie, stay. A little longer.*

My heart leapt from the words, but I wasn't sure if the Tromoal had just asked because it now knew my name or if it remembered something else. Was it really Alex?

I placed my hand on its surface once more and then allowed my inner calm and love to seep through. The inner turmoil of these eggs was much stronger than the others. I wondered why, but then answered myself. Because they were the new clan leaders—well, they would be.

Thank you, the words resounded together. I had no choice then but to step away. Placing my hand on the nearest wall to try to stop myself from falling over, tears burst free. The sobs, however, wouldn't abate, and I let my tears flow. I was sure Alex was no more. Instead, there was this new being. I tried to pretend it would all work out, that he was still in there, but my heart wasn't listening, and the sobs came quicker.

It was Steve who placed his hand on my shoulder, and although I knew nothing of this man before me. When I turned, he wrapped his arms around me and pulled me in tight.

When my sobbing finally subsided, he wiped away my tears and smiled. "This here is more than I'd ever expected from this world. I've never been connected to another life before, but I feel them, all of them. Like my mana allowed them to know and feel each other, but it also allowed me a deeper look into how they work as a unit. A family. Maddie, I know you're not an ordinary NPC, but do you mind if I look into who you are?"

I really didn't understand what he meant, but I nodded.

"Please. Take a seat for me. I'll have to try to touch your coding if that's at all possible."

"Why should I allow you to do that? I don't know you or what you could do to me."

"I just helped your friends. I want to help you. Please." He motioned to the floor. "Sit for me."

I crossed my legs on the floor and leaned against the wall for extra support. I could see Candice and the others still milling around the cave, and I looked at Steve. "Okay, I'll let you. Just don't try to change anything, I'm weird enough as it is without any re-programming."

Steve laughed and sat before me. "That's the weirdest thing anyone's said to me, let alone someone inside a game."

I wanted to laugh with him. I knew Riezella said there was something special about me, but knowing what that was... might make all the difference.

Steve took hold of my hands, and I felt a slight pinch, as though he were tugging at them. I could see he wasn't, but then a yellowing light glowed about him, and he whispered something I didn't understand. The energy from him started to cross over to me, and at first, I wanted to pull away.

Then, before my eyes, several screens popped up. And several sets of rules that flashed before me, there was no way I'd take in those right now. I gawped. I'd never seen this before. I wanted to, though. This was weird but amazing. To actually see what made me who I am, what also made me who I sometimes loathed.

Aspects -
Advantages -
Aptitudes -
Affiliations -

I clicked on Aspects, the numbers meaning nothing to me.

Body 1
Soul 1
Mind 1

There was a lot of things I could only stare at, not really understanding it at all, as it meant nothing to me.

I did notice the subtle differences that I thought made me strong. My body might have been lacking, but I was smart, and my soul made up for all of it.

Steve whistled as I clicked through to Advantages, we both stared at a long list. There were many pluses and minuses. Too much for me to take in.

"Maddie, that's a badass character sheet. I've seen advanced players with something like this in other games, but an NPC? No."

I cringed at his term for us, NPC. I hated it. He noticed and then I watched as his jaw dropped. "What is it?"

Steve pointed to the screen and I saw the flickering box.

Appointed Karma 27 – Unassigned.

"What does that mean?" I asked, seeing his face pale even more.

"You're twenty-seven years old, right?" On my nod, he continued, "It means the computer system hasn't put your generated birthday Karma into slots or used it for something important."

I let that news sink in for a moment. "But this system works on learning and developing."

"Yes and no. When a Visitor picks a character's age, they're also allowed a certain set of Karma to assign to their character. Along with their Affiliations, it defines who they can be in this game. For an NPC, the computer is supposed to do this." Pointing at the number 27, he added, "This shows the computer's been glitching from the day you were created. All your skills are learned abilities. Nothing you've been given has been assigned. Which means..." his voice trailed off.

When he didn't speak for over a minute, I pushed. "What? I don't understand?"

"It means you've got some serious in-game decisions to make."

I smiled, and tapped the screen, moving across to see my abilities and advantages.

Steve's jaw dropped once more at the shared view. "Maddie, you're not really an NPC at all, are you?"

The speculation had hit me before, but this confirmed it in a big way. "No, I guess I'm actually a Visitor, not an NPC at all."

He swallowed. "But you're not human, right?"

I shook my head. "No, I'm something else."

Steve's hands trembled in mine. "I won't hurt you," I said. "I'm discovering this, just as you are."

He nodded and flicked the screen over to the next one.

This was a list of Aptitudes and was pages long. I quickly read the top skill sets I had and moved to the next page.

"Hey," Steve said.

"You can study it all at a later date if you'd like."

"All right, I really do want to go over all of this in-depth. It's amazing." He nodded, and I clicked through to Aptitudes.

Combat 1
Diplomacy 1
Endurance 0
Faith 0
Logic 2
Subterfuge 1

They each had their own page and more information: Combat – The art of pain. Diplomacy – All interaction. Endurance – Pain Hurts. Faith – Belief in all things. Logic – Knowledge or lack of its power, and lastly, Subterfuge – Body Manipulation.

I stared at Subterfuge for a while. Then I pointed.... "Steve, do you see that at the bottom?"

I waited while he found what I was looking at. "How strange."

It read –

DATA ENTRY – 39TH ODEISTRA – 17:21
MADDIE VIES – DEAD

RESPAWN 17:22

DATA CORRUPT
RESPAWN INCOMPLETE

REBOOT INITIATED 17:25

DATA – PARTIALLY WIPED
MEMORY PARTIALLY WIPED

RESPAWN PARTIALLY COMPLETE 18:07

MADDIE VIES – DATA CORRUPT

COULD NOT RE-WRITE INJURIES

RESULT – DEBILITATING PAIN – REOCCURRING DEATH

POSSIBLE FIX – REINCARNATION
RESULT – MEMORY WIPE
DATA CORRUPT

39TH ODEISTRA – 00:12 – ZOFILEX SOUL INTEGRATION
STARTED
ZOFILEX SOUL INTEGRATION – STATUS COMPLETE
ZOFILEX MEMORY SEGREGATED
ZOFILEX MEMORY STORED

APTITUDES UPDATED – SEVENTEEN

MEMORY RESTORED
DATA REWRITTEN

39TH ODEISTRA – 01:14 RESPAWN SUCCESSFUL

Steve let go of my hands, shaking his head. "I've never seen anything like that before. You said Dresel was the game's programmer. I'd like to meet with him and see if he checked the code line by line before and after your respawn."

"I'm sure he knows his job," I said, pushing myself to stand. My hip was hurting more than ever at the moment. I tried to stretch it out, but it didn't ease off. I needed some of my potions back in the Hog.

"If you'll trust Candice and the others to catalogue things here, I'll go with you back to town."

"You really want the answer to that, don't you?"

"Don't you?"

I wasn't sure, did I?

"Let's get these eggs settled, then we should rest. I'll sort out plans with Josh and the others for us to head back to town in the morning."

Steve looked at Candice, and my eyes followed his. She was inside a clutch of seven eggs. I watched her for a while, then noticed how low her health bar was. "Steve!" I managed to croak out, but he was already rushing to his leader's side. I followed just in time to help catch her.

"What were you thinking?" he said as he pushed a strand of hair away from her face.

There I saw the tears streaming down her cheeks. "I couldn't help it, I..."

I touched her arm and squeezed gently. Turning to see where the others were, I shouted out to them. "Re-group now, please. You all need a break, maybe for the night." There were protests, so I added. "Now. No arguments. I don't want you having to respawn because of this."

HEALTH – 45%

Chip was the first to plonk down near us, his eyes red raw, his bravado gone. "We can't leave them like this overnight. I'll take a respawn if I have to."

Rose and Amanda joined us next. Their hard exteriors gone. I also

214

noted for the first time that they were holding hands. "We agree. This job needs to be completed tonight. They can't wait. It's not fair."

I stared at the group around us, as Mark also joined us, sitting on the floor and then helping Candice to sit better. "I don't know what to say," and I really didn't. They cared.

Steve seemed to pale, and he reported in. "With some food and a little rest, I don't think any of our lives are in danger yet. We're not even halfway through the cave. I think we should continue also."

Glancing from one to the other, I noticed they were all solid. I couldn't stop them even if I wanted. After all, it was their game life to risk. I sat with them while they recuperated, and then started to move off again.

Steve was the last one. "Don't go killing yourself for an easy trip back to see Dresel."

He laughed. "I don't intend on dying. These pain settings aren't nice, you know."

I watched as he trundled off to start connecting the Tromoal clutches once more.

The Savage Angels worked slowly, methodically. I could only watch them as they went from clutch to clutch. I felt totally exhausted. My pain levels were through the roof, health bar not at all happy.

HEALTH – 30%

Laying my head back against the wall, I fell asleep. It wasn't until I felt myself being lifted up and hoisted into the arms of Chip that I stirred. "It's all right, Maddie. I've got you."

I'd no idea where he was taking me, and I didn't really care. Exhaustion overwhelmed me as well as the pain. Pain? New pain. What was this? The world around me burned.

I heard Candice's voice next to him and felt a warm hand on my face. "She needs a healer. I can't do anything."

"We should get her back to town, to Dresel."

I didn't know why my health was on the decline. Maybe I'd done too much, maybe there really was something else going on, but all I felt was lightheaded and weightless, or was that because Chip was still carrying me?

Most of the next few hours I don't remember. Candice's face was above me, dripping water into my mouth. It made my throat sting a little but did nothing to regenerate my health. "Who's looking after the caves?" I tried to ask, but my words were just raspy bits of nothing. When she tried to drip in some of my potions from the Hog as well, my stomach wrenched, as if I didn't want any of it. But if it took the pain away, I really couldn't deny it.

Candice leaned over, whispered in my ear, "Whatever you're doing, you've got to stop."

I could sense it. I knew what it was, but I couldn't stop it. They needed the energy. I was sure they did.

Candice gripped my shoulders, and her voice became more firm. No, this wasn't Candice. This was. . . I was somewhere else. Where?

I tried to look around the room. The walls were white, the sounds around me were of clinking metal, whirring machines. I wasn't back at the camp. I was deep below the town, in Dresel's office. I squinted and could just make out that Steve and Dresel were hunched over a computer system and were discussing something. Me.

"Maddie, stop it, now."

HEALTH – 28%

"Maddie!" It was Candice. I had no idea as to why Dresel had let them in. This was his sanctum, no?

Dresel moved to my bedside. "The computer systems and your actual programming are telling me your body's shutting down. Maddie, you're putting your energy into something you don't need to. Stop it."

I tried to think about what I'd been doing, and as I focused on his face, I could see the tears brimming. "You don't have to do this," he said. "They will survive."

In the far distance, I could feel something pulling me away, but it wasn't what I wanted. I tried to smile at him, and I focussed inside. Stopping the exchange of energy.

The world around me blacked out. There was nothing. No sounds, no voices.

HEALTH – 25%

Then there was.

I saw light peeking around me, and I felt Riezella beside me. "Maddie, we're here for you. Do not fret."

The voices dimmed, moved, visions of many things around me. Then everything vanished, and there was nothing but darkness. Real darkness.

CHAPTER 3

The world around me shifted, lights exploded, here, there, everywhere. I glanced around at the horrors that beseeched my vision. I couldn't look. Death lay all around me, from the people I'd called as friends to those who I'd hated.

Up ahead was a shadow, a man. I knew him, but I had never met him. Not here.

HEALTH – 20%

Voices drifted to me on the winds. And I heard nothing but empty promises.

SYSTEM FAILURE
CODE CORRUPTED
FULL SYSTEM SHUT DOWN
DEATH IMMINENT

That was aimed at me.

"No," was all I managed to stutter out. "I will not leave them. I've made promises."

With a flash of bright white lights, I imagined a computer before me, like nothing I'd seen on this planet before. It's complex letters and algorithm sects, I had no clue to their talks, but I understood their content.

HEALTH – 12%

I reached out. My hands felt as if they didn't belong to me, heavier, and I had seven fingers. I almost blinked at them, but placing them to the computer's key system, they fit perfectly. It was made for me. There I began to type. Code after code line. Faster and Faster

SYSTEM FAILURE – PAUSED

The voices and messages popping into my head were strange, but I managed to understand the next sentence.

CORRUPTION RE-WRITTEN
SYSTEM SHUT DOWN POSTPONED
REBOOT INEVITABLE

Then something else happened.

- *Hello, Maddie.*

This came as a complete surprise. I replied with but a thought.

- Hello.
- *It is good to finally talk to you.*
- Who are you?
- *I am the governing entity behind the digital world you know as Puatera Online.*

- Artificial Intelligence?
- *No, I am real Intelligence, just as you are.*

I paused for a little while not knowing what I should say or ask. Or if I should actually do anything. But my inner mind had so many things I needed answers to, so I asked,

- You're like me, aren't you?
- *I am.*
- What are we?
- *We are survivors of a species called the Zofilex.*
- The last?
- *Of that, I do not know. I chose to integrate with this world directly, to govern and manage everything in her systems. You didn't want to join me. You said life was too short. That it was meant to be lived, not to live forever.*

There was something returning. Memories, destruction, death. Then there was running. Hiding, trying to exist without a world and without others. Then I found him, Tibex.

- Tibex?
- *You remember? That's a good thing. Because I need your help.*
- How can I help you? You're the one governing all of this, this world. What can I do?
- *You must return to them. Do not give up. You are much needed.*

I didn't feel needed, although I did feel that they liked me and maybe wanted me around.

- *All right, I'll word it differently. Alex needs you. You cannot leave him.*

That was all it took. My heart beat faster, and I found myself swallowing as hard as I could to stem and not push myself away from this vision. I had so much to think about.

- *No, we will talk again. I need you to remember everything first, and you don't. Return to Dresel and the Savage Angels. War is coming. A war you must win.*

That was it. That was all I got. My fingers moved quicker over the keys than I thought possible, but the keys themselves started to fade away. Instead of the place I'd seen, there was something else, bandages. My hands were wrapped in bandages?

I looked around. I was in a small bed in the back of one of the horse wagons. It seemed dark out, and yet, in here, everything was bright, too bright.

I choked out, "What the hell happened?"

And that was when I saw Chip before me, his dopey curly hair bouncing as he shot up and shouted. "Candy! She's awake."

Candice's face came into view as Chip helped me sit up. The pain bearable, but every part of me stung.

"What happened?" I managed to ask once more. My hands tingling, now feeling numb.

HEALTH – 10%

Candice sat before me, taking my hands in hers. "We'd just gone off to finish the last of the egg binding when you started screaming. The small fire we had going was just enough for you to stick your hands in. Steve pulled you out, but they were already badly damaged. Between that and your health has declined a lot, we had to finish the eggs quickly and get you out and to a healer asap."

"Why would I put my hands in the fire?" It made no sense at all.

She seemed to consider my thoughts and waited while I tried to remember.

Nothing came to me.

"Steve seemed to think you were trying to write something," Candice prompted, "maybe some kind of code."

But that was a recent thought, not while I'd been asleep. Or had Steve triggered something showing my code line to me? I tried to slap my head with the bandaged hands, but it hurt all the more.

Steve popped into view from the back of the wagon. He said, glancing at the other two, "Would you mind giving us a few moments?"

Candice clearly wanted to be in on this conversation, but she nodded and moved to walk away, Chip in tow.

I looked up at Steve wondering what was going on inside his extremely clever mind. The view of the wagon faded, my mind all confused. I really was in Dresel's after all.

Steve sat on the end of my bed. "Feeling any better?" He started to take off the bandages from my hands. I tried not to let the pain show, but they hurt like hell.

Steve was the one who winced for me. "They've not healed at all?"

I glanced to my health bar, it was so low it wasn't registering anything. A tiny, tiny mark.

HEALTH – 5%

Steve frowned and picked up an ointment. "There's something really wrong with your programming."

I let out a gasp as he covered my hands with the ointment. It stung, but it did ease the pain. His forehead crinkled in a soft way I now found cute.

I pulled my hands back from him, taking the pain like a trooper though I didn't want to. "It's not the programming," I said. "It's just me."

I motioned to Steve. "I've a couple of things to tell you." Steve edged forwards. "Where's my ring?"

Steve handed it to me, and never having felt pain like it, I slid the ring over my seared and burned flesh. I twisted it.

The faint pink glow shone around the room, and I felt the twinge of something happening.

HEALTH BOOST – 26%

The ring's pink glow turned blood red, and my hands started to heal. The redraw skin lightened and then grew new skin over it.

He watched. "Wow, that's amazing."

I knew what I'd done, not only using the power of the ring, but calling on the powers from the Tromoal themselves, and not the youngsters.

"I'm not just an NPC," I said. "I'm something very different than anything you'd imagine." What they wouldn't or couldn't know just yet was what I was trying to let settle into my brain. I couldn't compute it. If I wasn't programming, and I wasn't human, then alien?

Or maybe I was the one thing I'd always thought I hated. Visitor. Could I be a player? Alien or not? I laughed as he watched as my skin healed more. His face turned upwards, and he finally met my eyes with his. "What are you, Maddie?"

I didn't know what to tell him or how to even explain things to myself anymore, so I just shrugged.

Steve handed me a mug. When I sniffed it, I realised it was full of a warm healing potion. I sipped it, enjoying the sweet, fruity taste.

HEALTH – 40%

It was good to see my health bar going back up. I felt much better now.

I heard Candice outside the door talking with some of the others, and then she knocked, stepping in. Her long blonde hair fell around her face, and she beamed at me. One very beautiful woman. I wondered how many Visitors had the same physique in here as they did at home.

"Good to see you're feeling better," she said and moved to my side.

Her face fell, though, as she looked at Steve. "I'm afraid we have to leave for a while, though."

I almost took a double take. "You're leaving? Why?"

Steve locked eyes with her. "Me too?"

"No, I can get someone in to take your place for a while. You're needed here. There have been some complications back at the Mayor's farm. A quest came in for us to eradicate those zombie cattle and any others that might be infected, and we thought it best to take it, deal with them, and come back to you."

I would try to understand her reasons. They were players. They neither wanted or needed to babysit the Tromoal. As much as I liked having her around, I knew she also needed to go.

"It's okay, I said. I understand you should go. Get them sorted, make the world a little safer."

She reached forwards and placed a hand on mine. "We're not giving up on your fight, Maddie. We just realise the opposing team isn't going to come rushing in at you. The kind of war they're planning will take a little time.

"And you wish to gain more skills to help us?" Steve asked her. I hoped they were planning to come back.

Candice grinned. "Yes. The skills and rewards will not only help us with Maddie's coming war but also with continuing to play the game after."

I tried to sit up as I swung my legs over the edge of the bed. Steve helped me to stand. "You all right?"

I wobbled some more then finally found my strength returning, thinking I might not fall over.

"Please, let me get some fresh air. I'll not flake, I promise."

Candice led me out of the bay to the lift and then back outside and into the heat I was missing. No matter how much I hated the deserts, they gave me one thing—comfort and warmth.

The town was bustling. People ran here and there, getting things loaded onto carts and more.

"The town has really taken to the orders you gave them. I think the camp and the people stationed there will be fine."

I agreed. "You're taking Josh with you to the Mayor's?"

Candice nodded. "Never thought about having an NPC on our team before, but that guy can really fight."

"I hadn't known that about him, but I'm glad you trust one of us."

Candice's face flushed. "Oh, I'm sorry. I forget, but he really is someone not to mess with. He's also really warmed up to Chip. I think they're going to be really good friends."

I chuckled, unsure if she knew which way Josh liked his mates, but seeing Mandy and Rose together was enlightening. Candice never batted an eye, but I think she would have if Josh managed to get Chip away from his obsession with her.

On that note, I actually saw Josh heading our way. He had a huge grin on his face. "Good to see you up and about, Maddie. I couldn't believe you'd done that to yourself."

I frowned, still not remembering the actual injuries. But I knew the pain. Rubbing my hip, I quickly checked my health. I was okay, still. It was on the up, not headed back down. This was great news for me. The poison in my system really didn't like me using the ring.

HEALTH – 65%

Nothing out of place.

"What will you do now?" she asked me. "We're also prepping to leave."

"I'm going to take a trip to some of the other towns, try to get them to realise there's a war coming. The open quest call might have been enough to warn them, but seeing me in person will aid that. I don't know how many I can get to join us, but there's a greater need for weapons, people, and more."

Candice nodded. Josh held out a hand for me, and in it lay a key. "I want you to take everything you can from my lockup. Get it out of the camp. They'll need it and so will you."

"I'll get it to Sarah. She can distribute things easier." I took the key from him and stared at it. "Not planning on dying now, are you?"

His grin faded a little, but then he spoke clearly. "No. I'm going because I wanted to help. I also really think Chip and Candice need someone with a better lay of the land including monsters and creatures. If these zombie critters are as tough as they were a few days ago, then I think they'll need me."

I watched on as the groups all got together, and eventually, they moved on. Abel was the one who came and stood by my side this time. "I had something to ask of you," he said.

"Oh, what is it?

"With the others gone, and Dresel and Steve staying here to work out something, I had a new quest pop up."

"What was it?"

"It asked me to assist you, to stay by your side on your next job."

I glanced at my sidebar, and then there was a flash. A blinking box alerted me to something new. So I clicked on it.

QUEST – VISIT THREE LOCAL TOWNS. ENCOURAGE THEM TO JOIN YOUR WAR EFFORT

I could do that. I'd received a lot of attention already for the Tromoal. I wondered if I put out another call to arms if it would help. But maybe not.

As the last biker rode away, I thought about my next move. The nearest town to here wasn't really a town. It was a hold up for some of the most notorious criminals in Maicreol. "I guess," I looked to Abel, sizing him up. "We have a trip to Hell's Pass. If we can get them to join our fight, the other towns will seem easy."

The way things were heading for me, I thought I might need more pain meds. I struggled with walking. Abel didn't say anything, though, and walked with me at a nice steady pace to get in the Hog. It wasn't a long walk, but I was never going to do that without assistance. I felt it better for me to drive, so I opened the Hog up, and he got inside.

Driving off, slow and steady, I felt peace return to my being. I loved being in here, more than anything else. I thought about flying as we had with the Tromoal, but that was just too damned scary.

HEALTH – 75%

The best thing about my health returning to normal was there was less pain. Using my foot on the pedals now didn't hurt. Here in the Hog, everything was better.

I pondered many questions, though, and decided to ask quietly. "So does everyone know I'm not normal then?"

Abel shook his head. "No, and I think that it's best to keep that information to just those in your original quest. The runners have got your back, but they don't think there's anything different about you. They just want what's best for their families. It's the Visitors who were around at the time and could see there was something new going down."

"Oh, so it was a few things that let you know I was different then?"

Abel nodded, staring out the windows as the scenery passed us by. I drove for quite some time before he spoke again. "I'm honest when I say this, but Dresel's one of my closest friends in the real world. I'm here because he's the designer, and he also trusts me with many things he wouldn't trust with anyone else."

That made a lot more sense. "So you're a babysitter?"

I watched as Abel scrunched his fists up. "No, I'm not that. I still enjoy playing the game. I want to find all the flaws I can before it gets out of alpha testing."

"You don't think our world can be opened up anymore to the public, do you?"

"That's being debated right now, but the plan is still to go ahead with the first beta launch. It just means there's going to be a few things going on in here that we can't advertise."

"How many players are there already? And what's the next stage?"

"There are ten teams. I'm kind of the oddball. I don't have a team. I'm just a filler, a hole finder."

"And the next stage?"

"There's more than a few hundred. The tickets to getting in on this were so expensive that most people, most regular gamers can't afford them."

"So it's still very restricted in what happens in here?"

"That all depends on Dresel, and if he doesn't pull the plug."

I almost stalled the Hog as my foot slipped off the pedal, "What? he can't pull the plug, can he?"

Abel tried to look out the window again, but he wasn't fooling me.

"I'm sorry, Maddie, but yes, this game's only in development stages. If there are flaws he can't fix, then there's a cut-off point. Investors won't just keep plugging in money forever."

"What are you telling me?" I asked, finally stopping the Hog, letting the engine tick over so that we could talk.

Abel met my gaze, shifting in his seat. I'd not known him that long, or had I?

The way the world around me worked suddenly faded away from me. Like I was looking at all the code, the programming.

There was so much of it. Everything was codes, codes I couldn't see through, that made up Abel and the Hog, and as I tried to look at my hands... Me.

I tried to breathe in, but I couldn't.

There was no air. This place wasn't real!

CHAPTER 4

The ping came in loud and clear, and the words flickered across my eyes. I struggled all the more to breathe.

- *Maddie, calm down.*

I glanced at my interface, seeing the little tag and words creeping across. But I didn't want to type or talk to him. Flinging the door of the Hog open, I stepped outside, seriously trying to get the air into my lungs. My legs buckled. Abel was soon at my side. That's when I felt something else. Something around me started to change. No, it wasn't around me. It was me.

Abel's eyes widened, and I glanced at my hands. They flickered in and out of existence.

- *Maddie, if you don't listen to me, you'll blow everything!*

I blinked and stared at Abel's big stubbly chin. His hair wafted in the desert breeze, and sweat pooled down his forehead and ran off the end of his nose.

Finally, I was able to suck in a breath. The air tasted sweet. It's usually hot stickiness spread through my lungs and gave my body a second chance—again. I pushed myself back up and leaned on the Hog's bonnet.

"Sorry, that was just one heck of a shock."

"I probably shouldn't have said anything, but Dresel's really worried." He tried to smile, but it didn't come across as well as he had hoped.

"No, thank you. I needed to know this because I will do everything I can to fix it. This game can't be switched off."

"What do you think we can do to help?"

I thought for a minute. Letting the sun beat down on my face, I turned to him and said with the utmost confidence, "We have to do exactly what they want. We have to play the game."

Abel's eyes lit up, and he laughed. "I love it."

I moved away from the bonnet and opened the door once more. "Now let's get going again, shall we?"

Getting back into the Hog, I touched the pad to start the engine. It chugged, and a puff of black smoke billowed out the back.

"Crap," I said.

"Open the bonnet." Abel slid back out. There was something suddenly knowledgeable about him as he popped the bonnet to look into the engine. I started some basic diagnostics from the dashboard.

Joining him to look at the engine, he whistled down at what he saw. "This took some getting together, Maddie. These parts look original, but they're not. They've been handcrafted."

I could only nod. "The diagnostics will take a little while, which means we have to walk the rest of the way."

"Think you can manage, or do you need a ride on my shoulders?" He laughed.

I wasn't ever going to get on those shoulders—the guy was huge. I really didn't like heights. And that was way too scary for me.

"No, thanks. I'll be walking."

Abel watched as I pulled out supplies from the Hog, chucking him a bottle of water while I sucked on my potions. The silver flask was almost empty. So this time I popped it and found a refill, pouring the liquid into it, and then secured it on my belt.

"I'm good. Let's go. It's only about an hour now."

"That's okay. If you need to, I'm here."

I nodded.

I think the one main difference with Abel and Alex was I felt so strange being here now with Abel. He was the polar opposite of Alex, really difficult for me to actually talk to. But I did want to ask him questions, so eventually, when he didn't speak, I asked. "So, you were saying about the gaming system, the way things work for you. Have there been many problems?"

"Not really." He glanced at me. "A couple of rogue code lines left an NPC out in the desert with no way of getting or doing anything. The players that saw him wandering about wasting away alerted one of the team. They were slightly traumatised because of his condition, but we sorted it out pretty quickly."

The rubble from the roads hurt the bottom of my feet. I needed new boots as well as many other things. All this walking and stuff was really hard on equipment here.

Abel fell silent once more as we finally neared the first sign of entering Hell's Pass.

I hadn't expected the town to look so busy. People were everywhere... and not just their usual pottering and skulking about. They were flat out preparing for something big. I froze and glanced at the one place I knew I'd get some answers. A local knick-knack shop.

We wound our way through the bustling crowds. I got the tail end of conversations, and part of me hoped I'd not heard right. It came as no surprise, though, that they were planning the upcoming war.

I heard several of the locks click, and then Abel pushed the door open. "Always wondered what goodies were stashed away in places like this."

I paused. "Yeah, you're not kidding. There are some really decent weapons stashed in here, and then the potions. They're some of the finest you could ever come across."

Abel stepped inside and held the door open for me. I got a much better look inside the building. The room hadn't changed much, but this time, something felt different. Weird. Almost as if the owner really hadn't come home. I tried to push that thought away as I looked everything over, all neatly packaged in boxes and crates.

Abel perused some of the area, walking up and down the lines of weapons and equipment, then he turned to me. "This guy was more than serious about going to war."

And that begged the question—where indeed was the shop owner? "Hello!" I called out, but there was no reply. "Mr. Frankin?" I pointed to the back room. "I don't understand what's going on," I said to Abel. We moved towards it to enter another large display area, this one filled with lots of other goodies, some I really wanted for the Hog and myself. But now wasn't the time. There was something else calling us, a higher purpose, of the game and this war.

Once faced with the furthest wall, I placed my hand on it. I could tell now how fake it actually was, but there was also a heavy ward surrounding the wall. I tried to focus on thinking of everything good. But keeping us safe and then letting us in were two different things for this ward, and it didn't want to do either. I guess I did something wrong because the door didn't open. There was a loud snap of energy, and I was flung against the opposite wall. A moment later, Abel stood over me. I brushed myself off and moved to take his offered hand. He tugged me up without effort.

The door before us had not only opened but, instead, disintegrated.

"Interesting." I moved to look through the now open doorway. Abel stood beside me. Inside was dust free and very tidy. There were shelves lined with many different objects. Things I'd never seen before. "What is all this stuff?" I asked Abel as we moved around the room.

Abel picked something up, turning it over in his hand. "These are things from my world. Old things. They shouldn't be here." He looked at me, and his forehead crinkled. "This is a Walkman. They haven't been used for many years. There are other ways to store music digitally now."

"So how is it here?"

He shook his head. "I have no idea."

I moved around, careful not to touch too much or disturb anything that I shouldn't. I stopped before a desk and computer— well, what I could only presume was a computer. It looked like a basic set up.

"Abel, this looks like some kind of computer. You any good with them?"

Abel looked my way as I pointed to the end of the small space. There was a desk, keyboard, and something that looked like plain glass. Maybe when it fired up, the glass was the viewer—like a computer screen.

Abel sat, and I watched.

The screen lit up like I thought it would, but there was a language I didn't understand. "What is that?"

Abel looked at me. His face rarely gave much away, but then he said, "It's actually Italian. But I've no idea why it would be here. Since my father's Italian, he's the reason I recognise it."

"What's it saying?" I pointed to the largest part of the text.

"Lots of things. Some about Puatera Online."

I wish I could understand it, but I didn't. Maybe I could if I studied it, learned it.

"It mentions a portal...." he said.

He flicked through more screens, and I saw a town like I'd only witnessed when Riezella showed me Alex's Earth. "I've seen this place before."

"How can you have seen this." He pointed to the screen. "This is London, England."

"There are a lot of things you don't understand about me, but I've

235

seen this place. I walked through the rain and grasses, and I saw the signs advertising this game."

"There are references for moving through it, and then there are logs for every item in this room." Abel pointed to the Walkman. "That was taken from someone's bag in 1987."

"Stolen, and you think Mr. Frankin did that?"

"I don't know. It's not saying the name of the guy who's done all this. I find the whole thing bizarre."

"But this place belongs to one of the largest known criminal gangs. Who else could have been doing this?"

There was a cough at the door.

"That would be me."

I turned to see a woman. Someone I didn't recognise. Her clothes were of black silk, and she wore a leather armoured jacket and gauntlets.

Abel pushed up from the computer, and then the two of them started to speak in what I presumed was Italian.

Abel frowned before speaking. "This is Lidia Trovatto, a Visitor."

I stared at her. There was no tag against her head. "I don't understand?"

When Lidia nodded to the computer, she also tapped the side of her head. And there it was, her tag.

"You're a rogue?" Abel asked.

"Yes, that's how I like to play the games. I've been undercover here in the town for about six months."

"What happened to the shop owner?"

"He left this morning, and he hadn't known I was here at all."

"And Dresel doesn't know any of this is going on?"

"Dresel is the designer of the game. He's no detective. He might know where some of his people are, but there are some of us who were also asked to go as deep as we possibly could."

"You're working with others?"

"I am. There are three others stationed around the game because there were four portals opened up on the same day."

"Four? These portals…" I asked. "Are they real?"

"They're as real in the fact they let me go through to the past. To walk around and do things I never thought I could. However, I believe three aren't real—only one is."

"And you know which one?"

"No. There are similarities in all of them, so we're still investigating."

"Can you take me to see them?" Abel asked.

"I'm not letting you go anywhere without me," I said, suddenly feeling like he was about to up and leave me. "And we've some other pressing jobs to complete first."

He nodded, lowering his head. "Sorry, I just suddenly got too excited."

"Then I guess I'll take you both, as to how 'real' you think this Earth is, I am interested in that myself."

I already knew it was going to be very real, but what we'd do or how we'd do it when we got there… that was a completely different question.

We stayed for a while, looking through the shop inventory to see if anything there could help the Hog. There was nothing that could. Returning to the Hog had me frowning. Locked up and looking lonely, I palmed the doors open and checked the dash, hoping for an answer to the problems.

I blew out a sigh as Abel stood by my door looking in. "I can get him to limp across to the other side of town, but he needs some pretty rare parts."

"Can you fix him, though?"

"Might take a day or so. Means we're grounded here for a while."

"That's okay. We can do as you said and rally some of the other locals."

"It's not a town known for the locals to be friendly."

"You mean, I won't be welcome at all?" he frowned at me, his tanned face crumpling.

"No, Visitors aren't welcomed at all usually. It's one of the main towns where the underworld rules. But, if we're sticking around, I'll need backup. We'll have to make do."

I hadn't expected anything to go wrong so soon, but these things happen, and glancing at the hog, I had a feeling the day was going to get worse before it got better.

"How do they get the parts?" Abel asked as I managed to turn over the engine. Flashing lights lit the dashboard, and more black smoke billowed out behind us.

"Get in." I grinned. "It will just take a lot longer, but at least we'll get there."

Abel climbed in again, and I managed to get us rolling. This particular town was more than a few miles away. But it was also the only place I knew that would have the spare parts I needed.

"There's a small back garage that deals in specifics. I found Ian and his crew there to be very resourceful."

"They steal things then?"

I laughed. "No, they're crafters of the highest quality. That doesn't mean they don't do things they shouldn't. But they're the best at making something if I break something."

"Makes sense. Not been to that side of the county before."

"Then we're both in for a treat. Last time I stayed there, I was not only mugged but shot at and almost run out of town since their local vampire was a dab hand at recruiting all the wrong people."

Abel's hands clenched. "Well, if they hurt me, I'll respawn back at Dresel's now, but *you* have to be careful."

He was really worried about me, yet I'd never been that worried about myself. I'd always handled things my way. It was only the Tromoal that had me running scared, but now not so much since they were family.

I pushed the Hog on. Slowly.

~

It did take a lot longer to get around to the other side of town, a good hour more than it should have. Abel sent Dresel a message to tell him where we were heading, and when we finally pulled up across from the garage, I knew we'd be right here for a while. The sun had well started to set, and the busy town looked dim and dingy.

"Go across to the inn," I pointed in the direction of a sign. *Last Chance Inn.* "I'll get the Hog locked and meet you in the tavern for some food. We'll sleep tonight and then see where we're at in the morning."

"I'll be alright, big guy like me. They won't give me too much hassle."

I looked him up and down. "Just keep cool. I'll be in as soon as I can."

Abel nodded, his large frame sliding out and the Hog's suspensions returning to normal. He had been a big weight for my vehicle to carry in limp mode, but I kind of wanted his company. I was learning things the more I talked to these Visitors.

I was scared Tibex would pop back in to talk to me, and I didn't want to think about all the possibilities that were swarming around in my head.

CHAPTER 5

The garage was closing for the night. Ian watched as I chugged into a bay.

"Sounds rough there, Madz."

"Take a look in the morning, Ian," I said. "I've set the passwords for you for a couple of days."

"Nar, pop the bonnet now. I'll take a look at the diagnosis too. Might be able to put some feelers out before the night's end."

I palmed the bonnet open, and he took a quick nosey. "Yeah, not going to be a cheap one this time around." He poked his head in the driver door and tapped the dash a few times. "Might take a few days. Sorry, Madz."

"I knew that. Just get it sorted."

Ian nodded, and with a yawn, added, "Been a long day. You staying at Val's Inn."

I smiled. "As always."

"Then I might see you in there after dinner. Can't miss out on Ellie's cooking."

I turned to walk back into the town, allowing him to lock up. There was a lot of people around, a few I recognised, most looked my way with nervous dispositions and shifty faces.

What else was going on here? I was here less than a few months ago.

I pushed the thoughts to the back of my mind and walked into the tavern. It was busy as I'd expected it to be. The work crowd in and enjoying a quick drink before going home.

I spotted Abel and made my way over to him. His head was low, but he didn't look out of place. I was pleasantly surprised when I arrived, and he was actually chatting away to the barman, quite at home.

When I reached his side, the barman nodded my way, and Abel pushed a pint before me. "Was there room?"

"Yeah, though the town's busier than normal as there have been a lot of refugees heading this way from the other villages after the Tromoal attacks. Just got the last room, though. Sorry. We'll have to share."

I picked the beer up and tasted it as it's cool frothiness slid down my parched throat. "It's okay. I don't mind sharing. You seem like a decent guy who wouldn't try anything, right?"

"No. I'm not that kind of guy, plus Dresel already told me you sleep with your daggers."

I raised an eyebrow. "So, I like to cuddle with them at night."

Abel laughed, and I knew from then we'd be friends. "You hungry? The food's not so bad here if we order after the working crowd are out."

"Big lad like me eats a lot." Abel patted his stomach. "I'm always hungry."

I laughed and finished the pint before ordering us a few more. "You all right for cash? I can pay for this if you need."

"I'm good. I've been earning a small penny while here. It's not much, but it keeps me in food."

We talked for a while, letting the bar empty. But it was small talk, things about the local area that if anyone overheard us, it wouldn't be construed as wrong.

A short time later, we ordered food and moved to a small table at the far side of the room.

I stared into the eyes of the big man before me. I could see who he was here in the game and some of what he wanted me to see of his personality, but I didn't know who he was or what he really wanted from me, or maybe even Dresel.

"So you just work for Dresel. Is it money or something else? I'm trying to understand the reasons."

Abel looked away. "A lot of it's the money. I had a problem back in my world. Managed to finally sort it out, then came across Dresel. He offered me something of both worlds. I could play the games and not gamble with my home and life."

"There's something else, though. What?"

"I don't feel alive in my homeworld." He fingered the edge of his shirt. "It's like there's the day job, which pays some of my bills, people I owe money to, but nothing compares to logging in here, sticking around to find issues, and fix them. Working with the people here. It's more than real."

I could see he really felt that, and it made me feel better. Like this world wasn't just imaginary to him or to them.

"Everyone's experience in this game is very different, isn't it?"

He nodded. "Yes, take your friend Alex for example. He played because he was ill."

I swallowed and glanced away. They didn't know what Riezella had done with him. "Is he still alive in your world? Do you think you could find out for me?"

I hadn't even thought about this before to even ask. To know for sure if his life had passed on.

Abel seemed to look to the left, and I could only imagine he was accessing his interface. "I do have to log out later on tonight. I could ask. What was his full name?"

I wasn't sure if his name here was the same as there. "I don't know," was all I could manage. "His name here was Alex Dubois."

243

"Well, I'll try and find out anything I can, even if I talk to Dresel back at the main labs."

"Thank you." My head spun though, would it be news I could handle? I mean what if his body was still alive?

I forced that thought to one side when I noticed Ian enter the bar. He had two younger men with him, one still in slacks and an oil riddled shirt. I'd never seen them before, but they nodded my way. Ian grinned at me, and wandered over, leaving the other guys to find a table.

"Mind if I join you?"

"Course not," I said. "Pull up a chair. This is Abel. Abel, this is Ian, the man who will fix the Hog."

Ian pulled a chair over and plopped down, holding a hand out for Abel to shake. Which he did, strongly. "Any friend of Madz is a friend of mine. You're watching her back, right?"

Abel raised an eyebrow. Ian tapped the side of his head. "Implant. I'm able to see and read all Visitor quests and stats."

Coughing out some of his beer, Abel choked out. "What? How did you manage to get that kind of add-on?"

Ian grinned. "When you're smart, you can create most things you need. I wanted to be able to know who was what around me. There are only two prototypes of this in the world."

Abel looked concerned, but he didn't say anything else.

"Any thoughts on what we need for the Hog?" I asked as the barkeeper placed some of our food down for us. Abel dug in straight away, but I kept mine at bay, suddenly feeling sick.

Ian lowered his eyes. "It needs a new Rolestak."

I pushed my food away and swallowed down some more beer.

"Is that bad?" Abel asked, mouth full of food.

"There's only one place we can get a new one. We can't re-create it. It needs to be new."

"Where do we get it?"

I glanced to the barman who was serving a couple of other guys.

"Only one place around here that might have one."

"And he was the reason I was almost run out of town the last time I was here."

"Great. Sounds like we're in for some fun tomorrow then."

"No, if we're going, it will have to be tonight. He sleeps a lot during the day."

Abel looked to the friends of Ian's who now had food. "They are here so they can help us?"

Ian nodded. "Dec and Rai are good guys, but if you're heading into the dark forest, you'll need some extra eyes."

"Are we talking about vampires?"

"I'm not sure on your species clarification," Ian said. "But Doctor Foster is a Demon Lord."

"Oh, that makes it even more fun." I swallowed down more beer and picked up my fork. Since when had this lone vampire managed to obtain Demon Lord status? I highly doubted this was the case, but he was good at obtaining some of the things he wanted. He'd wanted me, but I'd declined and ran as fast as I could from the place.

When Abel then asked... "Do we get to kill him?"

I spat out my food. "Don't say things like that around here."

"Why? seems the place is pretty quiet."

Ian glanced around nervously. "There have been some local gangs that would love to have taken him out, but he's locked himself quite deep in a mountain lair."

Abel tucked himself closer in to Ian. "If we did manage to fend this guy off, would the Hell's Pass join Maddie's Quest Event?"

"Ah. I saw notifications for that." He turned to face me. "You started that?"

I nodded and finally managed to get food into my mouth without choking on it.

"Then we need to move this conversation somewhere private." Ian pushed his chair back and went to the bar. He spoke with the barman for quite some time, and I couldn't make out what they were talking about at all, maybe another language, but reading his lips wasn't working.

245

By the time Ian returned to us, Abel had almost finished his food. "Come with me," Ian said and motioned to Dec and Rai who started to head over.

I frowned at my plate of food, but Abel picked it up for me, and I followed with the beer glasses.

"Bring us in some more drinks before we lock it down, Val," Ian said to the waitress who sat at the end of the bar. She winked at him, and I kept on walking until we left that part of the bar.

We walked down for quite some time, the floor gently sloping away from us. Passing room after room, all the doors closed, locked, some with padlocks too. This confused and kind of scared me. Where were we going? Then, finally, at the end of the corridor, Ian knocked at the door and placed his hand to palm it open. He bid us inside. Abel checked out the room first before he let me in.

"It's got some heavy wards installed on it," Abel said. "I don't think anyone will hear our conversations in here."

I stepped inside, placing the beer on the table. The waitress had followed us with several other beers, along with a bottle of spirit with five shot glasses. "If you need anything else, just ping me." And she left.

I watched as Ian sat, followed by Dec and Rai. All three of them stared at me. "Meet, Declan Hoors and Rai Sal. Meet Maddie Vies and Abel Rimmer."

"Pleasure, Maddie." Declan held out his hand for me, and I shook it with a firm grip. Rai was a little more nervous. No maybe not nervous, but wary. He didn't hold out his hand.

"I'm not rude, Maddie," he said. "I have a gift that if I touch another's skin, I see things that they don't want me to see. So I prefer no physical contact, and I hate wearing gloves."

I smiled at him. "No worries."

"So what is this place, and why did you ask us down here?" Abel asked taking one of the shot glasses off the pile and pouring himself a drink.

"We knew Maddie would return one day for that part. Hoped it would have been a little sooner, but that's a different story."

"Wait, so you've been hanging around knowing I'd come back to do what?"

"Take out the new Demon Lord." Abel was right on the nose, and I knew it too. I wished he wasn't.

"I've been up against the doctor once before. He's not someone you mess with."

"No, we know that, and he's just been getting stronger each night he's holed up in there. He needs to go."

"So you think I'm the one to do that.

"Exactly. Declan and Rai are trained in many arts to aid you in this, and with Abel as well, you'd be a small fighting force that he wouldn't be expecting at all."

"I know I need the part for the Hog, but this is a little extortionate. A huge ask from me. Why didn't you guys just put up a job for it and call in any Visitors you could?"

"Because they'd take all the loot, and knowing you'd need it wasn't right. Those kinds of parts don't come along very often and last a lifetime. You had to come back when yours failed, and it was just a matter of time."

"But how many more has he killed or worse, kept trapped with him?" I shuddered at the thought of him keeping prisoners inside the castle he'd sequestered. But I knew that is exactly what he would have needed to do to survive.

"So, with all this time you've had on your hands, what's the plan then?"

Ian looked at Declan. "Go ahead."

Declan placed his palm on the table's centre and a large video screen popped up at the side of the room. We all moved to look at it and watched as the view switched to three separate screens. "There's only one way we're going to get in. Through the back door. The front has many guards, but the back has a couple less. There's no dungeon we can crawl through and no sewers. There are just two spots, the entrance and the back door where he gets deliveries. The plan would be to dress you up as..." He coughed, and I laughed.

"You want me to dress up as dinner for him?"

"Not very original, is it?"

"What would you suggest?"

I sat there pulling my plate of almost cold dinner to me and continued to munch on it. The root veggies were nice and crunchy just as I loved them to be. I paused, drank some beer, and looked at the screens again.

"I'm almost betting he knows I'm in town, he has eyes and ears everywhere. Especially after last time."

Ian nodded then with a sigh, admitted, "She's right."

"So, we walk to his front door and just take the fight to him. Even if he's ready, how much stronger can he actually be? There have not been enough missing people in the area for him to have massive stores."

Rai tapped the table and brought up the local missing people reports and the traffic watch they had on the 'backdoor.' They were at least well prepared.

CHAPTER 6

*P*lucking up the courage to head into the lair of a notorious vampire, and now supposed Demon Lord, was tough.

Ian wasn't coming with us, so the small party I'd be leading now consisted of Abel, our tank. Declan for damage and Rai for healing. I would probably do a little of everything if possible. I checked my equipment. I had nothing new, nothing extra I could use here to help either of us.

Abel's grin was huge, though. It went with the massive personality that accompanied his size. I would have said gentle giant, but he might take offence. He gave all the indications that he was a great guy to be around, but I also felt he was hiding something else. Maybe it was just me feeling cynical, though. I didn't want to trust anyone at the moment. Programming aside, I was learning how to be myself now—and to be around people without falling in love with everyone.

The grounds for the 'castle' weren't as I remembered. There was a great darkness that seemed to just envelope the whole area. I walked with Abel beside me, Declan and Rai behind us. There was no going back now. What I really wanted to do was turn and run, but that wasn't going to get my Hog fixed.

I noticed the two guards as I stepped into the eerie light from the porch. They were heavily armed, and they knew it. There was no fear showing on their faces.

"The doctor has been expecting you," one of them said as they moved to open the door. "He's asked that you go through and meet him in the main living room."

I glanced at Abel, who didn't look happy. I guess they all really did just want to go in guns blazing. However, I didn't think this would help our situation at all. To me, it seemed there was much more going on here than even the visitors could know.

I knew where the main living room was, and I also knew I didn't want to go there. It would mean looking at that ugly statue that he had on display. A living person, stuck forever, watching everything going on around them, trapped. Evil beyond measure.

However, when I stepped into the corridor leading to the main halls, I found the decor to be very different. White walls, clean wooden floors, not a splash of darkness, and certainly no carpet at all. I figured easier to clean blood off and shuddered.

Abel and Rai eased on ahead of me, and I let them. Declan caught my arm and pulled me to him, asking, "What do you think all of this actually means?"

The audacity of him grabbing me came with an instant reaction. I shoved him off and said. "I think he's done a lot more than become a Demon Lord."

Abel motioned for us to hurry and follow them through to the living space. I walked in and avoided the place where I had seen the statue, yet my eye was drawn to it once more, but there was nothing there. In its place was a cage, and within it, the most beautiful bird I'd ever seen. Drawn to it. I stepped forward and reached out, slowly so I wouldn't frighten it.

The bird sensed my approach and turned to me, it's bright blue feathers and flaming red ring around its neck something to behold. I couldn't look away.

Abel moved to my side, and we both stared at the creature while the other two wandered around the room. I didn't know what to do but stare. Then the creature started to sing. Its beautiful sounds echoing around the room in wonderful tones that moved me on such a deep level.

I turned to Abel. "Do you know what this is?"

He shook his head, obviously as mesmerised as I was. Then I heard a voice behind me, a cough. Doctor Foster. "Miss Vies," he said, and as I turned, he stepped into the room.

There was a strange glow about him, one that I couldn't put my finger on, and I tried to force a smile. "You know why I'm here."

"Yes." He grinned. "Beautiful bird, is she not?"

I glanced back to the bird who had stopped singing. Instead, she was perched on the end of a twig, staring at him. Her eyes seemed to reveal so much of her soul. I had to get her out of here. She couldn't be with this monster...

"Do not fret, I am not hurting her. She's to be locked up during the day, and I let her free at night."

"What is she?" I asked as Declan and Rai returned to join both of us.

"She's an Alerosa, a species native to Hikirio. She's a singer by nature, but she's shy around me. So I'm glad you were able to bring her out of her funk for a little while. I love to hear her sing."

I looked him up and down, noticing his attire, the long cloak and black clothes gone. He was wearing plain light coloured pants and a summer shirt. The deserts were always warm, but I'd never seen him warm. That confused me, and so did the pink almost glowing skin.

"What's been going on here?"

"A long story, my friend. Please take a seat, and I'll try my best to explain what happened since the day you ran out of this castle."

I tried not to panic as I felt the sudden need to escape once again, but I held back. There was so much that was different about the place. It shocked me. So I sat, and he did as well, reaching over to pour us all a drink.

"I didn't think you'd return quite so quickly. And I realise that my intentions to you, to keep you here were wrong. So I decided to change that. To become something different."

"How did you manage to do even half of this?" I indicated his change of wardrobe, the no carpets, and the re-decoration.

"I escaped the castle and went travelling. I found a portal."

"What?" I swallowed, my stomach knotting. "A portal?"

"Yes, there's one right under this castle. I didn't know about it, and we realised its potential shortly after that night."

"Where does it take you?" Abel asked.

"There's a city, but I find the word they use hard to say. It's something like London."

"London. Isn't that one of the cities we need to visit?"

I glanced at Abel my fear growing, "Yes, it is... But you said no, right?"

"Do you think it would matter if we went to take a look?"

"You want to see?"

I nodded at the doctor, but inside my twisting stomach turned to rising bile. "Yes, right now if we could?"

"I have a lot to tell you, but I think we can do that on the way down there."

He looked at the others. "Are you coming as well?"

Declan stared at me. "What is this portal and what is London? A new world?

Abel said, "Maybe it could be my world."

That would be very interesting.

I wasn't going to allow Declan and Rai anywhere near this other world, this portal. Just because there are NPCs that can cross over doesn't mean they should. I guess that would actually mean me too, but I just had to see it for myself. I mean I had no idea where Alex was from. Maybe it was London, maybe it wasn't. It could have been from any of the other cities the girls were trapped in. But I had to see it.

"Rai and Declan, you need to stay here. We need clear communication back to Dresel and the others. I'm afraid you're it."

They weren't too happy about it, but they agreed, and they were left with the other two guards by the main doors.

~

Doctor Foster moved through the house, and we followed. The white walls did recede, and the further we got, it was back to carpet and plaster. "So what did you discover in London that made you do all the remodelling?" I pointed back to where we'd come from. "The image, everything."

"There's a cure for vampirism, and it's not that costly. I've been taking the dosage of meds every day for the last few weeks. I'm not the same person I was, as you can see."

I did see, but I also wasn't going to be that easily fooled.

The further down we got into his world, the dingier it became. Abel looked back at me, and I nodded for him to keep following on, which he did. But I also got a bit of a bad feeling about this entire thing. My stomach churned. Was this a trap? Was he going to do something weird and horrid? No, I looked to Abel, and he wasn't looking the slightest bit worried. So I sucked in a breath and followed them both.

As we rounded a corner, I could see the light up ahead, golden glow that also hummed. "The portal is something to behold, but you'll need goggles, so it doesn't hurt your eyes. I can't do anything to protect your ears, though. It's quite a sharp pitch when you get into the room."

When he reached a doorway, we could see goggles hanging on the wall, and he handed us both a set. We put them on and then followed him out into the next room.

There before us was a large shimmering object. It seemed to float in mid-air, the size of the wall ahead of us. The humming indeed was quite loud and very high-pitched. It hurt my ears, but I held them closed and didn't let the noise win. I stepped closer to it, just like he did. And when Doctor Foster pointed and vanished through the gleaming object, I moved to do the same.

This wasn't like what Riezella had shown me. This was far different. There was a boisterous wind swirling from inside the portal, whistling and very strong. I turned to make sure Abel was following me. I couldn't actually see him or the room anymore.

Panic set in, and then I felt a hand on my shoulder. I still couldn't see anything, but there was a familiar presence.

- Tibex.
- *Yes, Maddie.*
- Is this a real place?
- *Yes, it is.*
- Is it where Alex's body is?

There was no reply, but then a soft whisper came to me. "Yes, Maddie. Your next task is to locate his body and turn off his life support."

"What's that?"

"There are machine's keeping Alex alive, you must stop them."

I stopped walking, and the hand that was on my shoulder squeezed gently.

"Maddie, closure is needed here. You need to see him, and you also need to finish what he's started with choosing to become more than human."

I actually agreed. I wanted nothing more than to see him be what was intended for him now. And if that was to do this one act, then I would.

I stepped forward once more, the wind in my hair settling down. Finally, I was able to breathe in and taste the air from this new world. This world that was something similar to Abel's.

Abel moved in beside me, his voice catching on the wind that was around him. He gasped and touched my arm. "That was some rush. Are you okay?"

I nodded and caught my breath. Doctor Foster was ahead of us and beckoned us on, but I needed a moment to do more than to catch my breath. I wanted to see where we were.

The green grasses around us were beautiful, the plants and trees, so much more than we had on Puatera. I wanted to touch them and smell them. Everything about it was meant for me to be here, and it was an experience I needed to savour.

I didn't allow myself to become too carried away with the new sensations. Doctor Foster urged us forwards.

I looked at him and then to where he pointed. There was indeed the largest building I'd ever seen. *Moors Memorial Hospital,* the label over the door said.

I then spat out the first thing that came to mind. "You knew about this? You knew about Alex? How?"

"Because I was given a quest by the game. To bring you here, to aid you, and in return, they took away the curse."

I swore under my breath.

"Maddie, what is this?" Abel said moving to stand before Foster and me.

"I'm here to end Alex's life."

"What?" his question said how he felt, but I could see with his shaking body and wandering eyes that he was freaking out. I knew I would, everything here felt real, but to him he should only be playing the game. "You can't be serious."

I was, and I knew it was something I could do. But I wasn't sure if I could do it on my own.

"There's a lot that I don't know, Maddie. This place, the way the game guides you and what it has asked of me. But I feel much better. I feel like I'm doing something for the greater good. I did so many bad things, and you know I did. I'm trying to make up for it, to help where I can, and to let my people survive."

I moved to whisper into Foster's ear, "You need to keep Abel out here. He can't see this, even if he thinks this place is a game. We know differently. Four portals—one is real, this one." I moved to go inside the building.

I expected Abel to put up a fight, and I could hear him shouting behind me. "You can't go in there, Maddie! You can't do what you're saying. What if this isn't the simulation? What if this really is his world and you're actually going to kill him?"

I turned to Abel and met his stare. His wonderful eyes now held such intense fear. Fear of something he knew nothing about.

I moved to him while Doctor Foster moved behind him, and I placed my hand on his cheek. "This is your world, Abel." I saw something else then, a shimmer from his nametag. "This is your world, Mark Langlos, age twenty-seven, born and raised in New York City."

His eyes faded, his shock evident as his jaw dropped. "You can't know that kind of information. It isn't stored anywhere. I have a fake name—even Dresel doesn't know that."

"No, he doesn't, but I do. I know your mother and father are dead, your sister works and lives with her boyfriend not far from you."

My hand started to glow, and I felt the energy coming from within me, no, not just me but from within the ring itself, from all the Tromoal and from even Tibex.

"You need to let me do this. You've seen more than your share of this game already. You're in our own world in a digital form while your body rests back in another country. That's not possible, but it's happening."

"Don't kill him." Tears started to stream down his face. I noticed several people giving him strange looks. I guess we were out of place. This world had vastly different clothing than we had. There probably was no need for armour, for goggles, or anything.

I glanced to Foster as I moved away from Abel. "He won't follow me, but take him somewhere he can start to believe in this, in himself. He's a special guy."

Foster nodded. "Will you be okay?"

"I'll be more than okay. This is a quest that only I can complete. For something to change in my world for real, it must end in this one."

When he lowered his head and began to walk away with Abel in tow, he didn't look back at me.

I made my way forward. All of a sudden, there was a bright flash and the clothes I wore vanished from my skin. I now wore something similar to the clothes I'd seen them wearing earlier with Riezella.

I moved to the door. It was made of glass, almost like something we'd have on Puatera but finer, easier to see through. I pushed it open. The ring around my hand started to glow, it's eerie pink sparkles lighting up the corridor I traversed.

I didn't know where Alex was, but I was listening to the one thing now that was inside me. There was hope, love, and more importantly, my instinct now to help and set him free properly.

I made my way through the building. People seemed to ignore me, which was weird. I didn't know if they could see me or not. I wondered if maybe it had something to do with the ring or who I was.

Tibex's words came through for me.

- *This is who you are.*
- I can traverse worlds and be seen or not be seen if I want to?
- *Yes, which is more than many can say.*
- Would Riezella be able to do this?
- *No, she cannot. Not in this way. She can see and view things, but she doesn't have a solid form that can swap between worlds. She's in digital form from her own world, and that's all she can do.*

I watched as several humans milled around. They stopped when they seemed to see something around me, but then they kept going once more.

I saw a box like what Dresel used on us and entered it. The lift started to move, and I went with it, following the path upwards towards the sky.

Once, there was a ping, and the door opened. I moved into a different corridor where there was a woman on a desk. She looked up at the empty lift but then went back to work. On the board behind her was a list of room numbers and names. Then I spotted it—a name. His name.

Alex Dubois.

I moved to the board and saw some of the diagnoses on there, understanding them, I sighed. Then I moved to leave the area and walked into the room where I knew he would be. Where I at least knew his body was, because his real soul, his inner person, was back on Puatera.

Sucking in a breath, tears flowing freely down my face, I paused, I wasn't sure I could go in to do this one thing to save him and to help save Puatera. I had killed people before, but I had never killed someone I loved.

I placed my palm on the door and opened it.

CHAPTER 7

The room was dark, but there was a little light coming from the window. I wanted to look straight to the bed, to see Alex. But I also needed light, so I moved to the window first and opened the curtains a bit. The world below us was immense, and I started to speak. I could hear breathing behind me, but it was mechanical, something I'd never heard nor probably wanted to ever again. It was the only thing keeping Alex alive in this world. What I was about to do to him was tearing me apart on the inside.

I watched as birds flew from one side of the building to another across the street, and I let my tears flow.

The sun on my face was warm, and finally plucking up the courage to turn, I faced my worst fear.

Alex lay surrounded by machines. They beeped and ticked and breathed for him. I knew they were the only things keeping him alive. He wasn't really with us. Not now.

Taking a step towards the bed, I reached out and placed my hand on Alex's hand. His skin was pale and clammy, thin, and he was so very weak. I picked his hand up gently and felt how real he was.

"Alex," I said, watching his face. "I know you're not really here, but

I am. I am here in your world. I wanted to see you, but it seems my task is greater than that. I'm here to sever the ties you have with your world."

The tubes and machines breathed for him, and the mask shook gently with each forced breath. I traced my finger up his arm. There was a mark there, something in ink. I looked at it and pushed up his shirt so I could make it out. There was a picture of a Tromoal, what he called a dragon. Stunning reds and blues, just like Riezella. I smiled. I knew he'd said they were mythical in his world, but seeing this version on his arm was something else. I leaned forward, placing my lips on his arm, and kissed him, letting out a breath, but then I sucked in quickly as my kisses turned to sobs. There on his bed, I cried, and I cried.

Cutting his ties to this world would have been hard for him, but it was even harder for me. Here he was still alive and still breathing, even if it were only machines. The machines are breathing for him. I didn't know if the transference would work. Would he still be alive there?

There was so much I wanted to say to him, and the words tumbled out as I moved from the bed to the machines. I had no idea what they were doing, but I did know they were doing the job of keeping him alive, and it couldn't keep doing it.

"Tibex?" I asked aloud. "I have to do this right now because the transference won't work, will it?"

There was silence for a while and then an answer.

- *You're correct, Maddie. There's not much time left for him to finish the process.*

I followed the leads to the machines from his arms and the mask on his face. Gripping the machine, I allowed my thoughts to flow through and into the machine. I could see the inside of the machine, the way it worked the rhythmical in and out. It was a lot, but it was also very easy to see where the mechanics were going, and where they went out of the room towards where that lady was sitting at a desk. I could interrupt the lines, and there wouldn't be any clues to what was going on. I did so, making the alarms silent. I then gripped his arm and tugged the lines out. There was a small spurt of blood, but it stopped with some pressure. I then moved to the mask and pulled it from his face. Lines and dark circles caressed his cheeks. I ran a finger down them as his body stilled. There was nothing now to keep him alive. Nothing here to keep him.

"Let yourself go," I said. "I'm here to be with you, listen to me, my voice. I am here. I won't let you down. I won't leave you."

Pulling his frail body to mine, I could feel his warmth, but then I also felt his body surge. His life was leaving him as he struggled for air even though he wasn't conscious. I focussed inside myself and allowed my energy to flow into him to help calm his struggling body. I knew it was working as I felt the energy inside him soothe.

Then he opened his eyes, and they locked with mine. There was recognition. I saw it. "Shh, my love. It's all right. I'll see you on the other side. I love you. I'll see you soon."

The light in his eyes started to fade, and I kissed his forehead, then his lips.

A moment later, Alex's body was still.

Tears ran freely down my cheeks, and finally, I was able to let out soft sobs. It wasn't long before those sobs turned into full-on wailing as I clung to his body. Still warm, soft. My heart was truly shattered, even with the hope that something of his essence would survive.

He'd gone. I'd helped him leave this world. I felt sudden and terrible guilt for my actions. My only solace was the egg and Riezella's words that he would become something different.

I sat there with him for some time, able to realise that while I'd done something bad, this was also a gift. I wanted to believe now that the soul inside the egg was his, that we'd have a chance at a relationship.

Tibex's message came through.

- *It's done. Return to the portal. Doctor Foster and Abel will be waiting for you.*

A little too cold, but I tried not to feel the hurt that pained me so much. I eased out from beneath Alex and moved to the door. I couldn't look back. I wouldn't remember him like this, an empty shell.

No sooner had I managed to get past the table at the front, my focus on the electricals in this world waned, and alarms sounded. I knew there wouldn't be anything they could do to revive him or to stem the pain to anyone who knew him in this world. I kept walking.

I seemed to walk for hours, but it wasn't. Eventually, the tiny flashing light in the corner of my eye annoyed me. So I looked at it.

A new quest had come through, but I pushed it away. Figuring out where I was on the human hospital grounds, I spotted Abel and Foster standing at the side of the road, talking.

I approached them, the icon in my view still flashing, this time red. This quest must have been super important. I glanced at the notification and stepped closer to them.

QUEST - TASK TO LOCATE THREE SISTERS WHO HAVE BEEN TRAPPED IN DIFFERENT LOCATIONS. RESCUE THEM FOR THEIR ALLEGIANCE IN THE WAR FOR MAICREOL.

What?

"Did you just get that?" I looked at both Abel and the doctor.

"Yes, I just don't understand it. How can Puatera send us a quest for going into another plane of existence?"

"There are some very strange things goings on here," Foster said. I couldn't agree more, but I wasn't allowing a stranger any information on the thoughts now whirling around in my head.

"Maddie, what are you thinking?" Abel asked.

"I can't tell you my thoughts. You won't believe any of them."

"Maybe I will," Foster said. "Please let us return to my home. Let me show you something that you won't have been able to see on your notification screens."

~

Doctor Foster moved to walk through the portal, and we followed him. Moments later, he sat and started to type away at a small touch keyboard. Then a screen popped up so that both Abel and I could see it.

Before us was a 3d hologram of my world. The five islands and two other mirror images of two other worlds. "This is what I've discovered so far. Puatera and its five islands. Follow this line, and you're taken to a VR world of Earth. On this Earth, my colleagues and I have noted several differences. They make me believe that it isn't real. That it is indeed just an alternate reality."

"So why is it there?" Abel asked.

"That, we don't know. If you follow this mirrored line, then there's also this alternative. We've discovered one almost desolate planet here, and there seems to be nothing other than a half-buried spacecraft."

I glanced at Abel. "What's a spacecraft?"

"A way of getting from one planet to another, like your Hog would from a town to a city."

"You can travel to other planets?"

"Well, not really, at least not in any sense that we have found other life out there."

I smiled. "I think there's plenty of life around you that you just haven't noticed."

This time I focussed on my hands and the energy I had within me.

- *Maddie, are you sure about this?*

I saw the pop-ups, and I ignored them. "This is who I am. I am not an NPC. I am not like you or from your world." I pointed to the screen, to the desolate planet. To that spaceship. "I believe I'm from there. That's another world, a world where many things have happened, where I ran from a very destructive being. Dresel discovered within my code that I was something called a Zofirax. I integrated

263

with this digital world as best I could. Myself and a friend. It's my friend who is managing a lot of the systems that Dresel thinks he created."

- *Your memories are returning? I'm glad.*

I saw the message and replied.

- Yes, I know what we have to do. We must play this game out, but there's a lot more to it than just this world. These sisters, do you know who they are, where they are?
- *I do not.*

QUEST - REWARD - RESCUING THE 3 SISTERS WILL AID YOU IN YOUR WAR FOR MAICREOL.

I saw that and immediately wanted to go. We were so close already. But Abel shook his head. "There are many things we have to do before that, Maddie."

Abel was right. "I know."

Travelling to another realm and these cities would have to wait. At least until I had the other villages and towns in on helping the Tromoal. I couldn't leave them as unprotected as they were right now. That would be death for them and for us all.

"Agreed, would you assist us in any way you can? A friend of ours is also researching these portals. Maybe you can confirm and work through this together."

"We must prepare quite a lot if we're to enter these other realms." Foster said. "This quest to save these sisters, you will attempt it, right?"

I nodded. The story of the sisters popped up on his screen, and Foster read it out.

"Breaking into their mother's laboratory, the sisters thought they were entering the hottest new game only to be thrown into the wilds of three different cities. Each of them now fighting for their lives. The power they contain will be a cast assist to Maicreol. Rescue them and return to Maicreol to defend the Tromoal."

REWARD - UNKNOWN

"Would be nice to know the rewards for this," I said aloud. "We'll go in as soon as the Tromoal have been secured."

"Then I'll gather all the information I can to assist you." Foster said. "Dresel must not be told about this just yet. Right?"

Abel nodded. "Whatever this is, it's something I want to see through, but I will have to report to him later on. I don't have the ability to stop him from watching my feed."

Foster grinned. "You don't think you got into this room with him watching, do you? That was well stopped. Don't worry. None of this conversation or the quest alerts has been seen by him. I can also block him permanently if you'd like?"

I had to think about this. I really wasn't sure it would help. The world of Puatera was already at risk because of the hints something else was going on. Maybe if all of this got out, it would stop the funding, and there would be no game. That meant maybe there would be no more safe haven for the Tromoal or for me.

"No, he needs to be watching me, he'll not let this kind of thing out into the game world. But I do think he'll want the war quest and the way things are going publicised. That's something gamers would like to be involved in. To play and help save the world you've created, so I like that side of things and so will he."

"I agree. Every gamer out there will be heading to your village right now, and to Port Troli, if there's promise of loot, fun, and making a new world for themselves. That's exactly what they're signing up for."

"Then we keep putting out those quest calls. Sarah, the gang. Together, we'll have to organise many other things."

"First things first, we need to go back to the Hog, visit Alstead and work from there. The others have their orders, so I'm good with that."

Foster held his hand out for Abel and then turned to me. "I'll come and see you in the morning, and we'll do some research here and in our world."

When we started to leave, Foster returned to the computer, and I asked, "Did she say anything else important?"

"Yes, but not for you to worry about just yet. We have enough on our plates."

I couldn't help but worry, though. Their world and mine clashed on so many levels. Abel and I moved to leave.

"There is something you do need, though." Foster reached down and plucked a bag out from under his table. "Here, this should be everything you came here for to get the Hog up and running once more. We're going to need everything you and that machine have to offer."

I took it from him. "Thank you."

CHAPTER 8

"*I* think the town there won't be as scared of me now that Abel can and will escort you back and inform the others of the changes I've been through," Foster said as we made our way through to the front of his home.

"I can and will do that." Abel nodded, then he lowered his voice. "Maddie, I'm not going to be here for a while, I've got to log out soon."

I tried not to feel bad for myself, to suddenly be thrust into being alone. I wasn't sure how often they needed to log out, so when Foster bid us farewell, and we moved to the door, I just asked simply, "How long will you be gone?"

That was when I saw the guard behind me suddenly move. He levelled his blaster straight at Abel's face and pulled the trigger.

I dove for cover, just managing to pull my daggers out of their sheaths before I rolled and slit the guard's right ankle. I managed to get a look at Abel's body as it sprawled out in front of me, and I turned to vomit. Just managing to wipe my mouth and move out of the way as other blasts fired towards me,

I heard Doctor Foster shouting behind me. Rai and Declan came rushing forward, pulling me away and retaliating fire. Doctor Foster took a shoulder wound but managed to get behind his front door as Rai and Declan took on the last guard in hand-to-hand combat. There was something strange about the guards eyes. They glowed orange, not like they had before. This was eerie, so very strange.

I pushed myself forwards, and with a quick flick of the wrist, I flung one of my daggers at the guard's throat, shouting 'duck' as I did. Rai ducked and the dagger embedded in the man's neck, blood spurting out as he slumped over and then fell.

Rai came to my aid. I'd been wounded, but it was a shoulder wound, just like Fosters. I wasn't worried. My health bar was still close to full, and I had potions back at the Hog. What did hurt was that Abel was dead. No doubt about it. I stared at his corpse. I knew it wouldn't stay there for long; the world around us would very quickly clean up. But, damned did it hurt.

"No worries. He'll respawn, won't he?" Rai asked. "All the Visitors do. That's why he protected you."

"I think he will. I hope he will," I managed to stutter back.

Declan was soon beside me, and between the two of them, they managed to get me up and to a more suitable place to assess my injuries. Rai was quick to start with some healing magic, and I started to feel better within a minute.

Doctor Foster came to my side, watching carefully as Rai treated me. "I had no idea they were going to try that. I don't understand. They were so loyal."

"Do you think someone else has gotten to them?" Declan asked.

"I don't know; I mean I don't think so. I don't know why they'd want Maddie dead."

"Only reason I know would be something to do with the war. Do they have any family or friends in the Port?"

Foster thought about it for a moment. "I think maybe they did. You're thinking they're against the Runners and that's all it was?"

"Maybe," I stretched my shoulder out. "I need a drink," I said, and of course, I meant something stronger than water. Within a few minutes, Foster returned with more ale, something nice and strong. I took it from him and downed it. I didn't care if I'd be driving soon. The Hog would be able to take me home on autopilot.

That's when I got a message from Dresel.

Maddie, what the hell happened? Abel just vanished from my screen.

I replied with a quick message back. *Someone just killed him, but he'll respawn with you, right?*

There was no reply and then came the biggest shock.

Get back here ASAP, Maddie. There have been some site-wide glitches. Steve and I are trying to look them over, but I can't make anything out. Abel's not showing on the computers at all.

I pushed myself up and forced myself forward. "I've to go back to Dresel. You can come with me to get the Hog started, then I'll need to leave."

"We can't let you go just like that," Rai said.

"Then you're coming with me back home." I wasn't arguing, and I wasn't going to hang around. I started back down the dark pathway and was almost at a sprint by the time the others managed to catch up to me.

Rai was pretty winded by the time we found the Hog. I quickly popped the bonnet and located where I needed to put the new parts. Ian was behind us asking what the hell had happened, but Rai and Declan didn't know the half of it, just that we'd been attacked on our way out.

The Hog's engine purred to life a moment later, and when I checked the dash, everything was lit green. "You coming with me or staying, it's totally up to you guys. If you have family here, I'd suggest you stay. This might be a much bigger fight than we know."

Declan glanced at Rai. "We're pretty strong. I think you could do with some backup, Maddie, now that Abel's gone."

I stared at the back of the Hog. "There are two empty seats. Get in," I said.

Ian nodded at them. "I'll let the safe house know you're not coming home tonight, maybe for a while. Good luck."

Ian held out a hand to me, and we shook. "I'll see you again," I said. "There are no hard feelings here. Just get the town to go see Foster. There's a lot of stuff he can show you and inform you of that you don't need to be afraid of. In fact, you need to see and learn about. Take a few of your other trusted people. Tell him that I sent you, and he can be honest with you as you've had my back all these years."

Ian nodded. "I'll take my wife. She's good at getting in all the right places. I am sure she'll slot right in there to see what he's been up too. Nosey woman." He laughed.

With a quick hop, I jumped into the Hog's seat, revving the engine and setting off.

I wasn't going to be telling Rai and Declan anything new, and they wouldn't get into Dresel's lair, but it was nice to have some real company for the drive.

It took far too long to get home, and I had to detour for fuel, too. This amount of running about in the Hog burned through a lot of my resources, and the twin tanks were on the dregs. My spares empty. We made it back across town and fuelled up with Ian. Then we were soon back on the road heading for Alstead.

I pulled up beside Dresel's office as it was going dark, and told the guys, "Go over to the bar and look for Sarah. She'll most likely be the one organising the front lines now." So they followed my orders, and I let them walk away. Thankfully, no more explanations needed—at least not yet. I wondered if all the locals, in the end, would start to realise and become as aware or as confused as I had been at first.

Dresel was waiting for me in the back of his office. I followed him as we quickly went out back to the barn, then down to the basement.

There was something about him and this entire situation that felt weird.

"Dres," I asked, "what is it?"

"I logged out to see what was going on with Abel and finally managed to get a hold of him. Abel said the whole system's frozen him out. At present, he's working on getting it back up and running on his end, but he's not looking good. He might not be back for a while."

I noticed Steve at the far side of the computer station. "It was a direct attack from Dail," Steve said. "I followed some magic back from your area, it linked up with the guards family in Port Troli. The guys were used as tools to take you out. Nothing more. Shame. They weren't bad people either."

"So Dail's resorting to magic to try and win this war? Really dumb if you ask me. There's not much more power than what you get from the Tromoal caves. Any luck in the cataloguing of everything down there?"

"There's been some amazing weapons and artefacts uncovered, but a lot of it we won't know what it's for some time the Tromoal are probably the only ones who can tell us where it came from and what it was used for." Steve said. "No one up to now has been able to use anything. Their magic levels aren't anywhere near as high as they need to be."

"Easy fix," I said with a wink. "They must train harder. In fact, we all must train harder."

There was a ping from a computer station, and Dresel walked over to it. On the screen came the image of a lovely looking shorter guy with blond hair, glasses, and a stubbly beard. I stared at the image for a moment and then smiled—that was Abel. Abel in the real world.

"Dres, I think I've got it running again," his soft voice came across. There's one thing I can't fix, though. It's telling me I have to respawn in Shiroth."

I coughed, and Abel looked at me. "Hey there, Madz. Good to see you're alive and well."

I moved so he could see me better, and smiled at him. "Thank you. That was very brave of you."

Abel grinned. "That's what I was there for. To take that bullet in the face. Won't say it didn't hurt, though, but you're worth it."

"So you can't return here?" Dresel asked.

Abel shook his head. "No, nothing I seem to be able to do here will change where I come back. I don't know why."

Dresel looked really worried for a moment and turned to me. "I'll have to re-assign Abel's duties to something he can help with over in Shiroth. That's a pretty big blow, but I think we'll be all right."

"How long will it take to get back over here from there?" I asked, not knowing that much about the seas. Maybe he could have used the inner portals somehow, but we also knew even less about them.

I leaned on the counter, suddenly feeling very lightheaded. This whole ordeal, the shooting and everything, was catching up with me.

Dresel was right by my side. "Maddie, you need to sit, take a few moments to think about things."

But I didn't have any more time. "No," I said. "I need to act now. This war isn't going to be stopped, but I do know the one person I can stop." I glanced back at the screen. "You saved my life for a reason, just like you let me do the one job I had to in London. Thank you, Abel. I'm going to do the one thing I can and know I can complete because I have all the backing of you guys. I'm going after Dail."

"Maddie, you can't do that." Dresel said.

I looked at the door. "I can and I will. I'm not going to let him do this. If he wants to see this world fall apart, it's not going to be with me in it. Steve, I know you can't recall the Savage Angels, and I wouldn't expect you to. But I am asking if you'll come with me? There are two guys I brought with me from Hell's Pass. They're both extremely talented. I believe if I ask for two more to join us, we have a chance at getting through the lands back to Port Troli. We might be able to finish at least this side of the war. With Dail out of the way, I think there will be a much better chance for us. As there's no one to spill our secrets and our tactics."

Dresel smiled. "I couldn't stop you from doing this even if I wanted to. I don't know what's worse, though—the fact you will go or the fact Abel can't be with you."

I placed a hand on his and squeezed. "We're doing this for you and for the world you built."

"Doesn't seem like my world wants to play at the moment. I don't have a clue what's been going on, but I am going to try my best to find out."

I nodded at him and moved to walk away. "I'm going to need more supplies from Josh's house, and I'll take a look at the list of artefacts from the caves. There might be something I can use there."

"I think there's some stored already over at Josh's. They also have the place under lock and key with some lady named Lidia watching over it."

I laughed. Lidia seemed nice enough. It was good to meet her. "I think she'll have something to say about Abel not being with us this time, though."

Steve moved to walk away from Dresel. "If you need me, just send me a message, and I'll answer as soon as I can." Dresel said.

Dresel looked back to Abel on the screen. "Good luck, Maddie," Abel shouted to us, and we left.

CHAPTER 9

 $\mathcal{J}$ osh's house was a bustle of activity, and I was surprised to see Lidia was the one leading it all. Her face frowned at the guy that was now walking with me. Rai and Declan met us at the front, and we all moved to go inside.

"What happened?" she asked, concern showing on more than her face as she crossed her arms.

"Long story, we need to get armour and weapons sorted out."

"Oh, I know where you're going." She grinned. "Count me in."

I was surprised at this, but I didn't disagree. "Do you know anyone else who might like to come with us?"

"That I do. How many do you want?"

"I'd just like to keep it to six, so just one more is fine."

"We really need someone else who can handle close combat. I know you're pretty good, but I have the perfect person. Let me message them, and I'll get them here as soon as I possibly can."

I moved to let her pass, and Rai and Declan perused some of the items in the room. I'd never thought about changing my daggers for something enhanced, but Rai moved to my side and handed me a beautifully carved box.

"These I think would be perfect for you."

I took it from him and opened it. Staring for quite some time at the ornate and stunningly carved twin daggers. They were more than beautiful. When I picked one out of the box, I was suddenly overwhelmed with the intense feeling of their power.

TRITHAOL TWIN DAGGERS
QUALITY – EXCEPTIONAL
BONUSES TO SPEED AND STRENGTH

"They're amazing. What other treasures are in here?" I asked knowing my eyes lit up as much as theirs had. I was sure there was a lot more than just these. This place was a victor's paradise. "Match yourself up with the items you can use the most, but don't be greedy. There are a lot of people here who will need things assigned to them."

Declan picked up a sword and shield. "This is the biggest find I've ever thought possible. The thought of it all being out in the world scares me."

I agreed with him there, but maybe once all this was over, it wouldn't be needed.

Rai, with a nervous smile, picked out a black onyx necklace and bracelet set. He swallowed when he showed them to me. "Do you think anyone would mind if I had these?"

I moved to his side and looked them over. They were more than exquisite. There were several displays for their usage and their power. "If you can use them," I said. "Then they're yours, especially if you can use them to heal or help one of us on this mission."

Rai lowered his head. "I'm honoured to assist you, Maddie. I won't let you down at all. I promise."

I had no doubts about that.

Lidia re-entered the room, and I noticed her move over to a rack of weapons. Once there, she plucked out a set of armour and then two smaller items. I wasn't sure, but they didn't look like daggers, but maybe some kind of throwing knives.

"I know you're unaware of a lot of what we've been doing in the background, Maddie, but we're here to help. If you believe that Dail needs to be taken down, we're with you. My friend Tanya is on her way. She's one of the best I know with a katana. She's also got some skills with fire and air. I'm surprised you've actually never met her. She does a lot of work for the Runners, though it's been a while since she's been in this part of town."

Maybe I'd seen her, somewhere. It could be that we've just never crossed paths, though. I didn't know everyone. At least I didn't think I did. Dresel had about seventy-two Runners, and then there were out-of-towners I knew he used. Maybe another hundred spread about. This could be interesting then.

I heard the door open, and a petite lady stepped inside. She seemed to shimmer in all white as the sun glinted off the sword she spurred. She wasn't afraid of letting anyone see she was armed and dangerous no doubt. Lidia waved her over. I noted that she wasn't just petite but extremely dainty too. Her light olive skin radiated the magic she held within.

When she reached us, she practically glowed. "I'm Tanya, I believe you've got a quest for us?" she asked directly as she looked up into my eyes. I stared for a moment, and then finally, embarrassed, I looked away.

"Yes, we're going to hunt down and hopefully take out the man who is plotting the war against us here. The only one who I think can do us damage. He might have the backing of Port Troli, but when I get him on his own, there's going to be nothing that will stop me from slitting his throat. He threatened everything I love, and I won't let him win."

"So where are we going then. You seem so sure that you'll be able to find him."

I knew Port Troli was a big place, but yeah, I had some ideas to where he might be holed up. If they were gathering forces to come at us, this would have to be the craziest place to do so, because there wasn't a lot of out of town room.

"Yes, I have a fairly good idea where they'll be, so that's where we're going to start."

Lidia grinned. "How are we going to get there? Not all of us will fit in your Hog."

That I'd also thought about, and quickly pulling my contact list up, I messaged one of the only other guys I knew who might be in the area with a working vehicle.

The voice message came in very quick. "Already in town, Maddie. On my way."

"How did you know?"

"Got an inkling that there would be some good jobs coming my way. No better place to be than right at the heart of it all."

I laughed. "Problem solved," I said to the others. "We'll have more transport in a few minutes."

"No way we can sneak those through under their eyes, though, so what's the plan for getting near Troli itself?" Tanya said.

"We'll drive in as far as we can. The rest might have to be on foot. There's a town I know which I think we can use effectively to hide the vehicles and sneak in under cover of night."

"Thought of it all, haven't you?" Lidia grinned.

"I don't think we have a choice. Bar dropping in on their heads with the Tromoal leading the way—this is the only way I think we can."

Lidia heard another engine and smiled. "Guess our ride is here. Three to a vehicle?"

Once outside, all kitted up it was easy to see why John was in town. His vehicle had a fair few bits missing. "Needed to get fixed up?"

John opened the door, and its creaking metal gave a terrible squeal. "Yeah, came across some really unfriendly folks when I left Troli a few days ago."

"I can't imagine why. They probably wanted the vehicle for themselves," Lidia said.

Quickly, I introduced them, and then, leaning on the door, I waited while they chatted. It was nice to have a group of such talented and strong people around me. This whole ordeal with the Tromoal and

Alex had taken everything I had away from me lately—emotion and resolve. I had vowed to try to do the best I could, and I wouldn't let anyone down. Dail had to die and die where he couldn't be resurrected by the game.

- Tibex, are you there?
- *I am.*
- What do I need to do to make sure that Dail isn't respawned by the game?
- *Good question. Only so many NPCs were given respawning capabilities, and he wasn't one of them. If he does die, do not worry. He will not be coming back.*

I thought for a moment then realised the whys.

- Dresel programmed my ability to respawn like a Visitor, didn't he?
- *He did so because he loved you. Once you took the role of Maddie, it was much more than that. I would have programmed it in for you, as well.*

That was good then. "We can really kill him. There's no coming back if I put a dagger in his heart."

Lidia smiled. "Then all we need to do is make sure you get to do it."

Steve patted my arm. "Time to go, Maddie."

I nodded and moved to the Hog. Once I slid inside, I punched in several command codes, and within a second, we had a live link up to John's vehicle. "Good to hear your voice too. This might come in handy as we get nearer to the Port. I think every side is going to be monitored, so we'll have to be on high alert."

Lidia's voice came over, "Don't worry. We'll get spotters out the back."

"I can do that," Steve said from behind me.

"Well, we've got some ways to go before we get that far. We'll make a quick stop at the caves, as well. Probably best to stay there during the day and then travel at night. You got good eyes in the dark?"

John laughed. "Had quite a few upgrades since we last conversed."

I grinned. That was good because his was way behind mine in tech. "Give it a name yet?"

"Sassy." He laughed. "And don't you be mean to her. She's got quite the temper if you don't behave."

Steve and Lidia's laughter could be heard echoing around both of us.

The desert drive this time wasn't as nice. I knew there was no real danger, and we passed several caravans of equipment and supplies that were heading for the Tromoal caves. I stopped only the once so the guys could use the toilet. After that, I found there was little chance the roads were very busy.

Steve asked, "Is all this heading to the caves?"

I didn't think they were, so rolling down the window, I asked some of the passers-by. "Where are you all heading?"

"Back to the Hanson's estate, ma'am."

Now that was something that made my heart soar.

"I presume it's safe and being cleaned up?"

The woman quickly explained the reasons why they were heading back. Simple, really, a mages guild ahead was planning to restore the lands to their former glory.

Candice might have gone off hunting monster ebolos or worse, but it didn't mean she hadn't set this in motion. I nodded to her ingenuity and rolling the window back up, I settled into the drive.

CHAPTER 10

*W*e arrived at the camp by the caves to the bustle of every one. It was Sarah who came over. How she'd managed to look like she was almost in two places, I had no idea. The gang was quick to disperse and get caught up, helping unload wagons and horses.

"You're doing a great job," I said. "Thank you. How is it inside the caves?"

"Few people have been let inside, don't worry. The movement around the eggs has been minimal, but several of our mages have taken it upon themselves to keep a very close eye on them."

I smiled. "I'll go and see for myself, but again, thank you."

She moved aside as I made my way towards the cave system. I was actually very impressed. There were two stationed guards now, and I paused before them. They smiled at me and bid me inside. "We're not here to stop you. Just the odd person who is too excited."

I thanked them too and headed in. There were several lights now that lit the pathway. I didn't need goggles.

I walked in silence, and eventually, I heard the rushing of water. The caves were warm and inviting.

But there was something different. I felt it. Almost as though the

Tromoal were at peace. This was comforting and made me feel much better.

I moved quickly to where I knew I needed to be. I just wanted to see Alex's egg once more. Hope filled my mind as I thought about being able to talk to him again. Would he know it was me, would he remember anything at all?

When I spotted Riezella's clutch, I let out a squeak. I couldn't help myself. The eggs still looked the same. There was nothing new about them, but I had hoped I could see something, maybe sense something new.

I moved in closer and allowed my energies to pool forward. I'd not known my mana capabilities before the other day, but I guess that was indeed what I was using right now to communicate with the young inside the eggs.

A voice greeted me. But not one I recognised straight away.

Maddie, I'm asking you to turn around.

Dalfol?

Yes, Maddie. Please listen to me. Do not go down any further. Return to the surface.

I wanted to ask so many questions, but I paused. I reached for the wall to steady myself.

Maddie, you're better than this. This programming doesn't make you who or what you are.

I love him.

Really, do you really love him?

I searched within, seeing my character sheet tabs. This time, I clicked through almost automatically to where I thought the programming for 'falling in love' was.

You see this... I tried to point at it with my mind, almost making myself laugh at the same time.

I see everything I need to, so yes, I do.

There, right in front of both of us was exactly what I knew to be the truth. Dresel had done the one thing I asked back when I learned he was the worlds' programmer.

FLAW – BOUNCES FROM RELATIONSHIP TO RELATION-SHIP – DISABLED

I smiled inwardly.

Then do this for me. He's not ready to talk to you, yet. Please, give him some space.

I placed my forehead on the wall, feeling the cool earth against my skin. That I could understand. The information given to me over the last few days had been quite enough, and yet I was still inside my own body. I couldn't imagine the internal processing of going through the kind of transformation he had.

I turned around and looked back to where I'd just came from. There was still a tiny amount of light. I made a few steps forward, not daring to look to the clutch of eggs, and returned to the surface.

Steve waited for me. "Everything good down there?"

I nodded. "I think so." I noticed the way he looked me over, then added, "And you? Why are you waiting on me?"

"Had some news from the Savage Angels."

I motioned towards the campfires ahead of us. I could smell food, and my stomach grumbled. "Oh, do tell me their news."

With a huge grin, he said, "The Mayor's camp is no more. But they lost Chip and Rose, they've both respawned back with Dresel."

I immediately thought of Josh, and Steve placed a hand on my arm. "He's fine. Chip took the hit that would have killed him. Candice is ecstatic. The zombie creatures hadn't overtaken the farm, so they're going to spend a few days organising it and making sure there are no zombie animals at all sticking around. There are a few tricks she said she's learned in dealing with the undead. Totally blew her expectations fighting for something that large, but their rewards have doubled their chances in a major fight."

I let out a breath. "That's good then. What are Chip and Rose going to do?"

"I think Candice said they were going to stay, but they're already on their way out here. They want to assist us in going after Dail."

283

"Putting together quite the little invasion army, aren't we?" I moved to pick out a cup from a pile, then filled it with water. Waiting in the small queue for dinner to be served. "Sarah's outdone herself in organising this little lot."

Steve picked up some water too and downed it before getting some more. "Yes, Chip said they'll be here before we want to leave tomorrow. So we should get some rest and be on our way as soon as they arrive."

Feeling the ring on my finger almost tighten in anticipation for the upcoming fight, I waited as a lovely lady smiled at me and then piled a bowl full of meat and stewed vegetables. "Thank you," I said and inhaled the aroma of the dish. It smelled divine. I moved away from them all and, finding a rock place to lean on, sat down to eat.

Steve joined me a moment later and tucked in.

I put my spoon down and stared at him. "How are Chip and Rose getting here if they don't have their bikes?"

I saw Steve raise an eyebrow just as something streaked overhead. The long shadow that followed it had me jump up and rush alongside everyone else to where Dalfol set himself down.

Dalfol? I practically screamed inside my head.

I rushed forward as he lowered his neck to the ground to let his passengers off safely.

What the hell are you playing at?

His eyes flickered, and his energy glowed around the edges of them, beautiful swirling colours. *I could not leave my Lady or my son any longer.*

I reached out and stroked down the side of his cheek. That familiar rumbling sound escaping his now spread lips. Almost looking like he was smiling.

You can't come with us. You know that, right?

I know what you are thinking, but that is my decision to make. If my son's protector is in danger, I must protect her so that she may continue to do her job.

I laughed, and Steve came up beside me. "I wanted to tell you right away, but he asked me not to. Sorry."

Dalfol's head slumped even more, and his body started to turn ridged. I'd not seen the transformation for a while, but the energy around us started to swirl together. Onlookers gasped and moved back as the dusty sands picked up, and there before them stood a young man.

Dalfol in human form was something. His strong muscular body and greying hair denoted, not only his age but his sheer strength.

I stepped towards him, and he embraced me. "Come, let's finish your meal, and we'll talk for a while before you rest. Tomorrow will be a long day for all of us. We'll need all the strength we can get."

It had felt so good to talk with Dalfol and the others.

We actually ate and drank for quite some time. Other people had stopped by to listen to his stories, and then they went on their way. The spirit of the camp itself had lifted once more with the arrival of just one Tromoal.

Now, I closed my eyes and rested, dreams flittering through my mind as I drifted in and out of sleep.

Before I knew it, the next morning was here, and we were packed and on our way. The heat of the desert made the ride uncomfortable, but within the confines of the Hog, bearable—at least for now.

"How close do you think we can get before we have to go on foot?" Steve asked once more. The proverbial child always wanting to know answers to things they can't understand.

"We're stopping not far from here. A small village called Spirit Vein. There are maybe a hundred homes there. If we stop on the outskirts, they won't see us with the vehicles or Dalfol, and while you stake out the area, I'll head in to see what things I can find out about them and their side of the war efforts."

There wasn't much of a response, but we pulled up beside a dusty outbuilding just as the sun had started to dip. John and I made sure the vehicles were hidden as best as possible, and Dalfol stayed well clear.

I didn't know who was best to take with me, but I wanted the best of both worlds. Someone I knew and trusted from Puatera and Steve. I watched as they all stood around, and I could clearly see the fun he was having in the situation we were in.

"John, Steve. You're with me. The rest of you hold up, wait for my signal. If you can come into town, I'll let you know. But we're on our own for now."

I pulled out some supplies, and John did the same, handing Lidia the main control to his vehicle. He didn't quite have the tech I had. His had an older locking mechanism.

When we started walking towards town. I saw the notification and read.

QUEST – LOCATE AND DESTROY – DAIL, THE HARBINGER OF WAR.
REWARD – 1 KARMA – TRUST WITHIN ALL OTHER MAICREOL CITY WALLS.

Steve's eyes gleamed. I knew more about the rewards given now than I did before.

"Only one Karma point? That doesn't seem like a lot," I stated.

Steve shook his head. "No, Maddie. Karma is the biggest reward for any of us. Remember when I said you had the gift of a lifetime in assigning yours?"

I did, but it seemed so long ago. I still hadn't made those decisions. I needed someone to help as it wasn't something I felt confident in doing. If I didn't understand the way things worked, how could I assign something to my personality when it could suddenly alter my whole being?

I saw that recognition on his face as he stumbled forwards. "You haven't done what I suggested, have you?"

"You mean assigning the Karma to my personality? No."

Steve stopped dead. "Maddie, you don't understand, I really need you to do something for me... no for us, right now..." I looked at the seriousness in his eyes. They were sharply focussed on mine. "Go to your character sheet and drop some extra points into your learned abilities. Anything that you can use here and now."

It wasn't hard to locate the items I knew I needed. The first screen itself.

Body 1
Soul 1
Mind 1

They were still all a 1. I swallowed my pride and dropped the required 3 Karma points into each to get my levels up.

Body 3
Soul 3
Mind 3

I was quick then to locate the debilitating poison in my system from Riezella's killing bites. Then I dropped 5 Karma into it, and the poison was no more.

The relief that washed over me from this huge upgrade was the most intense feeling I'd ever experienced. My legs gave way and nausea followed. I wretched, though nothing much came up, the food I had digested well. I just used over half my allotted Karma that in itself terrified me. *What have I done?*

Dalfol's voice echoed in my mind.

Maddie, what did you just do?

I have no idea. I guess I expanded.

Steve placed his hands on my shoulders. "It's okay, I'm here. Keep going."

I managed to choke out, "I can't. We need to get to the village, complete this quest. I'll make the other decisions soon, I promise."

When I looked up into his face, John was standing by him. "I've never seen anything like it ever."

I took Steve's offered hand so that he could pull me up. My legs shook, but as I tested their step, they felt stronger. I patted my thighs, my slacks now tight against the new muscles. "I feel like I've put on about ten pounds."

"What did you do?" Steve asked looking me over.

"I raised my Body, Mind, and Soul to *three* Karma each." The tightness around my waist actually dug in where the button was. I reached under my shirt and frowned as I undid it. "Hope I don't lose my trousers in the midst of battle." I laughed.

Steve's eyes widened. "No wonder your legs gave way. That's one heck of a jump in skill sets."

I looked at where the buildings started to clump together. "Come on. We have no more time for messing about like this. Let's keep going."

When I set off this time, there was no pain from my hip. I had a renewed amount of energy, and conquering Dail was the only thing on my mind.

CHAPTER 11

I didn't want to go into a bar, or in fact, any other shop or establishment. If my memory served me right, there was only one place I thought I might get some answers—a marketplace on the inside of one of the main buildings. Slap bang in the centre of the town. It was a good street market. One I had been to many years ago, but no sooner had we started to walk towards it, something ran across our path. I got a very brief view of him. He was about sixteen, well dressed, and quick. He stopped briefly before me and beckoned me to follow him. Then he was off again.

"Quick," John called and followed him. Where John got that quick blast of energy, I had no idea. With the walk into the village in the main heat of the day, sweat had soaked my clothes. But Steve was after the two of them with just as much speed, so I focussed and made my best attempt to keep up.

The young man flittered from house to shop then to the rooftops. We all followed until we finally stood panting and watching each other with careful glances to the streets.

John was the one to approach him first. I listened. "Why the goose chase, kid?"

The young man wasn't out of breath, his tanned and lithe form athletic enough to know where he was and how far to push himself. "I needed to be sure you were who I thought you were." He pointed out towards the skyline.

There in the distance, I could see Dalfol's shadow. "You know what that is?" I asked him, stepping closer.

He shook his head but spoke clearly. "I've never seen one in person. I've never left the village grounds. I've heard stories, though."

"So how did you spot him?"

The kid lifted his hand. On his palm was a mark. "I was born in the desert. My mother said I'd been gifted at birth with Tromoal sight. I've never been this close to have it spark to life."

Steve caught my attention. "There are several crowds gathering to the far left of the town."

"They already know you're here. There was a watch call put out in the village earlier today." The kid said.

"Yet you brought us up here?" I raised an eyebrow.

"I know they planned to trap you in the market hall. Bring in the Tromoal, kill him, and gain favour with Dail."

I sucked in a breath. "Dail's in this village?"

When the teen nodded, I felt a smile cross my lips and hope spread within. I looked at John and Steve. "We've got to do this now. We have to go in while they're still expecting us."

"It's a trap." Steve warned.

The young lad coughed. "I can tell you where his main guards are stationed. Dail's in one of our village's forges. He was going to stay near the main market, but someone persuaded him not to."

"Who was that someone?" John asked, his hand settling on his belt. I could just make out the sleek shape of his weapons hanging beneath his coat.

Lowering his head to John, he looked at me. "My name's Yehu. I am also the son of the village leader."

Steve frowned, and when I looked at him, he pulled me away from the conversation, towards where we could see the town folk gathering a street down from us. "Do you think we should trust him?"

I glanced back, seeing that John was talking intently with Yehu. I noted his strong back and the way he held his head high. He had noble intentions, so I moved away, back to their conversation. Steve whispered behind me, "I guess that's a *yes* then."

When I reached their side once more, John pointed to the far wall. "There are four traps as we'd have headed to the market. The largest one being just before where Yehu stopped us. Be thankful he was on the ball and managed to get away from his father's watchful eyes earlier today."

"Thank you, Yehu. I don't know if we'd have gotten this far without you."

I saw his face flush.

John slapped my arm. "Look what you made the boy do."

I laughed and glanced at Steve. "What?"

"Any guys around here would take one look at you and fawn all over the place."

I glimpsed down at myself not knowing what the heck they were talking about. "Maddie, I'm going to point you in the direction of the nearest shop window or mirror as soon as I can."

Yehu actually pointed back behind us. I turned around and could see where, at the top of the building, was a small door. There was a glass section to it. I ignored their calls as I stomped over to it. Expecting to see myself in the reflection but, when I caught the view, I almost took a step back.

It wasn't just that my trousers were tighter, everything was. I also took a double take at my hair, the length was still there, but the colour where it was dark and silken right through, now there were two shades. To my right, a fiery red and my left was pure white. Sitting on top of my head as it had usually wrapped around in a bun or plait, it had snaked through looking wild, and I admit, extremely different.

Steve came up behind me. "That's the first sign of a powerful mage, you know."

I looked back at him and once more in the mirror. "My whole physique has altered. My ass is bigger, my hips… even my…" I stuck my chest out pointing at them.

"And that's why you'd make anyone fawn over you, Maddie. You were stunning before, but now. There are no words."

I laughed. "Can I retract those Karma points?"

Rolling his eyes at me, John and Yehu came over. "We've got to go. The gathering at the end of the street is starting to move out. If we want to keep this small element of surprise, we need to hit them now."

I breathed out, feeling the zip underneath my button hitch. "Well, after this, you guys are taking me for some new clothes, right?"

They laughed and I reached for my daggers. I sparked the energy inside myself, feeling it flow into them.

It was time I learned how to use the new daggers, the feel of them slightly different in my hands than my usual set. I hadn't thought it would alter my fighting stances, but their weight felt better. The energy I was putting to them seemed to enhance the blade edges. I liked how they looked now, silvery glints and black shadows.

"Then, Yehu, take us as far as you can, then you need to turn your ass back home and stay clear of the fighting, you understand me?"

The kid looked like he was about to bust but he nodded. "I just want to help," he said.

I glanced through the door's mirrored section. "Seems this is a good way to get down. We'll find the street closest to where the mob headed off from, and Yehu can take us as close to Dail's men as he dares."

Steve's eyes sparkled. He'd already enhanced his mana capabilities with the black ensemble and the power oozing off him now was electrifying. "I hope we have a fighting chance, Maddie," he said.

"Don't worry. We have more than a fighting chance. We just need an upper hand as well, and a little luck Yehu's got the job right and not actually leading us into a trap."

Deep in my heart, though, I already knew this wasn't going to be what the young boy had hoped. His father and Dail would have found the best way to lure us in. Dail knew I had a soft spot for anyone who was different, for anyone who showed their true colours. And this boy was taking us right into the lair of the man we wanted to kill, and they were expecting it.

Steve watched me carefully, and John raised an eyebrow. They both knew what was coming, and I smiled at them. Then I opened the door and slowly, one by one, we followed the kid into the building and down the stairs.

The building itself just looked to be a storage facility. Once through and into the opening segments of the main structure, we could see out into the large rooms that the building housed. They were harvesting grain and other products. Storage for the coming winter months, I suspected. Something that would keep this side of their town in not only food but in trading goods, so they could ask for other needed items from their neighbours.

What baffled me was some of the machinery in here. I'd not seen anything like these before. They were huge. Much larger than the Hog. I wondered only briefly to their mechanics and purpose. Then I noticed something and had to do a double take. At the front of one of the machines protruded a large metallic horn. I stopped where I was and leaned over a small set of railings to get a better look. In the end, John leaned over with me.

"What is that, John?"

I saw the look on his face, and when his gaze met mine, there was a pure worry there. "*That* isn't something you want in this world."

"Why?" I asked. "What are they?" I noticed now that the building actually contained several of these things. They were larger than a house, and then it sank in. "They're for the Tromoal caves, aren't they?"

John tugged my arm. "Let's keep moving. We can deal with this later, but we need to get out of here."

The stairs around us lit up with flames and rapid gun blasts. I ducked just as a bolt of energy came hurtling towards my face. Ambushed. I thought about it, but I hoped this wasn't going to happen, either.

Yehu sank beside me, his face pale, flushed. "I don't understand?" he questioned shaking his head.

Putting a hand on his, I patted it. "Don't worry. I am not blaming you at all. This was going south way before you even came along."

John's eyes met mine. "You need to get back upstairs, my friend."

But Yehu's eyes changed colour. His face reddened all the more. "No," he almost shouted. "They think they can play me, and I won't retaliate."

Then I saw something else. The young boy was more than just talented. He was strong, very strong. And he had obvious skills as a mage. The irises of his eyes sparked with orange energy, and it started to spread out, like fire through his veins. In fact, I was almost sure there was a living flame passing through him. His hair seemed to burst free, fiery tendrils spreading outwards.

"You should come down *now,* son before you get injured with these traitorous fools." A voice boomed. Of course, I had no idea who it was, but I could take a guess. His father.

Yehu stood up, and two large fire bolts hit him in the chest. He didn't flinch, but all I could smell was scorched clothes and flesh. My nostrils twitched. "If you think I'm backing down, Father, then you're mistaken. There's no way I'm letting you take them in for Dail to just murder!"

Murder. Yeah, I guess he would if he managed to catch me. How had this turned so nasty? Someone I thought I knew and trusted just turned bad. I couldn't get my head around it no matter how much I tried.

"You're surrounded."

Yehu's energy sparked all the more, and with a flick of his wrists, he started sending out fiery blasts. Not towards the enemy men, though. Instead, he turned it on the machines that were inside the building. "I won't let you do this, Father," he screamed.

John and Steve both looked at me, and I motioned down the stairs. This was a perfect distraction. A father and son one-on-one, but it would keep all eyes on them, and hopefully, we could slip on past.

I did exactly that, hunkering down nice and low. Sneaking past.

Yehu was really going for it above us. The kid fought like a small demon. I was kind of blown away by the energy he contained, but the men surrounding his father were also pretty well protected. Yehu had the higher ground and was slowly picking them off.

We escaped to the far side of the building where there was a doorway. I managed to place my hand on it and pushed it open. The view of the street was clear, but this overwhelming feeling of impending doom sank in.

Steve poked his head out beside mine. "We've no choice, Maddie."

I smiled at him and stepped out into the street. Nothing happened.

Walking straight across and melting into the opposite cover of the street, I looked back at the building we had been in. It wasn't just big. What bothered me was that these machines were being stored there. Things that John looked very wary over. I guess I didn't need to worry too much about them anymore. The fiery blast from inside had started to increase.

Fire then burst out from the rooftop, and two men ran through the same door we'd just exited from.

One of them screamed out. "Damned kid's going to blow the whole street apart."

I pointed in the opposite direction to where they were sprinting too and started to run myself.

The explosion that rocked everywhere was intense. Fire burnt the back of my ass and sent me flying high into the air. The wind was sucked from my lungs, and my knees scraped the material from them as I finally skidded to a halt, bashing my head on the side of a wall. Blood trickled down the side of my face as the dust cloud hit. I tried to cover my mouth and eyes, but the blast was so furious, I wasn't quick enough. Something hit me in the shoulder, a brick or some sort of debris, and then everything around me went black.

CHAPTER 12

I don't know how long it took me to wake up. It was dark. I tried to move, but I couldn't. My hands ached, but the bonds that kept them from moving were worse.

I coughed. My shoulder hurt and so did my throat.

I forced my eyes open, looking around where I was. I could just make out Steve and John. They were both alive, but barely by the looks of it.

I coughed some more, spitting out blood.

Checking my health, I noticed I was more injured than I'd first thought.

HEALTH - 25%

What the heck had that kid done? Was he still alive?

I doubted it. If we had been blasted off the face of Puatera, then there were no survivors from the inside that building.

Outside, I could hear footsteps. I closed my eyes once more and waited.

A door creaked, and a light pinged on. It wasn't very bright in here, but I could see a little more as I peeked through my lashes.

The man that had us tied up was Dail. I could see the scruffy brown boots and the rip in his trousers that still exposed his burnt leg. So I opened my eyes.

"Good to see that you're awake, Maddie," Dail said. "The other two are drugged, but you I can't drug anymore without further risks to you or to what I'm about to try to do."

The voice, it grated on me. There was something different about it. I looked closer.

It wasn't. . . It couldn't be?

Above Dail's head was a Visitor tag. All this time, Dail had been a Visitor, someone who could change the face of my world, go home and not worry about a damned thing he'd done. How had he managed to keep that from me all these years? Or were they years? Was all of this just stupid programming?

I felt a hand on my cheek, and I looked up and into Dail's eyes.

"Oh, shocked, are you? Finally, you can see the truth. And know that I'm the one who has you tied down now, strapped up and at death's door once more!"

I swallowed, not quite wanting to believe what I now knew to be the truth. "You couldn't be... you can't!"

He laughed. "Can't what, Maddie? Want to get to the bottom of what you are? You've no idea how much investment I have salted into this. You've no idea how much you have ruined everything!"

I coughed again, seeing my health fall a little more. I must be bleeding somewhere internally. This wasn't happening. It couldn't be. I was dying though.

"Dail, what are you going to do with me?"

"I'm not going to do anything but let you die, Maddie. I'm doing nothing. Not one thing. Then I'm going to get one of my programmers, not Dresel, though, to drag your code through the ringer, and somehow manage to scrub every part of you from the system."

"Why?"

"Why?" he almost screamed at me. "Because you've been the biggest pain in my backside I've ever had to deal with. You didn't listen to my proposal the first time. I hoped to keep you clear of all of this. To stop your interfering in the plans to drill under the desert. I wanted to get in, get that loot, and sell it all for as much as I could out in the real world. My world."

"You're doing all of this for something in your world?"

Dail pulled a knife out. I watched it glint in the light, and cringed. He really was going to kill me I was sure of it. When he placed it on the side of my face, I was sure I flinched. I tried not to. I tried not to let him get to me. But he did.

Then, he placed the knife on my wrist, and he cut one of my bonds. With his other hand, he grabbed hold of me and dragged me up onto shaky feet.

HEALTH - 15%

It was falling fast. I wondered if he knew. If he could see how badly I was feeling. I coughed more blood. This time I couldn't do anything to wipe it off my face.

Pulling me behind him, Dail dragged me through and into a hallway, then down it and into another room.

The room itself was massive, and there before me was the same shimmering glow of a portal that we'd seen in Doctor Foster's home.

"This is why I'm doing it. Somehow, this is all messed up. There are portals that have sprung up around Puatera that shouldn't be. You are the reason for them, you are the problem, and when you die, so will they."

I looked out into the portal. There was a world before me that I'd not seen before. A large river and monastery? I wasn't sure. There were tiny boats crossing it, but they looked out of place. I wanted to reach out to touch the water, but Dail pulled me back.

"Oh, there's no way you're going through there. That place will die with you."

I thought instantly of the three sisters, trapped, and knew this was where one of them was. I couldn't let Dail win this. I just couldn't. I would not die.

HEALTH - 10%

There was that little problem, though, and it was waning fast. But. I still had my ring, and I still had some stat points. I could do the one thing I didn't want to—win this by using my brain.

I thought carefully about what I needed, not only the health to heal but that I needed more than the art of surprise here. I needed to be able to hit hard and kill him for good.

My character sheet pinged before me, and I quickly scrolled through what I wanted. There was a slot for the ring he'd given me, and there was an advantage for it. Could I stack Karma onto the ring? It looked like it was going to take everything I had to survive this, but I had no choice.

I dropped six Karma onto the ring and felt nothing. I knew I had to activate it, but it seemed the time just wasn't quite right. I needed to wait a little longer.

HEALTH – 8%

My focus wasn't quite right, and I noted a pool of blood beneath me, the injury obviously somewhere down below, my leg or stomach. Yes, stomach. I tried to breathe in deeper and felt it sting.

Dail dropped me, and I felt the shock as my knees hit the floor. Just about able to stay upright, though it was from sheer willpower alone.

"You can't destroy these portals," I said. "You have no idea what they're for or why they're here."

There was a tiny ping in my ear. Dalfol was close by, but he couldn't find me, his voice was panicked and pained.

Maddie, I need to get to you. I can help. I can heal you. Please, tell me where you are in the building.

I spoke back but warned him to keep clear. *You have to trust me, Dalfol. I can handle this. I won't let you down, ever. I need to do this on my own. I need to kill him.*

His voice seemed to back off a little, and I glanced up to Dail who stood over me, waiting for what little life I had left to fade.

"Was there any love between us?" I managed to remember some of the good times we'd had. But this programming had been just that, the only reason for it.

Dail laughed. "You were the best Runner in town and the only one who would do some of the most dangerous missions. You were a ticket to money, nothing more."

I fingered the ring behind my back, his words stung. More so because they meant my life before I became conscious and before things had changed meant nothing. The people in Puatera meant nothing to these visitors. That had to change.

With a quick twist, I activated the ring. The energy that shot through my veins filled me with fire.

HEALTH BOOST
HEALTH - 100%

I'd never felt this good before, ever. I jumped up, feeling the strength in every new muscle I had. Dail stepped backwards, the shock evident on his face. He reached for his knife, but I knocked it clear out of his hand.

"You see," I said. "The thing with you Visitors is you never listen. You always underestimate those around you."

Dail's eyes flickered to the portal. He was going to make a run for it. With a quick step, I managed to get myself between him and the easiest way out.

"Not only did you never know who I was, but the fact you kept using me, pushing me into things I didn't want or would never want is the only reason why I am who I am today." I felt the energy still surging through me, the wound in my stomach not only healed over, but there was no more pain.

A message popped up from Tibex.

- *That was some trick. Finish this. You're running out of time, and these quests are getting harder by the hour.*

I flicked it away, and glanced at the door. He wasn't going anywhere. I had no weapons, but if he came at me, I'd disarm and re-appropriated.

That's exactly what he did. Lunging forwards with his knife, he once again underestimated me. I slipped by him, twisting his arm out and snapping the knife from it. It clattered to the floor.

"How the hell did you manage this?"

"I listened to someone, a Visitor. I let him see who I really was, and we discovered many things about me. Maybe you could have been the one to discover them with me, but no, you chose the wrong side. Whoever you are, wherever you're from. Visitor, you will be no more. Dresel will see to that."

"He can't, he won't. I'm one of his largest investors!"

I pushed Dail closer to the portal. "He will because he's more invested in Puatera than anything. He might love money, but money isn't it all. Do you have any idea why I'm not just an NPC?"

Dail looked up at me. His face paled. "No...."

I pushed him further to the portal. I could almost smell the water across that river, feel the night airbrush my skin.

"No, Maddie, don't. I've never died in a game before. Please, don't kill me!"

The water bubbling ahead of me was very inviting. I wondered...

"You should have thought about that while you let me bleed out."

Then I didn't wonder anymore. I just did it. I pushed Dail's head through the portal while keeping his body here in my world.

He struggled, but I held on. I knew what was happening to him as the water filled his lungs and he could no longer breathe. Maybe the nicest way he could die—because if I had to really fight him when I had weapons, it would not be pretty.

One last jerk and Dail's body went limp beneath me.

Panting, I collapsed, letting myself rest while I tried not to let my emotions get the better of me. My thoughts flittered to Steve and John. Pushing myself up, I picked up Dail's knife and rushed back to the room. John looked to be the worst out of them both, I flicked the knife through his bonds and let him slip to the floor. His breathing was heavy, very laboured. Blood oozed out of a gaping hole by his right eye.

Dalfol, I don't know if you can reach us, but we really need some extra assistance.

Yehu's father is trying to get inside the building. It seems they're arguing over the password to the entrance.

Can you help them?

Didn't he just blow up a building?

Don't be worrying about that, I don't think they knew what they were doing. This was all Dail's plan to get me in here, to kill me, to stop this world from evolving.

Dalfol's snort came through quite sternly. I laughed, and moments later, there were rushing footsteps in the corridor outside.

Yehu was first through the door. I could only presume it was his father behind him. "Maddie, I'm so sorry," He glanced at John and immediately kneeled beside us.

"Can you help him?"

Yehu's eyes sparked with his fire once more. "Yes, but it will take some time."

I turned to Steve who was coming around. I was soon at his side, cutting his bonds. "Maddie, what happened?" he asked. His eyes struggling to focus.

"There's a lot that happened. How are you feeling? Will you be okay?"

Steve seemed to be accessing his character sheet. It was the weirdest thing to see someone else's eyes focus on something you couldn't see.

"Yes," he replied eventually. "I'll be okay. Just get me out of here."

"No." I looked at John and Yehu and then his father. "You're the town's leader. I need you to see this."

I pulled Steve to his feet and walked with him through to the portal's room. Dail's body was still there, but it started to fade. Pulsed and fade some more.

Yehu's father kneeled down and declared he was dead, which I already knew since I had just drowned him. Then his body vanished, and there were only several small items left behind. Yehu's father picked them up, and I nodded to him. "You keep them. I have no need for any more magical items or loot."

Steve stepped closer to the portal. "This is part of London still. I recognise the river and the buildings."

"I must continue this journey. Now more than ever."

"You want to go through it? The river will be freezing!"

I smiled at him. "I know. But there's a young girl in there who is terrified and needs someone to save her."

"That's your next quest?"

I saw the notification flashing up before my eyes, reminding me that time really was running out. "They have less than twenty-four hours to be reunited."

"Or what?"

I pointed to the building, it's eerie glow setting golden shimmers across the water. "I don't know the answer to that question, only that to help save Puatera and the Tromoal, I need their help. To get their help, I need to go find them and bring them back together."

Steve glanced back to the doorway. "And John?

"John will be fine. They can help with the town, start to gather enough protection for this portal. We can't have anyone finding out about it, coming through, or putting anyone else's lives in danger. You can do that, right?"

On the town leader's nod, he added, "I'm sorry. I don't know what came over me. It was like I was possessed. I've never argued with Yehu like that before. I always trusted him and his reasoning. Dail just seemed to come in here, place his orders, and it was like I had to do them."

I placed a hand on the older man's shoulder. "I know, don't worry. There's still a war coming, and we're on the wrong side of the desert at the moment. You need to keep your town off their map. You need to make sure your people and this portal are protected at all costs. Outside your town now is a Tromoal, Yehu can speak with him, trust that the two of them will have your best interests at heart."

Yehu's father smiled at me. "Thank you for your quick forgiveness Maddie. I will do everything you've asked." He looked at the portal. "The young girl you seek, do you think you'll find her?"

I looked at the river and its bouncing waves. "I have no idea where to start. It looks like a huge place to be."

Steve stepped forwards. "Yes, it is, but I have some ideas. I think I can help you find her, and together, we'll bring her back."

I glanced once at the doorway. This was it. I was going to step out of my comfort zone and away from my world.

I placed my hand on Steve's and squeezed it.

"For Puatera," he said.

"For Puatera," I reciprocated, and whispered. "For Alex."

Then, with a deep breath in, together, we stepped through the portal and into the unknown depths of the river.

The End

If you enjoyed this book, please consider leaving a review, they help keep writers motivated! :)

ABOUT DAWN

Dawn Chapman has been creating sci-fi and fantasy stories for thirty years. Until 2005 when her life and attention turned to scripts, and she started work on The Secret King, a 13-episode Sci-Fi TV series, with a great passion for this medium.

In 2015, Dawn returned to her first love of prose where she revelled in the world of The Secret King, Letháo and First Contact, as an epic prose space journey over 3 generations.

This year her experience of working with Producers/Directors from the US and AUS has expanded. From Drama, Sci-Fi, Action, to Litrpg. Dawn's built a portfolio of writing, consulting, publishing, and audio proofing.

You can follow on any of her public pages or her website - https://dawnchapmanauthor.com/

And her discord link if you're wanting to chat in real time is...(word hunting permitting) - https://discord.gg/3tmdnRE

Many Thanks!

    facebook.com/kanundra

    twitter.com/kanundra

    instagram.com/kanundra_

RECOMMENDED BOOKS

Here's some of my favourite authors!
Check them out! and if you do, let them know I sent you. :)

Michael Chatfield - Emerilia, Ten Realms and our co-written work in his world - Maurakian Wars
https://www.amazon.com/Michael-Chatfield/e/B00WCAOQME

K.T Hannah - Somnia Online
https://www.amazon.com/K.T.-Hanna/e/B00ZBPYU78

Bonnie L. Price - Deck of Souls
https://www.amazon.com/Bonnie-L.-Price/e/B079QM5LNT

Blaise Corvin with Delvers LLC and Nora!
https://www.amazon.com/Blaise-Corvin/e/B01LYK8VG5/

Printed in Great Britain
by Amazon

17161864R00182